Deception
A Phantom of the Opera Novel

Shirley Yoshinaka

Copyright © 2006 by Shirley Yoshinaka
ISBN: 978-1-4116-8296-2

Acknowledgements

I would like to thank the following people who have been so helpful in the writing of this book: Desiree, Jessica, Jill, and Tal. Your advice and support have been greatly appreciated.

I must also acknowledge Gaston Leroux for his original novel.

Prologue

~ *Paris, France*
March 1880

One step and this would all be over.

Erik stared down at the murky depths of the lake, a torch ablaze in his hand. His head was bowed, throat clogged with a bitter sense of loss. The water below was stagnant; a black mirror, yet it cast no reflection from its glassy surface.

He was grateful for that.

Closing his eyes, he swayed forward, then back, and forward again. It would be so easy to end his wretched existence, the exquisite pain that tore his breath away every time he thought of *her*. It had been two days since he'd last seen her and already, it felt like a lifetime. He longed to put an end to the torture. He had nothing left.

But he still had his pride.

Erik opened his eyes, the fingers of his free hand curling into a clenched fist. He'd survived worse than this in his life. It was only his heart that had been shattered, not his will. He didn't need her. He didn't need anyone. Fate had dealt him brutal blows at seemingly every turn, but he'd always managed to rise above the hardships. As a child, he'd been forced to endure whatever circumstances befell him. He'd sworn never to be powerless again.

He was in control.

Spinning around, Erik raised the torch higher and surveyed the remains of his lair. His lips tightened in a grimace. The mob had been thorough, ransacking and looting anything remotely valuable. He extended his gaze farther, toward the organ. It sat intact, though several pipes were dented in. If its size and weight hadn't been a hindrance, it would have been carted away as well.

This lair was no longer home. He had to make a fresh start.

Erik strode forward. He weaved his way around an overturned table. His boots crunched on fragments of glass. Fingering the edge of the mask on his face, he was lost in thought. Memories of *her* began to intrude once more, preying upon his mind. He stomped them down. If he could excise them with a knife, he would. Nothing, however, was ever that simple.

He would have to learn to live without her.

One

~ London, England
November 1881

Although she had expected these very words to be spoken, the finality of hearing them uttered aloud shook her to the core.

She was going blind.

"Are you all right, my dear?" asked the concerned voice of the blurred shape sitting a short distance away.

Melodie nodded, not yet trusting herself to speak. A moment longer was all she needed to regain her composure. She busied her hands by brushing them over the plain fabric of her skirt. "I'm fine," she finally managed to say. "Will I..." She bit her lip and tried again. "Will I lose my sight completely?"

"It's difficult to know for sure. At worst, yes, but I've encountered other cases like yours where vision exists but is terribly blurry and distorted. They did not go completely blind, however. They could still distinguish colours and light."

This gave her some renewed hope. She couldn't bear the thought of being plunged entirely into darkness. The prospect filled her with such terror, she refused to even consider the possibility. "Should I continue the liquid drops for my eyes? Or a stronger pair of spectacles?"

When the doctor failed to reply immediately, she knew the answer. Nothing was helping. In fact, her vision had worsened since the last time she had come four months ago. "Well, I suppose I won't be needing these any longer," she said, unhooking the thick spectacles from behind her ears and setting them down on the adjacent table. They were heavy, uncomfortable, and she was glad to be rid of them.

His voice was laced with regret. "I'm sorry, Melodie. I wish I could do more. Perhaps another specialist would – "

"You are the third specialist I've seen, and none of them have been able to help. You, at least, have been the most kind. Thank you for that," she said.

Melodie rose to her feet, a silent indication that this appointment was over. The doctor retrieved her cloak and the warmth of the wool soon enveloped her. She pulled on her gloves.

"Shall I see you to your carriage?" he asked.

Stiffening her spine, she drew herself up to the tallest height her petite form could manage. "Thank you, but no. Haven't I answered 'no' each time you have asked for the past year?" She kept her tone light, knowing he spoke out of ingrained courtesy.

He responded with gentle humour. "So you have. Forgive my politeness. It's always rearing its ugly head." He followed her as far as the door and opened it for her. "Please say hello to Henry for me," he said.

Melodie looked up, trying to gaze into the vicinity of the man's eyes. Even from two feet away, the outlines of his face were bleary. However, she knew his hair was greying, the skin of his face wrinkled and starting to sag.

"Take care, Doctor," she said.

She turned and moved down the straight cobblestone path toward the waiting carriage. The air was misty and chilled, threatening rain rather than snow. A weighted thud of boots jumping to the ground reached her ears, and the carriage door swung open. She accepted the proffered hand of the driver, stepping up into the cab. As always, the internal confines of the small space made her uneasy, and she pressed herself as close to the window as possible. Thankfully, the ride home would not be too long. With a soft nicker, the horses seemed to signal their readiness and she felt the usual jolt as they surged ahead. The rocking motion soothed her nerves. She settled back on the velvet-cushioned seat.

Her thoughts turned to the only home she'd ever known and the probability that she would be ejected from that safe haven. Although she earned her keep through housework and tutoring, she realized her precarious position. Henry Blythe was a trusted house steward, having worked for the Wentworth family almost thirty years. Since he regarded Melodie as a daughter, she too had been accepted into the family's home. But how long could she continue the ruse?

Her eyesight had been normal for the first eighteen years of her life. Then, ever so gradually, it had started its decline. The cause was a great unknown according to the several specialists that Henry had arranged for her to see – an infection or some strange condition passed along from a previous generation. In the past five years, she'd developed the ability to compensate for her failing vision by heightening her other senses: smell, hearing, and touch. She had so perfected the illusion of normalcy, no one save Henry suspected her sight was so poor. She was regarded as another servant, and thus, she kept her head down, gaze lowered to the floor. Now, with this prognosis, the future appeared bleak.

As the ride back home continued, Melodie hummed aloud. It was a mournful melody, befitting her sombre mood. By the time the carriage pulled up to the front gate, she decided the key of B-flat minor would work best. She was pleased with this little gem despite her current anxieties.

Melodie wound her way around to the rear of the house and let herself in. The kitchen was a beehive of activity. She recognized the servants mainly through voices, but sometimes in other ways. One young woman always smelled of rose petals. Another kitchen maid was an overly robust woman who suffered from laboured breathing. Melodie had discovered that everyone possessed something distinctive and unique. Once she isolated that characteristic, recognition was never a problem.

Calling out a greeting, Melodie inquired as to Henry's whereabouts. She held a wrapped parcel under her arm – the 'medication' she'd received for

Henry's stomach ailment. That was the ruse that had been concocted for her trips to the doctor's office.

Upon being told that Henry was in the drawing room, Melodie went up the back stairs. She found the stillness of the upper floor relaxing compared to the organized chaos downstairs. As she walked, she counted out the steps and turns in her mind, a routine that had become second nature to her.

"Henry?" she called out.

"There you are," Henry answered back. "I was getting worried."

Following his voice to its source, she realized he was seated at the piano. She bent to kiss his cheek and he took the package from her hands.

"I'm late, I know. The doctor is very thorough. He says hello. Did you finish Rebecca's lesson?" she asked. She tossed her cloak aside and sat beside him on the bench.

Henry's tone was impatient. "Yes. I believe she was offended that her beloved teacher wasn't here. But tell me, what did he say? Is there anything he can do?"

"No. He proved my suspicions to be correct. I'm going blind."

"Oh, Mellie." His hand rubbed her shoulder in a comforting motion. "I'm so sorry."

An aching pressure began to build behind her eyes, but she refused to give in to tears. "I don't know what to do," she whispered. She had no need to elaborate further. Having had several discussions regarding this possible prognosis already, Henry already knew what she referred to.

"Let me talk to Mr. Wentworth. He's a good man. A generous one. I'm sure he'll allow you to stay."

"Perhaps," she said.

As Melodie contemplated Henry's statement, she began to think of all he'd done for her, especially in her introduction to music. She remembered the day when he had seated her at the piano. Though only five years old, she had been fascinated with the instrument. Henry had some basic skills and had taught her to play. To his amazement, she had shown a startlingly accurate ear and a gift for music. By the age of six, she could play difficult, complex pieces. Two years later, she began composing waltzes, sonatas, and other piano works.

Henry had taken her to see her first classical concert on her ninth birthday. He'd known someone who worked backstage at the theatre, and they had been allowed to sit up on the rafters, off to the side of the orchestra. The glorious sound of Tchaikovsky's 'Piano Concerto No. 1' had pervaded her soul with joy and wonder. She'd never heard anything more beautiful.

One day, Albert Wentworth had discovered her playing the piano. She'd stopped immediately, certain that she would be scolded. Instead, he had sat down on a chaise and asked her to continue, applauding at the end of her impromptu recital. Impressed by her talent, Albert had encouraged her to play whenever time permitted. When his daughter Rebecca had shown an interest in playing, he'd asked Melodie to teach her. Most of the servants grumbled that Melodie was stepping above her place in the household but she didn't care. Rebecca was bright, eager, and showed promise. Melodie enjoyed tutoring the young child.

Albert had granted her more privileges than the average servant. While it was conceivable that Albert might allow her to remain in his home, Melodie expected his wife would object. To Ellen Wentworth, she was a housemaid and nothing more.

"Mellie?"

Henry's voice broke into her thoughts. "Let's not reveal anything just yet," Melodie said, her voice low. "I can continue on as I have. No one suspects anything."

Henry hesitated before speaking. "Are you sure? Mr. Wentworth adores you as if you were his own daughter."

"I don't know about that. But it's possible my sight will not worsen. Perhaps he is wrong. I don't want to be premature." While she knew she was clinging to false hope, the optimistic side of her rallied to her defense. Doctors were known to be wrong; they were only human. She would simply have to take care not to strain her vision. No more bedtime reading, struggling to focus tired eyes. She couldn't, however, give up her composing. She hadn't resigned herself to that fate yet. "Swear to me, Henry, that you will not speak of this."

"As you wish," he said, sounding reluctant.

"Thank you." She repositioned herself at the piano. "Now, tell me what you think of this. It's rather melancholy, but most suitable for the day I've had." Feeling at ease again with the coolness of the ivory beneath her fingers, she began to play.

After dinner and the completion of her evening duties, Melodie went up to the attic. During much of her childhood, this had been her playground. It was used as storage space for old, forgotten items – everything from books to furniture, dishes and toys. She had always found something to occupy her time.

She sat on the dusty floor now, her skirt swirled around her. Hunched over the top cover of her wooden chest, she scribbled at her newest composition. The tune from earlier this afternoon had become longer and more complex. Each time she dipped into the ink well, her hand raced to keep pace with the music flowing through her mind. She realized she should have brought more candles. In the dim light, her eyes were starting to itch and burn. Mere hours ago, she had vowed to stop straining her eyes. That promise fell by the wayside so she could record her new creation before it vanished from memory.

A sly voice startled her, stemming the flow of internal music.

"So this is what you do up here."

The nib of her pen jabbed into the paper; ink smeared and obscured the last two notes. Melodie quelled the flare of annoyance, and her heart thudded at the unexpected intrusion. She wasn't used to being taken by surprise; her concentration had been so absolute, she'd failed to hear the footsteps approaching.

She looked toward the doorway, seeing a shadowed form. Though she couldn't distinguish the exact physical figure, the voice was unmistakable – David Wentworth, only son of Albert and Ellen.

Melodie attempted to make light of the situation. "I'm afraid you've caught me." She began gathering the papers together. "It's nothing. Just scribbles."

"Let me see."

Although David voiced it as a command and not a request, she was intent on hiding her work. He crossed the distance in three steps and sat on the lid that she'd just begun to lift. She snatched her fingers away, barely avoiding having them pinched. The papers almost scattered from her grasp. "Not so fast," he admonished, grabbing the top sheet. "You're right," he said. "Scribbles indeed. Obviously they mean much more to you. This chest is full of such scribbles."

Melodie longed to throw him an accusatory gaze, but kept her head bowed. "Have you been spying on me?"

"Now that you mention it, yes. And I know it's not the only secret you keep." There was no mistaking the malice in his voice.

"What do you mean?" she asked, as casually as she could manage.

"Where are your spectacles?" he countered.

Thrown off balance by the abrupt shift of topic, she stuttered, "I...I have no need of them anymore." She inwardly cursed her foolishness. Casting the spectacles aside at the doctor's office had been an impulsive act. She hadn't thought of the questions that would arise from their absence.

"I see. You're suddenly blessed with perfect vision, then?" he asked.

Melodie drew back in alarm, becoming aware that he was leaning forward to inspect her face more closely. She turned away, and made an attempt to rise. "I should go. It's getting late."

David seized her forearm in a firm hold. "Am I so hideous to you? You're always running away from me. We used to be such good companions."

"We were children. It's hardly appropriate now. Please let me go," she said.

Instead of releasing her, he sank down to join her on the floor. His other hand cupped her chin, forcing her to look at him. His nearness unnerved her, but she tried not to show any fear. Within this close proximity, his face swam into soft focus. It had been a long time since she'd seen him so clearly. The features were still handsome, save for a slightly crooked nose. His blue eyes bore into hers.

"You *do* see me," he breathed.

Melodie jerked her head, tried to shake his grip, but failed. "Let me go," she said again. Any fond memories of their childhood were overshadowed by remembrance of the cruel nature that lurked within him. It hadn't reared itself often, but when it had, she'd been terrified.

David regarded her, his gaze relentless. "You see me now, but if I were to step away from you, you wouldn't be able to look into my eyes. Would you." His tone was flat, as if he knew he stated a fact.

Melodie's stomach clenched. He knew. Somehow, he knew. She stilled, her eyes riveted to his. As much as she wanted to look away, she remained locked in place.

"Your eyes hide nothing, do they? They never could. Yes, Melodie, I know you're going blind," David said, sounding pleased with himself for discovering her secret. "It's a mystery to me how you function as well as you do. I've had my suspicions for a while but they were confirmed today. I overheard you talking with Henry."

"Eavesdropping, were you? How typical of you," she snapped.

"Ahh, now that's more like it." He chuckled, lips curling with apparent mirth. "I much prefer to see the fire in you. You've become such the meek mouse these last few years."

"I suppose you'll take great delight in informing your parents about my predicament."

"I think delight may be too strong a word. But have no doubt that I will tell them. Unless…"

David's voice tapered off. Melodie wondered what he was scheming. When she felt the pad of his thumb caress her bottom lip, a chill slid down her spine. With strength she didn't know she possessed, she shoved at his chest with both hands. The grip on her arm slackened and she seized the opportunity.

Scrambling to her feet, Melodie attempted to run. She didn't get far. The front of her calves met an obstacle and she tripped. She tumbled downward, her elbow striking the floor hard. Pain shot up her arm. She felt David's hands yank on her shoulders, flipping her onto her back. Her wrists were ensnared and pinned to the floor on either side of her head. Incensed, she kicked and flailed against him. She knew that he had stuck out his legs, deliberately tripping her. The weight of his body settled over her. Her struggles weakened. Panting with exertion, she stopped fighting.

"Had enough? As I was saying, before that rude but enjoyable interruption, I will go to my parents. Unless, of course, you care to change my mind." David grinned down at her. "There's something irresistible about you, Melodie. Always has been. I've never had a shortage of women throwing themselves at me and leading me to their beds, but I've always imagined what it would be like to possess you."

Fear warred with disgust within her. "You're despicable," she spat. "Get off me."

"Not before I have a taste of you," he mumbled.

He leaned down to kiss her. His breath was hot on her face, reeking of brandy and stale cigar smoke. She averted her head. The muscles in her neck strained with the effort of avoiding contact. Her arms were dragged above her head as he attempted to transfer both of her slender wrists into one of his hands. But the exchange was clumsy, and she managed to free one of her limbs.

Fingers clamped over Melodie's jaw and her mouth was crushed against his. She couldn't contain the whimper in her throat as her teeth cut into the softness of her inner lip. When his tongue licked the edge of her mouth, she almost gagged. With her one free hand, she groped along the floor, hoping to find some miraculous weapon to help her. She couldn't believe it when her fingers closed around her pen, almost hidden beneath the folds of her skirt. She grabbed it and stabbed him on the back of his hand.

The howl of surprised agony was immediate. She pushed him away and this time, there was no resistance. Gasping, she swiped at her lips, desperate to be rid of the taste of him. She leapt to her feet and fled for the door.

"You'll pay for this," David cried out.

Melodie flung herself down the stairs, her heart pounding in time to her clattering footsteps. She was afraid she would vomit right in the stairwell. Tears welled in her eyes.

I will not cry. I will not.

Only sheer luck prevented her from breaking her neck as she careened down the steep steps. At last, she reached the lower level of the servants' quarters. She burst into Henry's room.

"Mellie? Good heavens, what's wrong?" Henry asked, alarm in his voice.

"I don't think I can stay here any longer."

Choked by tears, she began to cry.

Two

*~ London, England
March 1882*

The familiar sound of an orchestra warming up – the tuning of the string section, the occasional bleat from one of the horns, the trill of a lone flute – never failed to fill Erik's senses with anticipation and delight. Although he preferred the opera for its vocals, a symphonic concert was enjoyable for different reasons; one could appreciate the nuances of each instrument without the distraction of human voices.

He wondered if he would have company up in the rafters tonight. It had been a few months since he'd seen her.

As if on cue, she came into view, making her way up the rickety ladder. She was dressed in her usual attire of a white blouse and black skirt. Either her wardrobe consisted solely of this one outfit or there were several of the same style blouse and skirt in her closet. The only hint of colour was a blue ribbon that held back her straight chestnut hair.

Noticing something new, he frowned. As she reached the landing and stepped across the catwalk, she swept a long black cane to and fro across her path. Could it be the girl was blind? He watched with interest as the grey haired man followed behind her. They took their seats and turned to each other, speaking in low tones.

Although Erik had seen the woman many times from his hidden perch in the darkest corner, he'd never paid her much attention. He was intrigued, however, by the revelation that she was blind. He ventured a little farther out of the shadows, and strained his ears to catch any snippet of their conversation.

"I don't know if I'll finish on time," the woman was saying.

"But you must. Her birthday is less than a month away."

"I know, but these wretched headaches. Even after thirty minutes, the ache starts and it worsens until I'm almost ill. I don't suppose I'll be paid if I miss the date," she said.

The man shook his head. "No. Won't you accept my help? I can't jot the notes as deftly as you do, but it might be helpful."

"You've been more than helpful. I never would have received this commission without you."

Movement from below caught Erik's eye. The conductor made his way onto the stage and applause rang out around the theatre, including the enthusiastic claps of the young woman and older man.

Erik returned his gaze to her, fascinated by what he'd just heard. *Blind and a commissioned composer? And a mere female. How is it even possible?* He yearned to learn more. He hoped they would pick up the thread of conversation later, perhaps during intermission. As the first soft strains of the violins began, he shrunk back into his corner and settled down to enjoy the music. To his annoyance, he found his mind wandering. He was aware it was happening yet he couldn't seem to stop it.

Tomorrow would mark two years since he'd last seen Christine Daaé. His days were filled with such anniversaries: the first time he'd sung to her as her mysterious angel of music; the first time he'd physically touched her, leading her by hand down the passageways to his home; the first time he'd fallen in love – the only time.

Following the fiasco at the Paris opera house, Erik became a hunted man. As much as he loved Paris, he couldn't remain there. He'd amassed a tidy sum over the years, keeping it hidden in a secret chamber of his lair. It was so well concealed that the looters did not discover it.

After crossing the English Channel, he bought a modest home on the outskirts of London. But while he'd fled France, he couldn't escape his own mind. In those first few months, his moods swung wildly. Rage battled with despair, as he alternated between screaming and sobbing. He wished Christine were happy at the same time he cursed her soul and longed to see her rot in hell. His heinous thoughts consumed him with guilt until he begged aloud for her forgiveness. This went on for an eternity, a vicious cycle that nearly drove him mad. The internal battle eased after a time, perhaps because he exhausted himself. He then descended into a curious listlessness in which he ceased to care about anything. He wouldn't have been disturbed in the least if some unknown force struck him dead.

For a year, he only stepped out of the house when necessary, the hood of his cloak helping to obscure his face. Shop clerks gave a startled glance upon noticing his white mask, but they never commented on it. He lived a quiet, anonymous life; not that one could really call it living. In truth, he merely existed, until one day something unexpected entered his life.

There came a scratching at the front door. Erik tried to ignore it, but the sound persisted. Flinging open the door, he found a bundle of white and black fur huddled on the ground. Black, sorrowful eyes of a collie peered up at him. A whine escaped its throat. The animal had obviously been beaten. Erik hesitated, feeling a strange stirring from within. It had been so long since he'd felt anything that he barely recognized his pang of compassion. Sighing, he brought the dog inside. Its fur was matted, caked with mud and blood. One of its hind legs was broken. Its breathing was shallow, laboured, and Erik sensed the animal hovered near death. The beating had been thorough indeed.

Anger coursed through Erik as he cleansed the animal's wounds and set the leg as best he could. Although the process must have been painful, the dog periodically extended its tongue to lick his hand, as if giving thanks. Erik assumed it wouldn't live through the night; he expected to find a cold, stiff body to dispose of come morning. But when he awakened at first light, the dog lifted its head at the sight of him, wagging its plumed tail. Erik was pleasantly surprised. Like him, it seemed to be a survivor. Days melded into weeks as he nursed the collie back to health and in time, the binding was removed from its leg. Despite being cursed with a hobbling limp, its joy at being able to walk again was obvious.

On the day the collie took its first tentative steps, Erik named her Sascha. After weeks of having been nameless and only referred to as 'it', she deserved an identity.

That momentous day also sparked Erik's decision to live again. He started slowly, taking pleasure in small things. For instance, he'd been denying himself all but the most basic of food. For more than a year, he sustained himself mainly on bread, water, and the occasional slab of meat so he wouldn't collapse. He lost a significant amount of weight, dwindling his muscles to an unhealthy degree. When he finally indulged in some cheese, fruit, and a bottle of wine, his taste buds sang with bliss; he'd forgotten how satisfying a good meal could be.

He began going for walks at night, exploring the neighbourhood with Sascha at his side. There was a great expanse of green fields behind the house, complete with a bubbling brook. The next home was a half-mile down the road, so the location he'd chosen was ideal. Although he'd made the conscious decision to rejoin the world, he still valued his privacy.

As Erik's body regained its strength, he found himself craving music again. In his depressed state, he'd thought that part of his life was over. When he'd first come to his new home, he'd furnished it with the barest necessities to make it liveable. The lone extravagant exception had been a piano. He'd purchased it on impulse upon first moving in and yet, when it had arrived, the sight of it had seemed to mock him. Into the corner it had gone, with a cloth coverlet thrown on top. It sat there, silently gathering dust.

When the urge to plunge himself into music returned, Erik removed the cover and ran his fingers over the keys. His eyes closed as he revelled in the smooth, cool touch of ivory beneath his skin, reacquainting himself with the contours of the instrument. Then he sat down and played. And played and played. The music gushed out of him in an endless stream, at times fierce and pounding and at others, sweet and lilting. Time held no meaning as he lost himself in the glorious throes of his reawakening. When he ground to a halt, his chest was heaving, arms and fingers aching from overexertion. Wiping sweat from his brow, he sat hunched over limply, grinning like a fool. Sascha's high-pitched whines reached his ears, reminding him that neither one of them had eaten in many hours. She was treated to a fat sausage that night for her patience.

Soon, his own playing at home wasn't enough to sustain Erik; he needed to experience live theatre again. A fair number of venues in central London were his to explore. He shunned the city's transport systems – omnibus, the Underground, hansom cabs – preferring not to travel in such close quarters with the public. Instead, he made his way about the city on foot. Dressed entirely in black, from the tips of his polished boots to the hood of his cloak, he blended in with the night. Whenever someone caught sight of the mask, eyes widened with curiosity and fear, and invariably, that person would cross the street to avoid him.

Erik was aware that he struck a commanding figure, especially since he'd regained the muscles he'd lost. Better food and rigorous exercise had aided in filling out his form. He also projected an intimidating aura of danger that served him well; it warned others to keep their distance.

Erik roamed from theatre to theatre, slipping unseen into the backstage areas with ease. After climbing up to the rafters, he enjoyed many performances from his bird's eye view. However, it took considerable effort to find the one venue to call home. While variety was well and good, he was, at heart, a creature of habit.

Although this particular theatre didn't come close to matching the grandeur of the Paris opera house, it did boast one of the finest orchestras he'd heard in a long time. The maestro was infinitely more talented than the buffoon that had directed the music of the opera house. That fool had bowed to the misguided demands of Carlotta one too many times, shredding any ounce of respect Erik may have held for the man.

While the performances here did include opera, the main staple of this theatre was the orchestra itself. Erik's ears were treated to the genius of Mozart, Beethoven, and Liszt. The purity of sound was like a balm on his wounds, allowing them to heal by tiny degrees and giving him a measure of peace.

Then one night, a young woman invaded his sanctuary in the upper rafters. Erik stiffened with surprise and withdrew into his corner. On occasion, theatre crewmen came up here to adjust a backdrop or some other maintenance, never knowing an intruder lurked in their midst. Encountering a woman here was a first. Erik watched her with wariness, hoping she'd leave. But it soon became apparent that she intended to take in the concert. Considering the ease in which she hoisted herself up and walked about at this height, he surmised this was her regular seat. He guessed that she couldn't afford a ticket and must know someone within the crew who allowed her this free pass.

She possessed a calm, quiet nature and thus, Erik learned to ignore her presence. Over the next six months, she came on a fairly regular basis, often alone and sometimes with an older man. Their appearances ceased to bother Erik. In fact, when the last several months passed with no sign of either one of them, he vaguely wondered what had befallen them. Their reappearance tonight had been met with neutral indifference on his part until he noticed the cane in her hand.

The roar of applause roused Erik out of his contemplative state. Damnation, he'd missed the entire performance. As the conductor took his bows, Erik remembered that only one piece was in the programme tonight. There was no intermission. The evening was over.

A hum of voices floated up from parting members of both the audience and the orchestra. Erik's gaze returned to the couple that shared his unique box above the stage. They were lingering, appearing to be in no rush to leave.

"...wonderful, wasn't it?" the man was saying.

His female companion smiled. "It certainly was, though the piano could use some fine-tuning. It sounded a little off."

"I didn't notice. But your ears have always been sharper than mine."

"Ignore me. Just a minor quibble that didn't detract from the performance. The pianist had such nimble fingers. I'm quite impressed."

"I've been thinking. I could put in some inquiries and try to find someone to assist you. A music student, perhaps," the man suggested. "As long as the deadline is met, you could promise payment after completion of the piece."

Her lips pursed as she contemplated the idea. "That might work. But whoever accepts the position would have to agree to anonymity."

"I know. A student looking to earn some money might be our best option."

Very interesting indeed. Erik had stood and edged as close as he dared to the couple. He was a good twenty feet away and careful to remain hidden. He kept his head averted so no light could reflect off his mask. After talking a moment longer, they rose to their feet. She trailed after the older man, her left hand skimming across the railing as the other held her cane. Just before she reached the ladder to make her descent, she stopped. Her head turned to look over her shoulder and stilled.

Erik froze, resisting the urge to back away. She was gazing straight into his eyes. *Impossible!* He was sure he'd made no sound to reveal his position. He'd memorized each plank of wood that gave the slightest groan and meticulously avoided them. Even his manner of breathing changed when he chose to remain unseen, becoming so shallow that most men would faint from lack of air. In addition to his certainty that he remained cloaked in darkness, there was the matter of her blindness. While that might be some sort of ruse on her part, he could not fathom that any normal human being would be able to see him standing there.

And yet, she continued to seemingly regard him, a pensive frown marring her smooth brow.

"Mellie? Is something wrong?" the male voice whispered from below. He'd already descended to the next level down.

The sound of his voice apparently snapped her out of her trance. "I'm coming." She spun on her heel and soon disappeared from sight.

Though his tensed muscles relaxed, Erik didn't dare expel a breath. The moment of their locked gaze had been eerie and disconcerting. So her name was Mellie.

He had no doubt they would soon meet again.

Three

In her head, Melodie counted to five while the child before her refused to do as she asked. She imagined the girl was glaring at her, lips pouted and arms crossed belligerently across her chest.

"I don't want to practice these stupid scales. I hate them," the young girl declared.

Melodie spoke with quiet authority, showing no hint of her irritation. "I know you do. But they help to warm up your fingers so you can play better. Just five minutes on your scales, then we'll work on the piece you'll be playing at your recital."

"No."

She decided to try a different approach. "Grace, do you know why your mother insists that you eat your vegetables at dinner?"

There was a pause, as if the girl was contemplating the question. When she replied, the petulance in her tone was replaced by uncertainty. "Because they're good for me?"

Melodie nodded. "That's right. They're good for you, even if you don't understand why. I know you trust your mother, and I ask for you to trust me when it comes to music. No one likes to practice scales. Not even me."

"You don't?"

"No, I don't. But I know they're good for me, so I do it. Just as you should," Melodie said.

A moment later, the sound of the C major scale reached her ears, and she suppressed a smile. Grace Anniston was a stubborn, wilful girl of twelve. She had none of the sunny disposition of Rebecca, Melodie's former pupil, but Melodie was not about to complain about the challenge of dealing with the girl's snarly moods. Melodie was well aware of how fortunate her circumstances were.

She had left the Wentworth home four months ago. The night of David's assault on her, she burst into tears and sought the comfort of Henry's fathering arms. She almost withheld telling him what had happened. Henry held a soft spot for David, having watched him grow up since birth. But unlike Melodie, he'd never witnessed David's dark side.

Melodie had been frightened by the incident, yet strangely embarrassed as well. Most women her age were married and raising a family. While she had no burning desire to be wed, she wondered what it would be like to have a proper suitor, someone funny and charming that she could share her time with. She'd never even been kissed before. And she refused to call David's abominable attack on her mouth her first kiss. The thought revolted her.

When Henry pressed her to reveal what had happened, she blurted out the truth. He was furious, ready to charge upstairs and throttle David. She literally had to block the door, gripping the frame and refusing to budge until Henry calmed down. His next suggestion was going to Mr. Wentworth, but she wouldn't allow that either.

They talked long into the night. Various options were put forth and discarded until she made her decision; she would strike out on her own and attempt to find some independence. Henry thought a placement for her as a governess or music tutor might be possible. While he hated to see her leave, he agreed that she was no longer safe. Melodie feared that each time she turned a corner, David would be lying in wait for her.

The next morning, Melodie went directly to Albert. She confessed that she had been deceiving everyone in his household for more than five years. News of her blindness shocked him, but he kindly suggested that nothing had to change; she could continue living and working there. Had she received that same offer the previous morning, she would have been thrilled. In light of the situation with David, however, she stated that she needed to make a fresh start somewhere.

That evening, Albert called her into his study. He knew a family who was seeking a music teacher for their strong-willed daughter; the last teacher had quit after two weeks. On his recommendation, Melodie was invited to live in their home. Room and board would be free of charge in exchange for lessons and additional minor duties. Melodie was grateful for this turn of events.

The next day, goodbyes with the servants were uncomfortable. Melodie saw no sign of David or Mrs. Wentworth. Only Rebecca was tearful, clinging to her skirt and pleading for her to stay.

Melodie went to the attic to retrieve her compositions and opened the lid of the chest. As her hand swept along the smoothness of the inner wood, she frowned. She couldn't seem to comprehend what her touch was telling her. Her fingers fluttered with a frantic motion until they brushed against her pen. She brought it up to her nose and saw the red-brown stain on the metal nib. Dried blood. David's blood. For a full minute, she stared into space, numb with shock.

David had either stolen or more likely destroyed her compositions. The collection amassed from a lifetime of work was gone. What had he yelled before she'd fled? *"You'll pay for this."* He'd certainly taken his revenge in the most hurtful of ways. She could probably recreate much of the work, but the oldest pieces from childhood could never be replaced.

Melodie became aware that the rhythmic sound of the ascending and descending piano notes had ceased.

"Why have you stopped?" she asked.

"Because you're not listening," came Grace's snappish reply.

Melodie inclined her head. "You're right. I apologize. Let's start on the Chopin now."

Two hours later, the lesson was completed. Grace went up to her bedchamber, and Melodie wandered toward the kitchen to see if she could be of any assistance. While her presence in that area of the Wentworth household had been unwelcome, she'd become friendly with the cook here. Isabel was often sharp tongued, but the sting of her words hid a soft heart.

During her second week at the Anniston's home, Melodie had found Isabel railing at her kitchen maid. The girl had returned from the market with some fish that was far from fresh. Having explored much of the area around her new home already, including the nearby market, Melodie had volunteered to fetch a new batch. Isabel had been impressed when Melodie returned with a new basketful of fish so fresh, they seemed about to leap out.

There was no trick to it; Melodie possessed a keener nose than most, and by inspecting closely, she was able to discern the clarity of the fish's eyes. Since that day, she often accompanied Isabel on her market rounds.

Melodie now entered the busy hub of activity. An inviting scent of baking bread wafted to her nose. "Can I be of any help today?" she asked, steering herself toward the staccato sound of a chopping knife.

The sound halted. She pictured Isabel with the knife held mid-air, pausing to consider the inquiry. "No, dear, I think we're fine."

"I'll go out for a walk, then. Are you sure there's nothing I can get for you on my way back?"

There was another short pause before Isabel replied, "Well, I could use three more eggs."

"Consider it done," Melodie said.

She took a basket and stepped out the door. It was a lovely morning for early spring. She had no need for even a wrap. The rays of the sun warmed her skin and cast a yellow-tinted glow across her vision. Before letting herself through the gate at the front of the house, she reached into the deep pocket of her skirt. She removed her pen, a small well of ink, and folded papers. She placed them in the basket.

There was a park nearby. Melodie spent as much time as possible curled up on a secluded bench, jotting down music. The notes would later be tested on the piano, but she didn't like to be chained to the instrument when composing. She'd learned her creative muses were better served when she could feel the breeze on her face and hear birds chirping in the trees.

As Melodie walked, she contemplated her failing vision. The headaches had been mild at first, a pesky throbbing she could ignore. In the last few weeks, however, if she pushed herself to more than a half hour of writing, the pain would pound behind her eyes.

Melodie was startled by a shout of voices. She turned toward the commotion.

"Watch out! Runaway horse!"

She heard the panicked whinny of the animal and the clattering hooves of a fast gallop. The sound was getting louder, seeming to head straight toward her. She blinked, but could see nothing beyond the haze that clouded her gaze. People pushed past her, shrieking with terror. Unsure of which way to turn, she stood rooted to the spot.

Run! Her mind screamed at her. But which way?

Away from the wild horse that's going to kill you, you fool!

At last, the glue fell away from her shoes. Melodie pivoted to the right, starting to run from the thunderous noise that was almost upon her.

Something clamped onto her arm. She was then yanked backwards so forcefully, she thought her arm would pull out of its socket. The momentum spun her around. Her cane and basket flew out of her hands. The entire length of her body collided face first into a solid wall. She gave a muffled grunt on impact, her nose bent against fine, black cloth that smelled of soap and spice. Only then did she realize that a large hand was pressed to her back; the wall she'd been thrown against was a man.

Melodie laid one of her own hands flat against his chest, and slid the other upward. When she reached the slope of his shoulder, she almost sighed with relief, noting that he was tall, but not some sort of abnormal giant.

Although time seemed to have slowed and stretched with queer elasticity, only seconds had passed since she'd first felt the grip on her arm. It was terribly improper to be draped so intimately against a stranger. Before the rising flush of heat could reach her cheeks, she was released from his embrace.

"Whoa, there, steady. That's it, nice and easy," crooned the deep voice. It was low, musical, almost a purr in the man's throat.

As he continued to speak in soothing tones, the animal's squeals subsided to snorts of hot breath. The clopping sound of hooves against cobblestone stilled as the horse responded to the man's calming nature.

"Thank God! Thank God you was 'ere, guv," exclaimed a different man, sounding out of breath. "That damned 'orse could've killed…uh…em…"

Melodie frowned in confusion as the apparent owner of the horse went from gushing gratitude to a hesitant stammering, and now nothing, as if he'd been stunned into silence.

"What's going on?" she asked.

"N-nothin', miss. The guv 'ere saved your life. This idiot 'orse of mine was rearin' up on 'is legs, and you were right in 'is way. 'e woulda crushed you like a twig, 'e would. What were you thinkin', runnin' at 'im like that, eh?"

It was her turn to stammer. "Well, I…I suppose I…"

"She is safe. That's all that is important," interrupted the smooth voice of her saviour. "You need to take better care of this horse. His left hind leg is lame, and the bit is entirely too tight in his mouth."

When Melodie heard the retreating steps of the horse, she knew the man must have turned away. He hadn't responded to that last remark, so she imagined it hadn't pleased him.

"Are you hurt, mademoiselle?"

Mademoiselle? Oh, he's speaking to me.

Looking up, she viewed him as a large shadow that blotted out the sun. "No, I'm fine," Melodie said.

"I apologize for pulling you back so roughly. I had to react quickly."

"Please, no apologies are necessary," she said. "I cannot thank you enough. You saved my life."

"It was nothing, I assure you, but my pleasure all the same," he said.

Melodie was oddly lulled by his voice, just as the horse had been, and also intrigued by the trace of accent; it sounded French. She didn't realize her hands were clasped together until her cane and basket were nudged against them.

She hooked the handle of the basket over one arm, and then clutched her trusty stick. Although she'd only acquired it four months ago, she'd come to depend on it so highly; it was now a natural extension of her arm. "Thank you. I'm so glad it isn't broken."

"You're welcome. Is there somewhere I might accompany you? You still look shaken."

"Do I?" Her nerves were rattled, though she'd hoped it wouldn't be so obvious. She'd never been able to hide her emotions well. "Perhaps just to the park. It's a little farther ahead."

"May I offer you my arm?"

Melodie hesitated, chewing on her inner lip. Prior to using the cane, she'd allowed Henry to guide her when travelling in unfamiliar areas, but now she'd come to take pride in her newfound independence.

"My apologies if I've offended you," he murmured, his tone cool when she took too long in answering.

"You haven't. Forgive me. I'm simply accustomed to my independence." She tried to smile, but feared it was wobbly. "I would be pleased to take your arm."

They walked in silence. Melodie searched for something to say, but seemed to be tongue-tied. Fortunately, the park was a short distance away. After passing the gurgling fountain, she halted on the pathway and pointed off to the right. "Do you see the bench over there? It should be almost hidden between some trees."

"Yes, I see it," he said.

"That's my bench. I'm quite fine from here. I'm sure you have better things to do."

"Not today." He started forward again. Feeling the pull on her arm, she fell into step by his side. "I see you're a composer," he remarked.

Melodie didn't hide her surprise. "How did you know?"

"I couldn't help noticing the contents of your basket. They'd spilled out onto the road. Don't worry. Everything is intact," he added. "Luckily, the papers remained inside."

"Very astute of you."

"I also took a moment to admire your pen. Do you find it much improvement over the quill?" he asked.

This was much safer territory to converse on. "Oh yes," she said, with genuine enthusiasm. "It writes more smoothly and with greater precision. And one doesn't have to dip into the well as often, so it's more efficient. I would never go back to the quill."

"That sounds marvellous indeed. I shall have to look into procuring one for myself. Here we are." Coming to a halt, he cupped her elbow, and then guided her to the wrought iron bench. "Do you mind if I join you?" he asked, just as she settled onto the seat.

Melodie became flustered again. "I suppose not," she replied.

He sat next to her, keeping a modest distance. "I'm somewhat of a composer myself," he stated. "And I must admit my curiosity. Being blind, how do you manage to write?"

"I'm not completely blind. I can distinguish light and colour, but the world around me is a blur of distorted shapes. From a distance of several inches, however, I can see quite well. That is how I write." She suppressed a sigh. "But my vision is worsening, I'm afraid. If it continues to degrade as it has these last few months, it won't be long before even the distance of a few inches will become blurry."

"I see." He managed to convey a tone of sympathy in those two words. "I can't imagine how difficult that must be. I've never come across a female composer before. What an accomplishment for you."

Melodie wasn't sure if that was meant to be a compliment, but decided it would be wise to downplay her role. "Hardly. It's simply a hobby."

There was a pause before he spoke his next words, as if he chose them carefully. "Perhaps you should reconsider placing such a strain on your eyes for the sake of a mere hobby."

Oh, how Melodie ached to tell him that she had been commissioned to compose a piece for a prominent member of London society. It wasn't anything on a grand scale, but it had been as a result of someone finally recognizing her talent. There was also the minor issue of false pretenses being involved, but she didn't like to dwell on that aspect.

"May I take a look at what you're working on?" he asked.

Her first reaction was to refuse, but she batted that response back down. He'd mentioned that he also composed music. Perhaps it would be wise to get his opinion. "Please do," she said.

He rummaged in her basket, and she heard the crinkling of the papers being unfolded. Minutes ticked by at a snail's pace. A gust of wind caressed her face, and she brushed strands of hair from her eyes. Afraid of losing the ribbon from her hair, she pulled it off and tucked it into her pocket. Every so often, the rustling of paper could be heard as the man perused the next page. This wasn't taking a simple look at her work; he was examining every note and phrase. She sat for so long, she could have sworn she saw the shift of the sun in the sky.

At last, he spoke, but to her annoyance, he muttered unintelligibly, under his breath.

"I beg your pardon?" Melodie asked.

"This is good. It's very good."

She heard a strangeness in his tone, as if he was reluctant to give her praise. He then added, "There is one overly ambitious section for the harp you should tame. And a particular run of notes where the violin and cello will clash in a most unflattering way. Other than that, I can find no fault."

Melodie found herself bristling. He possessed an arrogance that she had not expected, and the criticism of her work irked her. "What is your musical background?" she inquired, almost wincing at the sharpness of her tone. She made her irritation too obvious.

"I've been composing almost all my life."

"Are you a student?"

"No," he said, pausing for a moment before pressing on. "I would like to offer my services to you."

"Excuse me?"

"Your writing. It can't be good to strain your eyes so much. It must be aiding the deterioration of your vision. If you would allow me, I could help you with the writing of the notes."

Melodie had never expected such an offer to be dropped into her lap. Before she had a chance to respond, he continued on. "No need to make your decision right now. Think it over and should you agree, come to this bench the same time tomorrow. Would that be agreeable?"

She replied without thinking. "All right."

"Good."

The man stood up. Before he could fade completely from her sight, she came to her senses. "Wait. What is your name?"

"Erik," he said.

She thought it strange, yet somehow fitting, that he should only reveal his given name. "I'm Melodie."

His darkened form grew distant and disappeared, leaving her in the midst of her solitary, hazy world. The papers had been refolded and returned to her basket. She pulled them out and rifled through the sheets until she came to one particular passage. Running the melodies through her head, her brow wrinkled. She hated to admit it, but he was right. The harmonics between the violin and cello, as she'd written them, would not blend well together. For him to have picked up on this flaw while glancing it over for the first time was remarkable.

There was no point in staying here any longer. Nothing else would be written this morning.

Melodie walked home in a fog, both troubled and excited by her meeting with this mysterious stranger. She supposed he was a stranger no longer, for she knew his name – Erik.

And tomorrow, she had an appointment to keep.

There was no real need of a fire, but Erik enjoyed the comforting warmth. He sat by the hearth, listening to the crackling flames, his stomach full from dinner, his mask and wig tossed on the nearby table. His mood was introspective this evening. For the second time in his existence, he'd invited a woman into his life. This new woman hadn't yet accepted his proposition, but he had the strong feeling she would. His instincts were rarely wrong. He kept reminding himself that he was doing this for purely selfish reasons; he needed the money.

Although he wasn't in dire straits yet, funds were dwindling without being replenished. It was tempting to fall into his means of income from his younger days; picking the well-padded pockets of the wealthy or travelling with fairs throughout Europe, displaying his astonishing vocal skills and sleight of hand. He could do those things, but he refused. He wasn't about to discard his chance to lead a normal life, or at least as close to normal as he could manage. Normal did not include base thievery or putting himself on display so people could gawk and swoon. And while he supposed his stealthy presence in the theatre rafters wouldn't be regarded as normal by most, he knew someone who might understand – Melodie.

She had not yet confessed her commission to him, but he anticipated she would. Payment for his services in assisting her would then be rendered, and he'd be on his way. Perhaps he could also attempt to sell his own compositions. Surely there were people who could overlook his disfigurement in light of the immense talent he possessed.

Erik pressed a weary hand to the right side of his face, the side that he was forever cursed with. *Who could ever overlook this monstrosity?*

Sascha lifted a paw to his knee and rested her chin upon it, gazing up at him. Erik almost chuckled at the uncanny timing. He stroked the delicate fur behind her ears. "Yes, I know you could, Sascha." At the sound of her name, she swished her tail in a show of delight. "Since the girl is blind, perhaps she won't mind either?"

Not a girl. A woman. Though petite and small boned, her well-proportioned curves had been evident, even for the few seconds he'd held her. But later, as he'd viewed her on the bench with her hair loose and flowing, her face clean and shining, she'd looked impossibly young.

Erik reflected on how he had followed her home from the theatre the previous night. His curiosity had been aroused, and finding her place of residence seemed a reasonable starting point in learning more about her. He was surprised when her male companion left her at the front gate of the townhouse, bidding her goodnight with a kiss on the cheek. He'd assumed they resided in the same household.

In the morning, Erik embarked on a quest for a few bottles of wine. There was a shop that happened to be located near the residence of his new friend. He was headed in that direction when he spied her walking. Without a particular plan in mind, he trailed after her once more. Even with her use of the cane, Erik had the notion that she couldn't truly be blind – not when she'd stared at him with such directness and was capable of writing. Perhaps she used the ruse of a disability to gain sympathy or, at the very least, she could not be completely blind. But in the face of impending disaster in the form of one runaway horse, she was as defenseless as a newborn babe.

The sight of the massive stallion charging at full speed toward her was cause for concern. But surely she heard the shouts of warning, if not the powerful hooves that hurtled her way. When she appeared to freeze, looking toward the sound but seeming confused, Erik's concern grew to a prickling fear. She meant nothing to him, yet he wasn't willing to stand there and watch her be trodden to death. Men and women scattered in all directions, cursing and screaming. They ran past her, practically knocking her over in their haste to flee. No one attempted to pull her to safety. Erik's temper flared. These heartless ninnies were so concerned with their own precious necks, they wouldn't lift a finger to save a young woman's life.

When the horse reared up on its hind legs, Erik's heart leapt into his throat. She actually turned into the downward thrust of those deadly, flailing hooves. At the last moment, Erik sprinted to reach her side and wrenched her back, safe into the circle of his arms. Stupid, foolish woman! He wanted to shake her but instead, thrust her aside to deal with the wild-eyed horse. The attention he focused on the animal gave him time to calm himself. The near death experience had been no fault of hers. And obviously, her lack of vision was very real.

As Erik retrieved her basket from the street, he spotted her composition inside. Insatiable curiosity pervaded once more. He was prepared to find a piece of work that ranged from bad to passable. By no means did he expect anything close to the beauty that lurked in her music. He told her it was 'good, very good'. But in actual fact, it was damned brilliant. Besides the monetary reward in assisting her, he suspected he would gain real pleasure in the development of her work.

Now, it was a question of whether Melodie would make an appearance at the park tomorrow morning.

He would be displeased if his plans were disrupted.

Four

What a change a day could make. Yesterday had been bright and warm. Today, the dampness chilled Melodie's bones, making her want to burrow deeper into her cloak. There was no golden glow in the sky this morning. Her surroundings were grey, dull, and wet.

Melodie strolled to the park at a leisurely pace, umbrella in one hand and her cane in the other. She turned at the entranceway, passed the fountain, and slowed as she neared the familiar clump of trees. Though she heard nothing but the drumming patter of rain against the umbrella doming her head, something made her pause. She swivelled around. She had an uneasy feeling of being watched. The same sensation had nearly overwhelmed her in the rafters of the theatre two nights ago. Although she tried to scold herself for her silliness, it didn't prevent the shiver that coursed through her. Of course, there could be a simple explanation.

"Erik?" she called out hoarsely. She waited with bated breath.

"I'm here," came the reply after a lengthy pause.

Melodie recoiled, startled by the close proximity of his voice. Erik was standing right in front of her, yet she had not heard any sign of motion. Was it possible he had also been hidden in the shadows of the rafters that night?

As quickly as the notion came to her, she discarded it. Her imagination sometimes stretched beyond reasonable borders. She had to gather her wits and remember why she was here. The wisdom of the act was already questionable enough.

"You move very quietly," she remarked.

Erik ignored the statement. "I take your coming here as acceptance of my proposal?"

"And you're very direct as well. Perhaps we could take shelter somewhere to discuss this more thoroughly," she suggested. "There is a lovely tearoom not far from here. In fact, it's right around the spot where we first met." When this garnered no reaction from him, she smiled, and prodded, "Remember? When you saved my life."

"Are you suddenly in the mood for tea, or implying that you would rather conduct our meeting in a more public place?"

There was an intentional bite to Erik's voice that wiped the smile from Melodie's face. "We *are* in a public place," she pointed out, matching his acrid tone.

"True. But I'm obliged to reveal the fact that not another soul is nearby. Not many people are fond of walking through the park in the rain, it seems. And we're quite well hidden amongst these trees."

Baffled by his surly mood, Melodie wondered if he was trying to frighten her. She didn't understand why he was baiting her this way. "I'm merely suggesting that we conduct our meeting in a place where we might dry off. And yes, a spot of tea would be nice," she said.

"I've never liked tea," Erik snapped. "Can we not talk about this here? A simple yes or no will suffice."

"But it's not that simple," Melodie said, her frustration mounting. "I'm sure you made your offer out of kindness or sympathy for my plight, but there are details you should be aware of. It will take some time to explain things to you."

He was silent for so long that she thought he might have deserted her, leaving as soundlessly as he'd approached.

Erik spoke at last. "Very well. But I insist on a location of my choosing. It will be dry, but I must warn you, we will be quite alone. I assure you, mademoiselle, you have nothing to fear from me."

Though niggling bolts of warning jabbed at her brain, Melodie found herself rationalizing out loud. "I would hardly think you'd take the trouble to save my life and then murder me the next day. So please, lead the way."

Melodie stepped forward, inadvertently tilting the umbrella. A gentle hand stilled her wrist, and the handle was plucked from her grasp. Erik placed that same wrist on the crook of his arm.

"Allow me," he said. A hint of humour warmed his tone. "I would prefer not to be stabbed in the eye. It wouldn't do much good for both of us to be blind."

She gaped at him, astonished that he would dare to make a joke about blindness. And to her great surprise, she laughed.

Since Erik was guiding her, Melodie took less notice of direction or landmarks than usual. She did perceive that the streets were less congested and noisy than they normally were at this hour of the morning. The inclement weather served to keep many people indoors. When Erik led her around to the back of a building, she realized they'd reached their destination. He handed the umbrella to her. Following the metallic sound of a lock turning, she heard the door open. She shook out the umbrella and stepped inside. In the semi-darkness, she gazed around. Feeble shafts of light filtered through the windows, barely illuminating her poor vision.

"Where are we?" she asked. Her senses were on heightened alert, tingling with nervous energy. "I feel this place is very familiar."

"It is," Erik said. He sounded rather ominous. "Follow me a little further, and I'll explain."

Melodie took his arm once more. They wound through corridors, and their footsteps echoed with a hollow sound. She was certain she'd been here before, but something seemed odd. As they turned down another hall, the realization struck her with resounding clarity. She halted in her tracks, tore her arm from his, and exclaimed, "We're in the theatre. The Empire theatre. I'm not taking another step until you explain yourself."

She was well acquainted with the area backstage, but had never been here during the day. In the evening, it was always crowded with people and brimming with activity. The absolute stillness now had been the strange element that had thrown her senses off balance.

"I ask for your indulgence a moment longer. Then we'll sit down and talk," Erik said, using his silken, coaxing tone.

Melodie found it difficult to refuse that voice.

An internal battle erupted in her brain. The logical half ordered her to make her escape now, return home, and forget that she had ever met this enigma of a man. The curious half of her urged her forward, lulling herself into believing that it wouldn't hurt to talk with him and hear his explanation.

Curiosity won, and she allowed him to continue leading the way. After rounding another turn, Erik stopped and said, "Wait here." Then he was gone.

Melodie stood rooted to the spot. Her thoughts whirled. Perhaps Erik worked here. Maybe he was a member of the orchestra. That would explain his musical skills, as well as the ease in which he'd entered the building. He certainly hadn't broken the door down.

Her nerves calmed. *Yes, that makes perfect sense.*

Erik returned a minute later and guided her through another doorway. She heard a whoosh, and several gas flames shot to life in the corner of her vision. Yellow-orange sparkles of light danced before her. She now realized where they were standing. Erik had lit a few of the lamps that dotted across the front of the stage.

With a touch to her elbow, he led her to a familiar object. "Sit here. May I take your cloak?" he inquired. Though he spoke quietly, his voice resonated in the cavernous space of the empty theatre.

Melodie shrugged out of the damp cloth. "Thank you." She set aside her cane and umbrella before sitting down on the piano bench.

After a brief shuffling of sound, Erik sat on a chair next to her. "It seems we both have much explaining to do," he said. "Since you wanted to engage in a thorough discussion, perhaps you could start."

"All right," she agreed. She folded her hands in her lap. "I wasn't entirely truthful with you yesterday. Composing has always been a hobby and just recently, I was able to secure a commission. It was actually Henry, a dear friend of mine, that made it possible. I have the piece completed up here." She tapped at her temple with an index finger. "Well, almost complete. With my eyes, I'm struggling to get it down on paper. This is where you can help me, and of course, I will pay you. Normally, I would give you credit as having assisted me, but in this case, you would remain anonymous."

"And why is that?" Erik asked.

"I was granted this commission under false pretenses." Melodie's fingers fidgeted despite her effort to keep them still. "Henry had been trying to generate interest in my work, but no one wanted to hire a woman. Two months ago, he found someone who liked samples of what I had written. When asked the identity of the composer, he gave the name of Michael Blythe."

Erik sounded puzzled. "I'm not sure I – "

"It's me," she interrupted. "Michael Blythe doesn't exist. It's just a name Henry created off the top of his head. It was the only way to sell my work."

When Erik roared with laughter, Melodie flinched at the unexpected sound. She didn't know if she should be relieved or offended by his reaction. Her lips compressed into a flat line. "I'm glad you find this so amusing."

He issued a softer chuckle. "Forgive me. But you've certainly managed to surprise me."

"I take it this deception doesn't bother you?"

"Not in the least."

"So I've made my confession," Melodie said. "Now I would like to know why you've brought me here. I assume that you work here."

"That assumption would be false."

Her uneasiness returned. "You're not a member of the orchestra?"

"No," he said.

Her forehead wrinkled. "I don't understand. Then how did you get in? You obviously know your way around the back corridors."

"We appear to have more in common than you realize, mademoiselle," Erik said smoothly. "I have my ways of letting myself in and making myself at home in the rafters. It's the only way I can take in the performance. Just as you do."

Apprehension shot through Melodie. "How could you know that?" she asked in a strangled whisper.

"I think you already know the answer."

"That was you, that night, watching me from the shadows," she accused. "I knew something or someone was there. I couldn't see you, but I…I felt you." She peered through the fog of her vision now, seeing nothing in this wan light. But she knew Erik was there, sitting and staring. Her pulse raced with an intensity that made her quiver. "What game are you playing? You miraculously save my life and then offer to help me. Now you've brought me here, broken in somehow, to…to…" she stuttered, "…I don't know what, but I don't want any part of this."

Melodie hadn't realized she'd risen to her feet. She'd reflexively stepped backwards, holding out a hand to steady herself. The surface of the piano was smooth and cold beneath her palm.

When Erik spoke, she took an acute breath. It was unnerving that he could move so swiftly and silently. Though he hadn't touched her, she was aware that he was looming over her, only inches away. "What did you say?" she asked, hating how weak her voice sounded.

Erik repeated his words patiently, as if dealing with a small child. "As I said earlier, you have nothing to fear from me. Yes, I was in the rafters that night. I have my reasons for hiding in the shadows. The same reasons have led us here for this meeting. To have gone to a tearoom, as you suggested, is impossible. If you look at me closely, you'll see why."

Melodie lifted her eyes. She saw only the vague outline of his head. "You're too tall. If you could incline your head…" Her voice died away.

As if ensnared in the web of a dream, she watched with fascination as Erik's face gradually became discernible. Staring into his eyes for the first time, her breath caught in her throat. Beautiful green irises gazed back at her with steady deliberation. His eyes held a cool appraisal, and she understood that as she studied him, he was judging her as well. Only after several heartbeats did her gaze slide to the pristine white mask that covered half of his face. Strange that it had not been the first thing to capture her attention. The mask served to hide a deformity, perhaps. She now thought it wise not to make any assumptions where this man was concerned. Next, she regarded the full curve of his lips and strong jaw before meeting his eyes again. It was impossible for her to view anything with clarity and sharpness, but even she could see the attractiveness of his features. He was older than she had imagined. And now he was waiting for her reaction.

"I don't suppose many masked men patronize tearooms. I understand why you would desire a more private meeting place," she said.

Erik drew back his head, and the handsome face receded from view. It was of no consequence; his visage was indelibly etched in her mind.

Melodie began to stitch the details together so she could comprehend everything thus far. "So what happened yesterday with the horse…it was just coincidence you were there?"

"Yes."

"And what of your offer to help me? At the time, you had no idea of the commission." Her eyes narrowed as a suspicion came upon her. "Unless you overheard Henry and me talking in the rafters."

Erik's lack of response spoke volumes, but she wanted to hear him say it. "Well?" she pressed.

"You've told me that I am astute. I return the compliment." He sounded irritated that she had found him out. "Payment for helping you is a factor. I don't deny it. But there are other intangible rewards."

"Such as?"

"Play for me," he said.

"What?" Melodie stiffened when he grasped her shoulders, but his touch was gentle. As if bending to his will, she found herself seated at the piano, her hands lifted to the keys. His head had lowered next to hers but this time, she dared not look at him.

A hot breath caressed her ear as he spoke. "I want you to play." He paused, and softened the demand. "I ask you to play."

And so she did. She had never played a grand piano before. The rich sound was glorious. She didn't put any thought into choosing which piece to play; her fingers began to fly of their own accord. When her hands finally stilled, she belatedly recognized the music – her unfinished commission.

Glancing up, she felt Erik slide next to her on the bench. She started to rise, but he laid a restraining hand on her arm, silently requesting that she stay. She sank back down and sat motionless, entranced by the notes that surrounded her; they glided through the air, washed over her skin, flowed through her as well as around her. The music was haunting, beautiful, filled with aching sorrow. Her eyes brimmed with unexpected tears. When the final chord was played, it faded into the air, as if drawing its final breath.

They sat in hushed silence. Aware that something extraordinary had passed between them, Melodie feared that speaking would disintegrate the magical moment. But at last, she couldn't contain her curiosity. "Did you write that?" she asked.

"Yes."

Words could not describe how moved she was by his music, but she had to say something. "It was breathtaking," she murmured.

Erik did not respond to her comment. She gave her head a slight shake, and forced herself to return to reality. "You're more than 'somewhat of a composer', as you so clearly understated yesterday. I would be a fool to turn down your offer. I need someone to help me, and if you still want it, the position is yours."

"I do," he said in an even tone that betrayed no trace of emotion.

Melodie usually read people well, but this man gave away nothing. "There is the issue of where we can work," she mused out loud. The Anniston's home would not be possible. They were not aware of her commission, and she could only imagine the reception that Erik would receive at the door. *No, that would not do at all.*

Erik's voice broke into her thoughts. "Why not here?"

"Here? Are you mad?" she scoffed. "We're trespassing as it is. I keep expecting someone to burst in here and discover that we've broken in. You can't be serious."

"I'm quite serious. I wouldn't have brought us here if I hadn't been sure of our safety. I know the running of this theatre as if I managed it," he assured her. "The maestro is scheduled to be a guest conductor in Vienna next month. There won't be any rehearsals here until after his return."

"But what if someone comes in unexpectedly? The owner or someone else who decides to make a surprise visit?"

"Highly unlikely, but I concede it's a possibility," Erik admitted. "Unless you have another idea in mind, I can only offer one other alternative."

Having run short of other options, she would gladly hear his. "And what's that?"

"I have a piano at home. We could work there; however, it's a one-hour walk from central London. I wouldn't think it feasible for you."

"No, I suppose not." Melodie's hopes deflated. She couldn't afford to hire a coach every day for the next few weeks either.

She had to make a decision. Henry might find a student to help her, but she was nervous about delaying the work. Even with an immediate start, they would be rushed to meet the deadline. And while she wasn't sure of how trustworthy Erik was, he knew his way around music. At this point, she couldn't afford to refuse his offer. She reasoned that the situation suited her current purpose. After completing the commission, she could find someone else to work with on future projects.

Squaring her shoulders with firm resolve, she stuck out her hand. "I agree to your proposition. We'll work here." She waited until the warmth of his palm enveloped hers. She tried not to dwell on the fact that her hand felt lost within his grasp – or that the contact lasted a fraction too long. She disengaged her hand and adopted a note of professionalism in her voice. "So let us go over some details, such as the amount of your compensation. I'm prepared to be generous, as I wouldn't be able to accomplish this on my own."

As they continued their discussion, Melodie had the distinct feeling that she had no idea what she was getting in to. The next few weeks promised to be very interesting indeed.

Five

Erik swore to himself that he would keep his distance while he worked with Melodie. He didn't want to repeat what had happened the first time they had sat down at the piano together.

That morning, he had wanted to hear her play, almost demanded that she obey his wish. He had been deeply touched by the music that had risen from her fingertips. A locked chamber of his heart had slid open. With his defences lowered, he'd shared a passage of music that he'd written ages ago. His passion and loneliness had been wrapped in every note. When he'd finished, he'd been horrified by how much he'd revealed. Getting too close to Melodie and her music was a dangerous path – one that he had no intention of taking, no matter how strongly an undeniable part of him longed to.

Erik found it amusing that Melodie had achieved her commission through the deception of being a man. She claimed that it didn't bother her, so long as her work was appreciated. One day, she'd explained how it had all come about.

Colin Grayson, a member of parliament, had been invited to the Wentworth home for a luncheon. Henry overheard his remarks about planning a musical gift for the birthday party of his wife. Although he was overstepping his place, Henry approached Colin as the gentleman was leaving. Along with the man's hat and cloak, Henry passed some samples of Melodie's work. Colin's surprise was obvious, but he accepted them. In a few days, he returned to seek Henry out. Colin had asked someone to look over the excerpts and the recommendation had been glowing. When Colin asked for details about the composer, Henry used his imagination for guidance.

Apparently, Michael Blythe was a gifted composer, but a total recluse. All dealings and communications were done through Henry. The intriguing air of mystery may have served as a bonus. Colin hired Michael Blythe for a generous sum, considering he was yet an unknown name. He was commissioned to write a piece for a chamber orchestra, comprised of Mrs. Grayson's favourite instruments – harp, piano, violin, and cello.

Erik and Melodie worked long hours, side by side, on a daily basis for over two weeks. The score was essentially finished in that period, and just the final touches remained. To account for her time away from home, Melodie told the Annistons that she'd acquired a teaching position at a local music school. As long as it didn't detract from her lessons with their daughter, Mr. and Mrs. Anniston did not seem to mind.

Erik sat at the piano in the theatre, waiting for Melodie to arrive. Today would be their last day together. He tapped at the keys, his thoughts drifting. His only previous experience of working with someone had been in the role of a teacher. He had shaped and nurtured Christine's voice, coaxing her vocal chords to reach soaring heights. Manipulating her voice and susceptible mind had been far too easy.

With Melodie, the situation was different. She was the master of her composing, while he merely recorded the notes – or at least, that was what he had expected. On several occasions, she had asked for his suggestions. Though flattered, he hadn't outwardly shown he was pleased. He'd offered his critique when asked, but otherwise retreated to his role as recorder and nothing more.

Erik heard a noise. His head shot up, fingers halting in mid-air. He relaxed as he recognized the light fall of footsteps and the sound of a cane scratching against the floor.

Melodie appeared from the right wing of the stage, her face radiant even in the dim light. With a sense of detachment, Erik noticed that her choice of a chocolate brown dress did nothing for her appearance. Blue would be more flattering to her skin tone. Over the past fortnight, he'd learned that she indeed owned garments other than the standard issue white blouse and black skirt, but not many.

"Hello, Erik," she called out.

Her smile was open and friendly. Erik, in turn, closed himself off to her charm. "Good day," he said. He stood to allow her access to the piano bench.

After removing her cloak, she settled onto the seat. She hefted her leather case with some difficulty. The sheets of music were no longer stuffed into a basket. She'd indulged in the purchase of a proper casing so the papers did not have to be folded. During the course of completing the composition, the case had become bulky and heavy.

"Isn't this exciting?" Melodie continued to grin, and her eyes crinkled at the corners. "We'll be finished today. Then I'll take it straightaway to Henry, and they'll still have sufficient time to rehearse. I think Mrs. Grayson will be very pleased with her surprise."

"Let's get started, shall we?" Erik urged, wanting to dispense with conversational pleasantries. He was in a particularly foul mood today. And although he was self-aware enough to know the reason, stopping to think about it only worsened his ire.

Melodie blinked at him, her head cocked as if puzzled by the gruffness of his tone. For a moment, he thought she would question his abrupt attitude, but she seemed to think better of it.

"Certainly," she said. The single word sounded clipped. She pulled out several sheets of music from the case and spread them out on the top cover of the piano. "We left off yesterday debating about the closing section. Forte or pianissimo. Have you rethought your position?" she asked.

Erik's answer was blunt. "No."

They had opposing views on how the final bars would be played out. He felt the piece should end dramatically, with a strength that commanded attention. She thought it better to fade away, with a lone violin trailing into the distance.

Melodie puckered her lips, forming a perfect bow. "Not even in the slightest?" Irritation clouded her voice.

"No. Because I know I'm right," he said with a confidence that made him sound smug. He added, "Of course, you are the composer, not me. My opinion doesn't matter."

"I wish you would stop saying that. It *does* matter." She considered the issue. "But in this respect, I believe you're wrong. A strong finish is always expected, but what I've written for Mrs. Grayson calls for a more delicate hand. Pianissimo it shall be. I think I will even write it down myself."

She looked pleased with her decision, and turned her back to him. Erik emitted a soft snort.

"I heard that," she stated dryly.

Despite his brooding, he had to bite his lip to keep from chuckling.

They spent the next few hours going over details, finalizing all the loose ends. Melodie reworked phrases while Erik hunched over the scattered pages, pen flying to match her pace. He took no notice of the ink smearing his fingers or the kink in his lower back.

Whenever she stopped to mull something over, he found himself staring at her. Her dark, wide-set eyes were expressive pools, incapable of veiling her emotions. Whether they flashed in annoyance or shone with happiness, they never failed to reveal her inner self. Her complexion was fair, but a smattering of freckles across her nose and cheeks marred her otherwise creamy skin.

"Erik?"

At the sound of her questioning voice, he ripped his gaze away. He gripped the pen so tightly he was surprised it didn't snap in half.

"What?" Erik muttered. He rebuked himself for giving in to the distraction of her. This was precisely why he was thankful this relationship was ending. He recognized how ironic it was that he had been the one to pursue her so diligently; now, he couldn't wait to be free of her.

But that's not true, his mind mocked. He was also loath to leave her. While he'd found pleasure in her music, as he had suspected he would, he'd also enjoyed her company – enjoyed it far too much for someone who was destined to be alone. And therein lay the contradiction of his emotions. He didn't dare expose his heart again. No good could come of it.

"Is something wrong?" Melodie asked. Her eyebrows were knit with concern.

"No. Continue." Erik bit off the words, practically hurled them at her.

After twenty minutes, Melodie folded her hands in her lap. An air of satisfaction emanated from her.

"I believe we're done," she announced. "Can you think of anything I've overlooked?"

"No." Erik flung down the pen and rubbed at his fingers. He only succeeded in spreading the black stains, the ink setting into the grooves of his skin.

"What is wrong with you?" Melodie burst out. She whirled toward him. Tendrils of hair fell across her eyes, and she whisked them away with an impatient hand. "Have I offended you somehow?"

"No."

"You've done nothing but give me grunts and one-word answers," she said in exasperation. "I've made it clear that I value your views, yet I have to force them out of you. I don't understand your aloofness."

Erik closed his eyes briefly, shutting out the sight of her hurt and bewildered face. "I'm not a man of warmth and manners, mademoiselle. I've done my duty, and now our work is finished."

"Why do you not say my name?" she demanded.

He stiffened, taken aback by the question. "What?"

"My name. In all the hours and days we've spent together, it's never once crossed your lips. I find it odd."

Erik said nothing. He resorted to staring at her again. She remained oblivious, of course, looking at his general direction, seeming to regard the area near his ribs – where his heart should have been. At a loss for words, Erik remained mute. His muscles were rigid, making him feel akin to a marble statue.

They both flinched at the muffled thud of a door from within the back corridors of the theatre.

Someone was inside.

Melodie inhaled sharply. Erik snapped into action. He gathered up the papers and crammed them into the case. When Melodie leapt up to reach for their cloaks, her hip knocked the cane that had been propped against the piano. Erik reached out with lightning speed, snatching it up before it clattered to the floor.

"The lights," she whispered. She clutched the cloth bundle to her chest, her knuckles white.

Cursing under his breath, he lunged for the long handled snuffer and eliminated each flame. Wisps of smoke made his eyes sting. Thrown into darkness, he gave himself a few precious seconds to allow his vision to adjust. He could barely make out the shadow of Melodie's form. Grabbing her arm, he led her across the stage and through the opposite wing. He felt her stumble once and tightened his hold, raising her arm higher to help keep her upright. He didn't slow the pace.

The first door Erik found was locked. He raced to the next, fumbled with the handle, and exhaled with relief when it turned beneath his hand. He shoved his way into the room, pulling Melodie in after him. They were plunged into blackness when the door closed. Although light was visible at the bottom and one side of the doorway, it didn't permeate through the inky darkness.

Erik adjusted his breathing to shallow, indiscernible depths. While his breaths diminished, however, hers grew harsher with each second, as if she were choking. Frowning, he knelt down to lay the cane and leather-bound music at his feet. Then he grasped her shoulders and nudged her closer to the door. The vertical slat of light was so weak; he doubted that her poor eyesight could perceive it. No doubt her world had been submerged into a nightmare of complete blindness.

Melodie's head was down. Placing two fingers under her chin, Erik tilted her face up. She appeared to be struggling to breathe, though it was difficult to judge her exact expression.

"Calm yourself," he said, the order emerging as a rasp from his throat.

She jerked her head away, dropped her face from view again and bent forward, almost doubled over. Her head tossed back and forth. "I can't do this." Her voice was reedy, tremulous, woven with panic. She strained against his hold, as if about to launch herself at the door.

Voices were approaching. Words weren't distinguishable, but the source seemed to be two men.

Erik hauled her up against him more roughly than he had intended. "You're fine," he breathed in her ear. "Just hold onto me."

Taking his advice literally, Melodie's hands clutched at his shirtfront. The fine linen yanked so hard down his shoulders, he thought it would tear. She finally stilled in his arms. He felt her heart fluttering madly. Her cheek was flattened against his chest; quick puffs of hot breath penetrated his shirt.

His head lowered against his will, drawn by the alluring citrus scent of her silky hair. She always smelled fresh and intoxicating; one of the reasons why he avoided sitting close to her.

The voices and footsteps neared and then floated past their hiding place. Erik heard one of them mention retrieving something that had been forgotten. The sounds from the hallway became fainter, receding into the distance. Erik crept to the door. He opened it less than an inch, paused, and listened. Only silence met his ears.

"Wait here," he said. He kept his voice low. "I'll make sure they've gone."

"You're leaving me alone?" Terror edged into Melodie's voice again.

Erik opened the door wider, allowing more light to spill through. He could now discern the haunted expression in Melodie's rounded eyes. It was a look he was all too familiar with, yet it troubled him to see it reflecting from her.

"Stand by the door. Keep it open a few inches, but no more. I'll return shortly." He took one step and halted, a twinge of amusement curling his lip. "I'll have to ask that you release me, my dear."

Twin spots of rosy colour suffused each of her cheeks. She let go of his shirt and crossed her arms against her chest.

Erik slipped into the corridor. He stopped every so often to listen for any sign of the visitors. But it appeared they were alone in the theatre once more. Just to be certain, he circled the ground floor of the entire building. The Empire was a small theatre, so it only took a few minutes. Although it was possible the men had retreated to a room or some other corner of the establishment, it didn't seem likely.

Coming full circle to where he'd started, Erik was surprised to find the door shut. Melodie must have heard his approach. He mused that perhaps he wasn't as stealthy as he imagined himself to be. Easing the door open, he said, "All is clear. You can come out."

He expected her to meekly peek her head out, and thus wasn't prepared for the flash of brown that shot forth. When the small whirlwind slammed into him, he rocked backwards but managed to remain on his feet. She spun around before he could reach out to her, and hit the wall with her back. Sucking in air with gulping breaths, she sank to the floor and drew up her knees. She hid her face in the folds of her dress.

As Erik watched her tremble and shudder, he felt a stab of pity. It was an emotion he usually reserved for wounded animals. She, however, was a fully capable woman. "You're behaving like a child," he rebuked, his tone cold.

Melodie's head lifted just enough for her to speak. "I'm well aware of that. Thank you very much." She enunciated each word, sounding incensed. "Just give me a minute." And down went her head again, her forehead resting on her knees.

Leaving her to calm her own demons, Erik walked into the room to gather up their belongings. It was a tiny enclosure, bare of any furnishings. Aside from a lone bucket and a mop propped against one corner, it was empty. It was filthy as well, judging by the coating of dust and grime that marred his cloak. He retrieved it from the floor with a grimace, and swiped at it ineffectually. He completed the task slowly, giving Melodie time to collect herself. When he exited the room, she was on her feet, waiting for him. Her face appeared drawn and pinched, but he detected no trace of the frightened child that had clung to him in the dark.

Erik draped Melodie's cloak about her shoulders, and pressed the cane and leather case into her hands. She marched down the hall toward the back exit. Erik threw on his own cloak and trailed after her. Once outside, he used his version of a key to lock the door; it was a handy stick of metal, about four inches long with a curved tip. He'd used it countless times to manipulate the inner workings of locks and bolts – another skill that didn't endear him to respectable London society.

With eyes closed, Melodie turned her face up to the sky like a flower seeking the sun's rays. The afternoon was overcast. They stood in a gloomy alleyway, yet she seemed grateful for the freedom, breathing deeply. Erik supposed she was comforted by the daylight despite their dreary surroundings.

"I'm sorry for what happened back there," Melodie said. "You must think me a silly goose."

"Considering your situation, I suppose it's understandable," he said generously.

"My situation?"

He assumed he was stating the obvious. "Your blindness."

"Oh. Yes. I suppose there's that too." She seemed pensive, lost in thought.

Erik didn't understand her cryptic response. Before he could question it, she spoke briskly. "Well, it appears our work is complete. I'm not sure if I'll receive payment upon submission or after the performance. How shall I contact you?"

He considered his options and said, "There's a young lad that I sometimes hire to run errands for me. I'll have him go to you the morning after the performance."

"All right. And his name? You do know his name, I hope."

Erik couldn't believe she was baiting him. He spoke through gritted teeth. "It's Peter."

"Henry has been invited to the Grayson's for the party, and I'll be accompanying him. I don't suppose you would consider joining us?" she asked.

"I think not," Erik said. He had no desire to be the centre of attention at a party.

"I wanted to extend the invitation anyway." Melodie cleared her throat. "It's been good working with you. It truly has. You've done more than simply write down the notes. Your advice has been invaluable. I hope that someday you'll be able to share your gift with others. Good luck to you, Erik."

Although Erik wondered whether her speech had been rehearsed, it at least sounded sincere. He drank in her features for the final time. "And to you," he said softly.

Deciding he did not wish to watch her walk away, he pivoted around and departed from her first. Each step that increased the distance between them firmed his resolve. He'd been complacent for too long. It was time for a change.

When Erik thought about what he would miss the most about Melodie, the first thing that sprang to mind was so ridiculous, he grunted with self-derision.

Her freckles.

Six

Standing in front of the full-length mirror, Melodie placed her hands on her waist and tilted her head, pretending to admire her form. It was a pity that she could see nothing beyond a golden blur. She leaned in for a closer look, and her gaze fell to the neckline of her dress. Her eyes popped with surprise as she noted the swell of her bosom; it had never been so prominently on display before.

At the knock on the door, she snapped back to an upright position. "Come in," she called out. The door opened and a single clap of hands reached her ears.

"Melodie, you look wonderful," Trina Anniston exclaimed, the delight evident in her voice.

"You really think so?"

"I do. While I always loved that dress, the colour made me look washed out. But with your darker hair, the yellow suits you perfectly."

Melodie smoothed one palm over her hip. The richness of the silk felt exquisite, yet odd. She felt out of place wearing such a garment; she might be a swan on the exterior, but still remained the gangly duckling on the inside.

She traced the neckline with her index finger. "Do you not think this is too low?"

"Nonsense," Trina told her. "It's an evening gown. And a modestly cut one, at that. Come and sit here. I'd like to arrange your hair."

Melodie took a seat in front of the vanity. The older woman's hand ran lightly atop her head. "Lovely and thick," Trina murmured, gliding a brush through the tresses. "Grace never sits still long enough to permit me to do this. That child has the most unruly hair imaginable. Takes after her father, I'm afraid."

"This really isn't necessary," Melodie began to say.

Trina interrupted her. "Shush, or I might accidentally jab you with a hairpin."

Melodie gave in and held herself as still as possible. She would have been content to wear something from her own wardrobe, but when Trina had heard about tonight's party, she set her own plans in motion. This morning, Trina had gathered up an armful of dresses in a rainbow of colours. The silks and muslins had been deposited on Melodie's bed with the instruction that she choose one; a seamstress would drop by the next hour to make any necessary alterations. Though Melodie had protested, her words had fallen on deaf ears.

"One last pin should do it," Trina announced. "There. You look much more elegant with your hair upswept. Would you care to take a look?"

Melodie took the hand mirror and perused her image. With the hair up, she looked more mature, and the line of her neck seemed longer. She wasn't able to regard the whole effect of her transformation, but of what she could view, she thought she might pass for pretty tonight.

Smiling, she patted Trina's arm. "I adore it. Thank you so much."

"You're welcome. Now, I want you to know this dress is yours."

Melodie almost dropped the mirror. She set it on the vanity before risking her luck for the next seven years. "What? I couldn't possibly – "

"Hear me out, dear," Trina cut in again, her tone gentle. "I know you wouldn't feel comfortable tonight wearing a borrowed dress, so you need to know it's your own. And don't be concerned by a stain or two."

"Stain?" Melodie questioned, appalled by the mere thought of soiling the dress.

"Oh yes. It's a party, and that means food and drink. It's almost inevitable that someone will spill a drop of wine on you, or a clumsy gentleman will step on your hem and cause a tear. But don't fret about it." Trina's voice became wistful. "In any case, I don't have the figure of my youth. It's silly of me to keep all these dresses. I thought Grace might wear them one day, but they'll be horribly out of fashion by then. You've been wonderful with my daughter, so I'm pleased to do this for you."

Melodie was touched by the gesture. "You're too kind."

After a final tweaking of a stray hairpin, Trina bustled about once more. "Don't forget your gloves. Henry is waiting for you in the parlour. Oh, I almost forgot."

Another item, this one tiny and rounded, found its way to Melodie's palm. "Dip your finger in this," Trina instructed, "and put some of it on your lips. It will give them a hint of pinkness and shine. It's very subtle, I promise."

Trina exited the room, the door clicking shut behind her. Intrigued by this mysterious substance, Melodie picked up the mirror once more and carefully applied it to her lips. It felt a bit waxy, but as promised, its effect was not overpowering. As she regarded the reflection of her mouth, a sudden vision of Erik's curving lips swam before her.

Horrified, Melodie hurled down the mirror, grateful when it didn't shatter to pieces. She refused to think about him tonight.

Melodie pushed back the chair and sprang to her feet. Every time she recalled their last day together, her face burned with humiliation. She'd made a fool of herself. Besides which, the man was completely maddening. She had been excited by the fire and vivacity in his music, and had anticipated their partnership would be equally stimulating. It hadn't turned out that way at all. Erik had been aloof and abrupt, not quite to the point of being rude, but erecting an effective barrier that kept her at bay.

She wondered whether anyone would ever take the effort to peel away his complex layers. And what would one find at the core – a buried treasure or a hollow, desolate soul of a man?

Why am I still thinking about him?

"Honestly, Mellie, you're hopeless," she stated out loud, aggravated with herself.

She sought out her gloves, and then proceeded to greet Henry in the parlour.

Melodie had been surprised to find not only Henry, but a carriage waiting for her as well. Albert Wentworth had been delighted to learn that she would be accompanying Henry, and insisted on hiring a separate transport for them. He was often generous that way and treated his loyal head steward very well.

The carriage came to a halt at their destination. As the coachman jumped down and opened the door, Melodie could hear a mingling of voices and trills of laughter from outside. Henry stepped out first. She was thankful for his steady hand as he guided her down. Her dress was more voluminous than what she was accustomed to, making her feel awkward. Combined with a corset that sought to implode her ribs, she was breathless and uncomfortable.

Melodie slipped her arm through Henry's. They took their time walking, surrounded by other guests that were also converging on the country manor. The evening air was cool and refreshing. "I didn't think politicians made this much money," Melodie commented, her tone wry. "Describe the estate to me, Henry."

"Apparently, he comes from a wealthy family," Henry explained. "It's a little too dark to see clearly, but the grounds seem very large indeed. It took a good two minutes to arrive here from the main road. We're just passing a fountain now. We'll be at the house soon." Henry paused in his narrative, and then added, "It's quite massive. I hate to think how many rooms there are to clean."

Melodie chortled softly. She squirmed as the dress tightened across her chest. "Don't make me laugh. I'm ready to burst at the seams as it is."

They joined a queue at the door, and shuffled their way to the front.

"May I see your invitation, sir?" the butler intoned. He sounded bored, indifferent to the liveliness of the partygoers around him.

A booming shout carried across the front hall. "It's all right! Send them through."

Still linked with Henry's arm, Melodie followed him inside. The man with the frantic voice led them aside. "Henry, thank God you're here. Something disastrous has happened."

"What's wrong?" Henry asked.

"Some idiot coachman managed to crush the pianist's hand in the carriage door. The poor girl was beside herself. The doctor's been here and patched her up. I've already sent her home." He spoke in a heated rush. "I thought you might know of someone who could replace her. I know it's next to impossible at this hour, but I'm desperate."

"Erm, well…"

"Or could it still be done without a piano?" the man asked.

Aghast at the suggestion, Melodie said, "It doesn't work that way. Forgive me, I don't mean to be rude."

Henry intervened with haste. "Allow me to make the introduction. Melodie, this is Colin Grayson."

Her hand was lifted and kissed, judging by the slight pressure on her glove.

"It's a pleasure to meet you," Colin said. "Excuse my manners. I'm not normally so abrupt. I'm just terribly disappointed. Everything had been going so well, and now this."

A plan started to brew in Melodie's mind. It was bold. It was perhaps foolhardy. But it could work.

"I think I can help you," she said.

"How?" Colin asked.

"I'm Michael Blythe's assistant. I'm familiar with this piece and am confident that I could fill the role of your pianist."

There was an acute tugging on her arm. "Mellie, could I speak to you for a moment?" Henry interjected. "Excuse us, Mr. Grayson." After taking several steps to one side, he murmured, "Do you really think this wise?"

Melodie wasn't sure that wisdom had anything to do with it, but she was determined. "I came here tonight to hear my work performed in public. I have no intention of leaving without that satisfaction, even if I have to do it myself."

"I understand. Really, I do," Henry said. "But...Michael Blythe's assistant?"

Melodie heard the questioning tone in his voice. She had not planned to concoct another deceitful tale. "I had to give some explanation for knowing the music," she said, bristling in defense. "I can't very well say I'm going to sight read."

"True," Henry conceded. "I suppose there's no harm in it. And you'll certainly save the evening. I'm sure Mr. Grayson will be most grateful."

Colin was indeed happy with the turn of events, though he expressed it in a restrained way. Melodie assumed he must be skeptical of her claim. Considering her blindness, she couldn't blame him for any reservations he might have.

As Colin guided them down another hallway, he stated that the remaining three musicians were anxiously waiting in the ballroom. They weren't sure if they would still be performing or if their duties would be cancelled.

Melodie tried to calm herself as she entered the large room. She wished she could take in her surroundings. She'd never stepped into a ballroom before. A buzzing of voices from across the room faded as their small party approached. Colin introduced everyone, and Henry led her to the piano.

Melodie stripped off her gloves and set them aside with her cane. She took a few seconds to steady herself, and then began to play. Ten bars later, she stopped at the touch of a hand on her shoulder.

"Thank you, Melodie," Colin said, sounding earnest. "I believe you're hired."

Colin departed to attend to his guests and Melodie talked with the others. There was some concern over the fact that they'd never played together. When one of them suggested a brief rehearsal now, the idea was rejected. They did not have enough time, and they couldn't risk being overheard; the element of surprise was key, after all. Melodie pointed out that any faltering in their playing would probably not be discernible to the general public.

The guests would be ushered in to the ballroom at eight o'clock; that left a half hour to fill. Feeling restless, Melodie walked with Henry to the area where refreshments were being served. He fetched her a drink, and she sipped at the glass of punch. Henry then offered her some type of hors d'oeuvre that smelled like sausage. She wrinkled her nose with distaste.

If she attempted to eat, with the combination of bone-crushing corset and jittery nerves, the consequence would not be pleasant.

Among the throng of invited guests, David Wentworth stood with a drink in hand, almost bored to tears. The room glowed with a combination of gas lamps and an array of candles. A long table covered with a lacy white tablecloth held an assortment of delicacies. Everything was polished and carefully arranged, designed to impress the finicky crowd.

David regarded them with a critical eye. The stodgy old men strutted around like peacocks full of hot air and self-importance. Their matronly wives twittered around them, glittering in their finest jewels.

David exhaled a pained sigh. This could possibly be the most boring party he'd ever had the displeasure of attending. *At least the liquor is good.* Throwing his head back, he gulped down the remainder of his second glass of brandy since his arrival.

He raised his empty glass to a nearby server. "I'll have another," he ordered.

Without looking, he could feel his father's glare of disapproval. "I know what you're thinking, Father, but allow me this one indulgence. You dragged me here against my will, after all."

Albert's back was ramrod stiff, and when he spoke, his tone was equally hardened. "It would have been rude of you to refuse the invitation."

David grimaced. "Yes, and appearances mean everything. We're just the perfect family. Isn't that right?" Sarcasm dripped from his voice.

His mother touched his sleeve. "Please, can we be civil for one night?" Ellen pleaded. Her gaze was beseeching, her eyebrows winged in an arch.

David resisted rolling his eyes. "I promise to be on my best behaviour."

He resumed scanning the room. Surely there were some women closer to his age milling about. His eyes flitted from one female prospect to the next, finding a fatal flaw in each of them. *Too fat. Too tall. Too ugly. Laughs like a horse.*

David shook his head with disgust. *Too depressing.* His father's ire be damned, he should have stayed in tonight – or even better, gone to Diana's salon. He had a standing invitation there.

Where is that blasted server? If he was going to survive this evening, he needed another drink. *Hold on. What have we here?*

David's gaze focused on a solitary woman standing apart from the crowd. She caught his attention, perhaps for the very reason that she wasn't huddled in a group, prattling on about the latest scandal. *A little on the short side. Slender, yet deliciously curved in all the right places. A black walking stick. Interesting.*

Her face was in profile, and when her head swung toward him, he thankfully noted that she was attractive. She seemed rather familiar as well.

David's mouth fell open at the precise moment that he realized who she was. With the elegant hairstyle and fancy gown, he hadn't recognized her.

He turned to his father. "You didn't tell me she was going to be here."

Albert broke off his conversation with Ellen, looking distracted. "What? Who do you mean?"

"Melodie."

"Didn't I? I'm sure I must have mentioned it." Albert swivelled his head. "She's here, then? I must say hello."

David glanced over in her direction again, just in time to see her hurry away. "Don't bother. She's gone now," he said. "So why is she here?"

"Henry brought her. And I distinctly remember telling you why Henry was invited. If you don't remember that, I suggest you clean out your ears or remain sober for a change."

"Albert," Ellen said, sounding dismayed. She patted her dove-grey hair and darted her eyes about, as if worried that someone had overheard her husband's remark.

Though David stiffened, he was an expert at pretending his father's jabs failed to wound. He kept his head high, and said, "It's all right, Mother. No harm done. If you'll excuse me."

David couldn't get away fast enough. Every word from his father was coloured with a thinly veiled insult. He had endured criticisms and negativity all his life, yet to everyone else, Albert Wentworth was magnanimous to a fault. David had learned long ago that he would never please his father, so he'd given up trying.

The guests in the reception hall began to disperse. They headed through the wide French doors to the hallway. Apparently, it was time for the surprise event. David surveyed the room, searching for a servant. He hoped to squeeze in another drink, but all the servers had disappeared.

David grumbled under his breath and followed the crowd. If the sight of Melodie hadn't intrigued him, he would have had their coachman take him back to the city and drop him off at Diana's. Now, he supposed he would have to endure the evening a while longer. After this next dull interlude, he would find Melodie and learn what she'd been up to since making her escape.

Escape.

Another bolt of envy rippled through him. He found it infuriating that a slip of a servant girl could make him seethe with jealousy.

David strode into the ballroom. Chairs were set up in rows; the guests took their seats. He sat down and craned his neck, trying to locate Melodie. He didn't see her anywhere. He noted the small stage up front where musicians stood with their respective instruments. David gave way to a yawn. His assumption had been right; this would definitely be boring.

Taking a closer look at the figure seated at the piano, his mind boggled with surprise.

Melodie...What on earth...?

Erik patted the sleek muscled neck of his horse. He'd acquired the stallion two days ago. Considering the distance they had traversed, he was pleased that the animal had barely broken a sweat. Erik tethered him to a nearby tree, and gave the animal a final pat before heading across the grounds of the estate. His boots sunk into the soft earth with each step. The moon shone brightly tonight, bathing everything in a liquid shimmer; even the shadows weren't as dark as he preferred.

It hadn't been difficult to find out where Colin Grayson lived; what had been difficult was making the decision to come. In the end, Erik couldn't resist this one chance to hear 'Celebration' performed to an appreciative crowd.

He was approaching the rear of the vast house. He vaulted with ease over the low stone rail surrounding the terrace. Pressing close to the wall, he drew near the open glassed doors. His timing had been excellent. The introduction was just being made now.

Erik leaned back, allowing himself to relax as the music started. He swayed slightly to the music. The piano sounded striking. And strangely familiar.

He edged closer to the doorway and took a calculated risk by briefly exposing his unmasked eye. Recognizing the face bent in concentration over the piano, his lips tightened. *Did she plan this all along? Why did she not mention performing the piece as well as composing it?*

Before withdrawing, Erik's gaze roamed over the ballroom in appreciation of its sheer beauty. He found it gratifying that the performance was being held in surroundings of such elegance. It was a world that he feared was forever beyond his reach.

Breathe, Mellie.

Melodie sat at the piano and waited for the doors to open. She tried to control her ragged breathing. Her palms were damp with sweat. Wondering if anyone was watching her, she discreetly brushed at her dress, as if smoothing out the wrinkles. The man next to her – the violinist – coughed and shifted his feet.

At last, the doors were thrown open and a thrum of voices could be heard as the crowd was directed to their seats. Melodie sat up straighter. She swallowed with difficulty. She had never performed before an audience, and this was not exactly the general public, as she'd so casually stated to her fellow orchestral group. This was an invitation-only private party for friends and colleagues of a government official.

Colin's voice rang out above the hum and the noise hushed immediately. "Ladies and gentlemen. Friends. Thank you for joining me today in honour of my wife's birthday. We are both delighted that you've come. For the highlight of this evening, I'm pleased to present my gift to her – the commission of a new work by a talented but unknown composer named Michael Blythe. I daresay after tonight, he won't be quite so unknown. Without further adieu, here is the debut of 'Celebration'."

Melodie had never thought she could consider blindness to be an advantage until this moment. Unable to scan the intimidating sea of faces, she imagined she played for herself alone. She was fine once her trembling hands touched the keys. The next twenty-three minutes rushed by in a blur. It was wonderful to play within a group and hear her composition come to life. She relished every note, not wanting to miss a fraction of the experience.

And when the violin's final lone note receded into thin air, Melodie realized it was over.

Several belated seconds later, the audience erupted into clamorous applause. Melodie flinched at the sudden uproar. She was soon swept up in hugs and the shaking of hands by each of the musicians. Congratulations were extended all around and she thanked them for allowing her to join them. She reached for her cane and held it tightly, finding comfort in its familiarity; all this attention was overwhelming.

"Mellie, that was smashing! I'm so proud of you."

Melodie smiled in recognition of Henry's voice. As he embraced her, she nuzzled against the crook of his neck and inhaled his faint scent of peppermint – another warm and familiar comfort.

"Could you tell I was nervous?" she asked.

"Not at all," he assured her. "You were the picture of serenity."

Another voice joined them. Colin spoke loudly to be heard above the din of the crowd. "Melodie, you saved the evening. I can't thank you enough. May I present my wife. She wanted to meet you."

Feeling stilted, Melodie dipped an awkward curtsey. "It's an honour, ma'am."

"The honour is mine. My husband tells me you're blind. How extraordinary that you play so beautifully," Mrs. Grayson said with genuine warmth. "I couldn't have asked for a better gift. I would love to meet Mr. Blythe sometime. Do you think it might be possible?"

"I'm afraid not. He values his privacy," Melodie said. The falsehood slipped off her tongue with ease.

Colin made an odd sound in the back of his throat. "But surely he realizes that anonymity will do nothing to further his career."

Melodie's mind twirled as she tried to concoct a reasonable tale. She was becoming such a master of deception, she almost believed in Michael Blythe's existence. "He thinks his music should speak for itself. And he feels that should others be interested in his work, they'll come to him." Aware that she was painting an arrogant picture, she hastened to add, "Of course, he's grateful for the opportunity you've provided him tonight. Hopefully word of his talent will spread."

Colin's ruffled feathers seemed to subside. "Your Mr. Blythe isn't much of a business man, but there's no denying his talent. I wish him well. This, Melodie, is for you."

Melodie accepted what felt like a velvet bag. It was heavy and jingled, as if filled with coins. "What is it?" she asked.

"Payment for your services tonight."

Surprised, she had to protest. "But you've already paid me. I mean, you made your payment when the score was submitted."

"Yes, but that didn't include your unexpected role tonight. This is for you, not Mr. Blythe," Colin said, emphasizing the point. "I insist you accept it. I would be offended if you didn't."

Well, I don't want to offend the man. And Melodie supposed she'd earned it. "All right. Thank you very much."

After a last curtsey, she waited until she was sure the Graysons were engrossed in another conversation. Turning to Henry, she gave in to her excitement. "The bag is so heavy, Henry. Do you think it's a good sum?"

"I don't doubt it."

"Would it be terribly vulgar to count it out here, you think?" she asked in a serious tone.

"Mellie," he admonished.

Giggling, Melodie thrust the bag into his hands. "I'm joking. Would you take it for me, please? Oh, excuse me," she said, jostled to the side as someone bumped against her. It was becoming too warm in the room. The air seemed to grow thicker with the dense clustering of bodies. She squeezed the cane until her fingers grew numb. "Do you see a terrace nearby?" she asked.

Henry replied after a beat of hesitation. "Yes, I see one. Are you all right?"

"I'm fine. It's just a little stifling in here." She waved her fingers in front of her face. "Could you lead me to the doors?"

Melodie reached the open doorway. As she gulped in the night air, her sense of suffocation subsided.

"Shall I get you a drink?" Henry offered. "Water, perhaps?"

"Yes, thank you," she replied.

Lured by the breeze, Melodie stepped outside and walked across the terrace. Once her cane bumped against an obstruction, she put out her hand and felt smooth horizontal stone beneath her palm. She'd reached the outer perimeter. She set down the cane, propped both elbows on the flat surface, and leaned forward. Humming to herself, she gazed out into nothingness, trying to imagine what lay beyond her – a garden, perhaps, with lots of trees and greenery. She imagined it would be a divine place to do some composing.

A male voice sprang out of nowhere. "It appears congratulations are in order."

Melodie whirled around. Though she felt a sudden chill, the cause wasn't the night air.

He didn't have to identify himself. She would know that voice anywhere.

Still hidden from view, Erik listened with a satisfied ear to the resounding response of the audience. It appeared that 'Celebration' had been a great success.

Erik risked another glance into the ballroom. He watched as a congratulatory crowd engulfed Melodie, and he soon lost sight of her.

Lingering for a while, he replayed the music in his mind. Finally, afraid that someone would wander outside, he decided to make his retreat. He crossed the terrace, lifting his eyes to the towering statue at the far end. He paused to admire it. *Apollo, god of Music. How fitting.*

At the sound of footsteps behind him, Erik lunged forward and ducked behind the protective shelter of the bronze god. When he peered around it, he found himself gazing at Melodie. She looked charming, though her gown had too many frills and ribbons, making her seem girlish. A plainer dress would better allow her subtle loveliness to shine. The colour choice of buttery yellow was flattering, at least. As for the upswept hair, it served to elongate her neck, but he preferred to see it loose over her shoulders.

He considered going to her; she had extended an invitation for him to come. But he'd already said his goodbye once, and that had been difficult enough; it would be torturous to repeat it here.

Ready to slip down to the grassy lawn, Erik froze at the sound of a man's voice.

"It appears congratulations are in order."

Erik turned back around and fastened his eyes on the intruder. A well-dressed young man approached with twin champagne glasses in hand. Fair skinned, with sandy blonde hair tied at the nape of his neck, he ventured forth with confidence.

Erik stared at him. The man reminded him of someone.

Raoul. He looks like Raoul.

A flash of memory flared through Erik. *The rooftop of the Paris opera house. Raoul and Christine. Betrayal, despair, mindless rage.*

Emotions from that devastating scene bubbled up once more, seeped through every fibre of his skin. The pain of it took his breath away so sharply, he almost missed Melodie's reaction.

"What are you doing here?" she asked.

Erik tossed his head, trying to shake off the cobwebs of the past so he could concentrate on what was happening right before him. He moved beyond the edge of the statue. He knew he was partially visible, but was beyond caring.

"I could ask you the same thing," the man countered.

Melodie looked apprehensive. "I don't wish to speak with you. I came out here for some privacy, so go away."

Erik was pleased that Melodie did not welcome the man's attentions. His keen eyes flickered back to her partner in this wary dance.

As the young man bent to hand her a glass, he said, "But I've brought you a drink."

"What is it?" she asked, closing her fingers around the stem.

Erik wondered what Melodie was up to. The fact that she had accepted the glass surprised him.

"Champagne," the man replied.

The word barely left his mouth before Melodie threw the liquid in his face. Gasping, blinking madly, he swiped at his sopping cheeks and chin.

Erik snickered under his breath. *Clever girl.* Melodie had used the man's voice to reveal the exact location of his face. Her precision had been remarkable.

Bravo, my dear.

"You little bitch!" The spurned suitor grabbed hold of Melodie's arm, yanking her toward him. He drew back his other hand.

Erik darted out even further from his hidden post. He growled from the depths of his throat, sounding feral and threatening. "*Salaud,*" he cursed. If that bastard struck her, left one bruise on her fragile skin, his life was finished.

Though Erik had spoken softly, the relative silence of the outdoors allowed the minutest sound to carry through the air. As the man's head jerked up, Erik retreated slightly. His cloak billowed out, caught on a gust of wind. He stilled it with one hand.

The man dropped Melodie's arm as if he'd been burned. His other hand fell limply to his side. "Did you hear that?" he muttered. "I thought I saw something move."

Melodie replied with disdain. "You drink far too much. It's affecting your brain."

The man didn't comment. He gazed at the statue once more, his expression discomfited.

Erik thought the man might come over to investigate. *Let him come.* He almost welcomed the confrontation.

A new voice entered the tense arena, disrupting the moment.

"Mellie, sorry I was delayed. Oh…David. Good evening."

Erik recognized the older gentleman – Henry. He also came bearing a drink, though it appeared to be harmless water. His greeting was polite but cool.

David did not seem to be a popular man.

"Henry," David acknowledged. "You must be proud of your Mellie. I didn't know she'd be performing tonight."

"I'm always proud." Henry peered at the younger man. "Are you ill? Your face seems rather damp."

David brushed at his cheek with the cuff of his dresscoat. "It was overly warm in the ballroom. That's why I strolled out for some air. Melodie, it's been a pleasure getting reacquainted, but I should get back. I bid you both goodnight." With a bow, he turned and stalked away.

"What was that about?" Henry questioned, sounding concerned. "Was he bothering you?"

Melodie's shoulders slumped forward, as if finally able to relax with David gone. "No. He was congratulating me on a job well done."

Henry's expression was one of disbelief. "I'm not sure I believe you. Not when your glass is empty and his chin was dripping."

Erik had to resist the urge to laugh at Melodie's obvious glee in hearing that observation. She was grinning, her eyes lit with mirth.

"Really? Was it dripping? It must be terribly embarrassing to literally drip with sweat. Poor man," she crooned.

"Indeed," said Henry dryly. He took the long stemmed glass from her hand and replaced it with the goblet of water. "Since I doubt you've actually imbibed any liquid, you must be parched. Drink up. Now, I have the most exciting news for you. It's why I was detained. I believe I may have secured your next commission."

Melodie almost choked on the water. "What? How?" she spluttered.

"Two gentlemen just approached me. They're in the midst of building a theatre and want to commission a new work for the opening night gala." Henry spoke rapidly. "They were impressed by what they heard tonight and want to hire Michael Blythe."

"I can't believe this," Melodie said, fingers fluttering at her throat. "It's what I hoped for, but I didn't think it would happen so soon. What are they looking for?"

A smile spread across Henry's weathered face, as if he knew the answer would please her. "A symphony."

Melodie's squeal of joy caused Erik's lip to curl upward; she'd been reduced to a little girl, ribbons and all.

"A *symphony*! Henry, you know that's always been a dream of mine." Melodie threw her arms around the chuckling man. Water splashed across his shoulder. She stepped back, her expression contrite. "Sorry."

Henry extracted a handkerchief from his pocket and blotted at the darkened spot. "Quite all right, although you're a bit of a menace tonight."

Melodie sighed. "What a night. So much has happened." She brushed at her bare arms with her hands, and shivered. "It's getting chilly. Shall we go back in?"

After retrieving her cane, she took Henry's proffered arm. They headed for the doors, continuing to chat until they disappeared from view.

Alone once more, Erik stood motionless within Apollo's shadow. Minutes passed, and an itch began to plague him, just below his right eye. The irritation swelled, needling him, until he almost ripped the mask from his face. Instead, he stood there, back to back with the statue, imprisoned by his own harsh breathing.

His goal tonight had been accomplished, yet he felt no sense of satisfaction. Seeing Melodie again had ruined the pleasure of simply enjoying the performance. He had thought she would be an unseen face in the audience. Even then, perhaps he wouldn't have been able to resist searching her out for a last glimpse. But he certainly had not predicted the drama that had played out on the terrace stage.

Erik told himself he should be happy for Melodie. Her deception had proved to be successful and her next work had already been commissioned. Yet, if he was honest, he admitted a twinge of envy. Her future appeared to be bright and promising. His own path led to a great, gaping black hole – an unknown void.

A road he was destined to travel alone.

Erik slammed a fist into the unyielding base of the statue, disappointed that his leather glove softened the impact. *Useless, weak self-pity.* He'd already wallowed in it for far too long and had vowed never to step foot in it again. *Putain!*

The mental curse roused him out of idleness. With a running leap, he jumped over the rail and landed on the lawn below. He slipped through the shadows, avoided patches of ghostly light, and blended in with the cover of night. A faint fragrance of roses teased his senses as he passed near the garden. The scent invoked some unnamed emotion from deep within, but just as it began to stir, he roughly shoved it back down. He'd done enough reminiscing for one evening.

His waiting horse nickered at his approach, its sensitive ears flicking back. Erik greeted the animal with a gentle stroke on the sloped head. He untied the rein and led the horse by foot through the trees. He didn't want to start riding until he reached the main road.

The front area of the house was packed with carriages. Coachmen and valets mingled about, chattering and guffawing as they waited for the party to disperse.

As Erik passed by, his attention was caught by a small disturbance. A coachman stood next to his carriage with arms crossed against his chest. A taller man was in front of him, his back to Erik, hand waving about in agitation. They appeared to be arguing.

"I'm telling you, they'll be starting to come out any minute. The answer is no," the coachman was saying, undisguised irritation in his voice.

"I'll double the price," exclaimed the other man.

"Mr. Wentworth, please. Just go back inside and wait for your parents," the coachman implored. "If you still want to make your visit, I'll drop you off on the way back. I'm not about to leave now."

"Bloody hell," came the muttered oath.

Erik regarded the petulant boy with contempt. *David Wentworth.* Melodie hadn't revealed much about her past, but she had mentioned previously living with the Wentworths and that Henry remained on staff with them. Erik could now tie some of the loose threads together.

With a jolt, Erik realized that David was heading his way. Erik angled further into the nest of trees. He threw the hood of his cloak over his head.

David was mumbling and staggering, holding out an arm to help balance himself.

As David ventured deeper into the secluded area, Erik had to wonder what his purpose was. When he received his answer, his eyes rolled and he quickly averted his gaze; the man was relieving himself.

When David finished, he turned and stumbled, steadying himself with an outstretched hand upon a tree trunk. Propping himself against it, he fished inside the inner breast pocket of his dresscoat. He withdrew a small flask, tipped his head back, and gulped the contents. He appeared to be in no hurry to leave.

As Erik stared at him, he was aware the itch beneath the mask had returned. His breaths grew shallow as an icy calm descended upon him.

How easy it would be to kill the boy.

It would be swift, painless, perhaps too merciful for one who dared to harass an innocent woman.

He needed no weapons, not even his trusty lasso.

Not when he had the use of both of his capable hands.

Erik stood motionless; only his hands twitched, flexing within the confines of his gloves. He was locked in an internal battle. Yes, the boy was arrogant, foolish, and needed to be taught some manners. That didn't mean he deserved to die.

But seeing his blood spilled would bring you satisfaction. Isn't that what you were seeking tonight?

The unbidden thought confused him. Cold sweat popped out on his forehead. No, that wasn't what he'd sought in coming here. What was wrong with him?

As Erik recognized what was happening, pinpricks of fear stabbed at him; it was the beginning of that sickening downward spiral that reduced him to blind, murderous rage. In the past, he'd allowed the fury to consume him, like a fire blazing through a forest and leaving nothing but smouldering ash in its wake.

It would be so easy to succumb to that slippery descent.

Squeezing his eyes shut, Erik fought against the seductive call of madness, for that was what lay at the bottom of the well. If he were to fall into its black depths again, his fate would be sealed. He struggled to think of something good, something filled with light that would ease his mind.

Christine…

No, she was dead to him. She couldn't help him.

Think of something comforting.

He almost laughed. Almost sobbed. There had been no comforts in his life.

A woman sits at the piano; brown eyed and freckled, her hair spills in silken waves down her back. She smells like a clear, spring day – sunny and warm. Her graceful hands fly across the keys and the beauty of her music wraps around him, giving him comfort and peace.

Erik opened his eyes, dazed, weary, as if he'd just trudged off the battlefield. He had no idea how much time had passed. A minute or an hour? His gaze came to rest on David, who remained slumped against the same tree. *It couldn't have been overly long then.*

Erik regarded the young man and was relieved to find his emotions on a more even keel. There was no question of his intense dislike, but the blood red haze that drove him to kill no longer possessed him. Erik emitted a shaky breath. It was time to head for home.

A twig snapping beneath his foot sounded like a gunshot.

Even as David's head swivelled toward him, Erik had spun around and jumped onto the saddle. With a swift jab of his heels into the stallion's flanks, they galloped away. The hooves kicked up clomps of grass, then great clouds of dust, as they veered onto the path that led to the road.

Although voices of alarm were raised, they soon faded into the distance. Erik's hood had blown back off his head. His cloak snapped behind him. He pressed his face closer to the straining muscles of the horse's neck, but didn't look back.

He should have learned that lesson long ago.

Seven

"Isabel, what time is it?" Melodie asked. She hoped she sounded nonchalant.

"Ten minutes since the last time you asked me," Isabel replied, wry humour evident in her voice.

Melodie sat at a table in the kitchen, keeping her hands busy by folding a pile of linen napkins. She was waiting for Peter – the boy that Erik would be sending to collect his earnings. She'd asked the butler to have him come around to the back door when he arrived. It was past eleven in the morning now and still no sign of him.

She heard Isabel bustling about amidst the metallic clanging of pots. "No, not that one," Isabel directed one of the kitchen maids. "No, no, on your right. Yes, thank you. So when was this boy supposed to come?"

Melodie realized the question was directed at her. "Sometime this morning," she said, her response deliberately vague.

By way of explanation, Melodie had told Isabel that she'd recruited a new student. He would meet her here, and then they would go together to the school. It was a weak tale, but so far, no one had questioned her about it.

As Melodie's nimble fingers folded the squares of cloth in a repetitive motion, her mind wandered. Last night had been such an eventful evening. The thrill of her moment in the spotlight hadn't quite left her yet. She'd caught herself several times this morning with a dreamy smile on her face.

At the knock on the door, Melodie pushed to her feet. The door creaked open, and Isabel's voice rang out. "What can I do for you?"

"I'm looking for Melodie," piped up a child's voice. Not having reached adolescence yet, the pitch was high.

Melodie gathered up her cane and reticule, and rushed to Isabel's side. "Are you Peter?" Melodie asked.

"That's me," the boy confirmed.

"Thank you, Isabel. I'll see you later." Before any questions could arise, Melodie stepped through the doorway. Stretching out one hand, she found a rather bony shoulder and steered him away. "Come, Peter, let's go."

"But I – "

Melodie cut off his protest. "No arguments, please. Follow me." Waiting until the door closed behind her, she halted on the path and knelt down to his level.

"Are you blind?" Peter asked. He was forthright in a way that children often were.

"Yes, but not completely. If I get close, like this..." Melodie paused, leaning forward until his face came into focus. He was thin, with cheekbones that were prominent beneath his skin. Intelligent blue eyes filled with wariness looked back at her; the bright colour was striking compared to the curly black hair that framed his face. "...I can see quite well. You're a handsome boy."

Peter grinned. Twin dimples puckered his cheeks. "You're pretty, too. Can I have the money now?"

Melodie patted the reticule dangling from her arm. "I have it here, but there is a slight change in plans. You're going to take me to Erik."

Peter's smile vanished, leaving a troubled expression. "He won't like that. He told me to get the money."

"I know, but it's important that I talk with him in person. He'll understand." Melodie knew she was trying to convince herself as much as Peter. Erik did not strike her as being particularly understanding. She wasn't sure what sort of welcome she would receive.

Pursing his lips, the boy looked doubtful at that statement. "He'll get angry. He's not very nice when he's angry."

Melodie had never witnessed Erik's temper, but apparently Peter had. She suspected it must be an unpleasant experience. "I'll make sure he gets angry with me, not you. I'll tell him that I wouldn't give you the money unless you took me to him. How does that sound?"

Appearing to be at a loss, Peter shrugged.

Melodie interpreted the motion as acquiescence. "Good. It's settled then." She stood up and brushed the dust from her skirt. The top of Peter's head came to just below her shoulder, so there wasn't a vast difference in height; she could take his arm comfortably. "I'll be counting on you to lead me, Peter," she said. "Remember, I can only see up close, so as we're walking, I really am blind. I'm putting my trust in you to guide me safely. Can you do this?"

She waited for a response, but none seemed to be forthcoming. "Are you nodding?" she asked.

"Oh, sorry." He sounded sheepish. "I forgot. I can do it."

She gave his shoulder a light squeeze. "I knew I could count on you. Let's go."

Melodie knew the journey would be long, as Erik had once warned her. After having walked for an hour, Peter told her they had thirty minutes left in their travels.

The boy had proven to be good company. Though a little shy at first, he'd soon grown to be quite the chatterbox. He described the sights to her as they walked along, telling her of landmarks they were nearing and anything out of the ordinary. A carriage with a broken wheel by the side of the road made for interesting commentary. His animated description of the hapless coachman surrounded by sniping old ladies made her laugh.

Melodie also learned something of his life. His full name was Peter Bain, and he was ten years old. Since his mother had died several years ago, he lived alone with his father, about a mile away from Erik's home. He'd been climbing a tree on Erik's property when they first met. Erik had not been friendly, chasing the boy away. Then, upon passing the recluse's home one day, the masked man had ventured out and asked Peter to go into the city to fetch him a few items. That's how their little business arrangement had started.

"Now he's teaching me how to read," Peter said with pride.

Melodie's eyebrow lifted. "You don't go to school?"

"No. I help my dad with the farm."

"I see." Melodie mused that Erik must have some kindness in him after all. "What else can you tell me about him?" she asked.

"He used to live in Paris. He's always playing the piano. He has a dog that used to be my dad's dog, but now Erik calls her Sascha." Peter paused in his narrative and then added, "Oh, and most important, never ask why he wears a mask. That makes him really angry."

Melodie made a mental note to remember that piece of advice.

"We're almost there," Peter informed her. He tugged on the sleeve of her blouse. "There's the gate. He's probably watching us."

Melodie's heart began to pound, and she licked her dry lips. All the words she had rehearsed so carefully last night seemed to have leaked out of her ears. *Maybe this wasn't such a good idea.* It was impossible to turn back now, however, so she marched on with a stiff spine.

Peter left her side to unlatch the gate. It swung open with what sounded like a groan of protest. Taking her arm once more, he guided her up the walk.

"Is he at the window?" Melodie asked, speaking out of one side of her mouth.

"No, he's at the door," Peter replied. "Hello, Erik."

Melodie imagined Erik framed within the doorway, tall, imposing, and probably scowling through his mask.

When Erik responded, his voice was as brittle as she'd feared it would be. "This wasn't our agreement," he said.

The icy waves emanating from him were almost tangible.

Melodie suppressed the impulse to shiver. She spoke with haste. "This was my doing, Erik. I needed to speak with you, so I told Peter I wouldn't hand over the money unless he brought me to you. If there is anyone to be upset with, it's me."

Another drawn out silence ensued.

Melodie swallowed and managed to remain still, though her insides were churning.

"Peter, come here," Erik ordered at last.

As the boy's familiar little arm slipped out of her grasp, Melodie asked, "What do you intend?" Although she didn't want to believe the boy was about to be punished, the thought sprang to mind.

"It's none of your concern," Erik barked.

Left alone, Melodie could only stand there, waiting, worrying. The door was open and she could hear murmurings from inside. It seemed to be a civil interaction, but she kept her ears alert for any sign of anxiety on the part of the child.

When Peter emerged, he sounded excited. "Look, Melodie! Sorry, I keep forgetting. Erik gave me money and some books. He's going away."

"Peter, you should go," Erik said gruffly.

He's leaving? A dozen questions flitted through Melodie's mind. Her task today would be even more difficult than she'd anticipated.

"Are you coming back?" Peter asked.

"I don't know." The man's response was surprisingly gentle. "Go on, now. Don't let your father see those books. And don't forget the coach."

Melodie's ears perked up at his last statement. "What coach?"

"The one that will be taking you home shortly," Erik advised her, the hardness returning to his tone.

"But I've come all this way," she said. "Don't you want to know why?"

"Not particularly."

Melodie could feel the radiating heat of her cheeks. "I refuse to be turned away like this. We have unfinished business to conduct, and I simply had to do it in person." She took a breath, willing herself to calm down. "I realize it was rude of me to come unannounced. I apologize for that. Please give me twenty minutes of your time. That's all I request."

Yet again, his answer was delayed in coming. "Very well." Erik sounded reluctant. "Twenty minutes. Peter, make sure the coach isn't late."

Melodie felt the brush of a body run past her. She turned as Peter called out his goodbye, and raised her hand in a wave. Then she pivoted back to face the man who was no doubt staring daggers at her. She grew more uncomfortable as each second passed by. It had become a battle as to who could hold the silence the longest.

Deciding to give this victory to Erik, Melodie said, "Are you going to invite me in? I'm tired and would like a drink of water."

Erik's reply was cool and clear. "Enter at your own risk, mademoiselle."

Erik left the door open and strode away, trying to keep his jumbled emotions in check. Not long ago, he'd been pacing back and forth, wondering why Peter was delayed. The cynical side of him had been convinced that the lad had betrayed him, taking his share of the salary from Melodie and scurrying away with it. His more rational side had argued that Peter wasn't capable of such a deed; it was more likely that he'd been robbed or met with some unforeseen incident.

That unpredictable event had been Melodie's interference. Once again, she'd managed to catch Erik by surprise. When he'd spied her approaching the gate on Peter's arm, his entire body had tensed. Any ounce of pleasure in seeing her again had been overridden by anger that she would dare to invade his privacy.

Erik glanced about his abode now, attempting to view it through the eyes of a first-time visitor. He had never bothered to add any decorative touches. Compared to the opulence of his former lair in the opera house, his current home was stark. Only belatedly did Erik realize it would not matter much to this particular guest.

Erik stood with arms slack at his sides, shoulders tightened with unease. Melodie came in and shut the door behind her. After snapping open the clasp of her reticule, she withdrew a bag and held it toward him.

"Your portion of the commission," she said.

Erik took it from her, avoiding contact with her slender fingers. She cleared her throat, sounding croaky as she asked, "May I have that glass of water?"

Erik obliged by heading to the kitchen. He flung the bag onto the table where it fell with a dull thud. Reaching for the pitcher and a glass, he poured a generous portion of water that he'd collected from the brook this morning. He had to admit, his curiosity was piqued by her visit; in fact, it was nearly overwhelming him. But he drew back into his shell of detached disinterest.

Erik found Melodie in the sitting room, perched on the chair by the hearth – his chair. Considering it was the only one in the room, he allowed it. He'd chosen this particular chair because it was big and overstuffed, holding his large frame comfortably. Poised on the edge of it, her face pale and lips pinched, Melodie looked anything but comfortable.

"Water," he advised, pressing the glass to her hand.

She grasped it with eagerness. "Thank you."

As she drank with unladylike gulps, Erik said, "Need I remind you that time is running short?" He made his impatience obvious.

She did not reply until she finished the entire glass and set it down on the adjacent table. "I'm sorry. It seems that everything I'd thought out last night has escaped me. I'm not sure where to begin." She hesitated. "Actually, I do know where to begin, but I must insist that you be truthful. I need to know I can trust you."

Erik's mouth twisted in a sardonic parody of a smile. "I find it amusing that you insist on truthfulness when you've become an expert in deception."

Melodie's eyes narrowed. Erik assumed his verbal arrow had struck its mark.

"I'm not proud of the lies, but they were borne out of necessity. However, I won't tolerate anything but honesty between us if we're to – " Cutting herself off in mid-speech, Melodie sucked in a breath. She looked dismayed. "I'm getting ahead of myself. Erik, tell me the truth. Were you at the Grayson's estate last night?"

Erik was taken aback by the question. Had Melodie guessed that he was the phantom that had plagued David Wentworth's liquor-induced hallucination? Or had David revealed his sighting of a figure cloaked in black, riding like a madman with the devil at his heels?

Erik was surprised by his own reply. "Yes, I was there."

Melodie's face remained pensive. "Thank you for being honest. Did you take in the performance?"

"Yes." Although Erik had been both impressed and moved by her playing, he wasn't about to mention it.

"You must have wondered what I was doing at the piano. The pianist injured her hand so I volunteered to take her place," she explained. "I was petrified. But once I started playing, it was gloriously thrilling. Did you happen to view the inside of the ballroom?"

"I did," he said.

"Describe it to me."

Once again, Erik was thrown off guard by the direction of their conversation. "I hardly think we have time to – "

"Please," Melodie interrupted, her voice beseeching.

But it was the eyes that drew him in – velvety pools that gazed upward with warmth and longing. Erik's hold on his anger slipped a little farther from his grasp.

With a disgruntled sigh, Erik moved closer to the empty hearth. He leaned back against the mantel and cast his mind back to the previous night. "High, vaulted ceilings with a curving arch. The walls adorned with a rich mixture of deep reds and glinting golds. The floor, a polished cherry wood, so smooth and gleaming, one could glide effortlessly on its surface."

As Erik spoke, the ballroom seemed to come to life before him. He continued on, imagining that he was walking through it. "White marble statues stood at their posts in each corner. Angels took flight among the clouds on the painted mural. Three crystal chandeliers hung from the ceiling, the reflecting light sparkling like starbursts all around."

Erik thought of Melodie at the piano, immersed in her musical creation. His voice softened. "And then there was music that infused the room, building to a stunning climax before trailing away on a single sweet note of the violin."

That was as close as Erik could get to admitting that Melodie had made the right choice in how to conclude her composition. While he had a flair for the dramatic, it sometimes swayed on the side of heavy-handedness. Her touch was more sensitive.

Melodie's wide eyes were transfixed in a dream-like state. She blinked, and seemed to pull herself back to reality. "Thank you. You're very eloquent. You were inside the ballroom?"

"No. I stood by one of the doorways on the terrace."

"The terrace." Melodie's forehead wrinkled. "So, you saw…did you see…" she stammered.

"I saw everything," Erik stated. *More than I wished to see.*

Melodie's hands furled in her lap. "Everything," she repeated. "You already know about the next commission, then."

"Yes. Congratulations." Erik bit off the words, sounding wholly insincere.

Melodie pressed on with another inquiry. "Peter hinted that you're leaving. Is that true?"

"It is." He had made the decision before they'd finished the work on 'Celebration'. With their business arrangement completed, there was nothing to keep him here.

"Where? For how long?" she demanded.

Erik supposed her questions were reasonable, and yet he could provide no solid answers. "I'm not certain. I've always held a fondness for Italy. I may start there and see where fate leads me."

"But why? Why leave? What are you running away from?" she persisted.

Erik stiffened. His mouth flattened. Her prying was beginning to grate on his nerves. "There is nothing that compels me to stay," he said.

"What if I gave you a reason? I need assistance in writing the symphony. Not just the physical writing of the notes." Melodie waved a hand in the air. "Any capable student of music could do that. But I've thought long and hard on this. There are far more technicalities involved in something of this scale. I'm afraid I may have gotten in over my head."

Melodie bent forward in the chair, and spoke in earnest. "I propose that we work together as a team. Co-composers, if you will. Our musical styles are different, but I think they would complement each other. You're also more experienced. I could learn so much from you."

Erik couldn't help sneering at her last statement. "Your attempt at flattery is much too transparent, my dear. It's a ridiculous notion. If this is the reason for your uninvited visit, you've wasted your time."

Melodie was not easily deterred. "If it makes a difference, there's a great deal of money involved. Especially if…" Her voice faded.

Erik's irritation blossomed into full-blown annoyance. "If what?" he snapped.

"If Michael Blythe makes an appearance at the gala," she pronounced in a rush.

He made a sound, a cross between a grunt and a snort. "There is no Michael Blythe."

"On the contrary," she informed him, "there was quite the flurry of speculation last night that he was seen galloping away from the Grayson's property. It seems he couldn't resist the debut of 'Celebration'."

It took Erik a moment to piece together what Melodie was hinting at. When the connection was made, he stared at her with blatant disbelief. "What are you suggesting? That I assume the identity of this fictional composer?"

Her chin lifted. "I know it sounds mad, but it could work."

Erik burst out laughing, a harsh sound that held no humour. She was either idiotically naïve or an insane fool.

In two strides, Erik closed in on her, broad hands gripping the armrests on either side. Melodie shrunk back in the seat, trapped within the confines of the chair as he planted himself inches from her nose.

"You've forgotten that I possess a face that does not condone itself to public viewing," he snarled.

Though her eyes reflected startled discomfort, she held her ground. She gazed back at him without flinching. "I haven't forgotten. But your mask has already been seen, and even added an air of mystery to the gossip. Everyone was talking about it last night. If you don't want to do it, however, I understand. It's your decision."

Her tone became coaxing. "I still hope we can work together. Do you not think we could write something exquisite between the two of us?"

Erik had invaded Melodie's space in order to intimidate her, but he was the one caught in the pull of those bewitching eyes. She was so close; he could hear her rapid intakes of breath – a sign that she wasn't as calm as she outwardly projected.

Wrenching himself away, Erik retreated to the safety of the mantel. He rubbed at the throb in his left temple. "You don't know what you ask," he said, letting the weariness creep into his voice. He struggled to regain some semblance of logic in order to prove how unfounded her request was. "Where would we work? Have you thought of that? I can't imagine you'd want to return to the Empire after the last episode."

"I have thought of it," Melodie said. "You once offered your home as a possibility."

"Yes, but it's too far for you to travel. I presume you found it so today. Unless you mean to take a coach?" he asked.

"No, it wouldn't work. I've already started to neglect my lessons with Grace." Regret entered her voice. "I'm not giving her the full attention she deserves in order for me to continue living with the Anniston's. Writing this symphony will be a full time endeavour. So…I…thought I could live here…with you," she said softly.

Erik had been regarding the bare wall with unseeing eyes. Now, he whirled around to gape at this audacious woman. "What did you just say?" He couldn't believe his ears had heard correctly.

Melodie's next words gushed forth, as if she feared she would lose her courage in voicing them. "I'm aware of how incredibly forward this sounds, but please, just consider it. I spent all of last night thinking about how to make this work, and this makes the most sense. We would keep our relationship strictly professional, of course," she assured him. "The commission shall be split evenly between us. And should you decide to make an appearance at the gala, the extra money would be yours."

Melodie stood up and stepped toward him. She continued her fervent speech. "You've been aloof with me during our time together, but I've seen the genius in your work. And though I've tried to convince myself that I could hire anyone to record my notes, it's not what I desire. I want this symphony to be something special. Extraordinary. We could do it together if you're able to open up and trust me."

Erik realized his mouth was still parted with shock. He clamped it shut, ground his teeth until his jaw ached.

How ironic that the previous night, thoughts of Melodie had been able to calm the stormy seas of his soul. Now she had tossed him back into an ocean of writhing emotions.

He was leaving tomorrow. He had already set plans into motion and resigned himself to whatever fate awaited him on his journey. How dare she come into his home and tempt him with this outrageous proposition. There was no question that he was tempted; to focus solely on composing again would be wonderful.

But even as Erik's heart lifted in contemplation, an inner voice mocked him with scorn. It could never work. He could never allow Melodie to see him for what he really was.

"Erik?" Melodie's voice was almost inaudible.

With a muted roar of frustration, Erik launched himself at her, grabbed her arms and hauled her against him. Piercing her with a glare filled with fury and agony, he spoke through clenched teeth. "Don't presume that you know me. You think me a musical genius? You're right. But these hands of mine have done more than write music."

His voice was low and ominous. "You don't want to know what I'm capable of. And you damned well don't want me to 'open up', as you so delicately put it. If I truly revealed myself to you in all my glory – not just what lies beneath the mask, but within my soul – you would run screaming into the night. Is that what you want? Is it?"

As Erik rasped the last two words, he shook Melodie like a rag doll; her head bobbed precariously on her neck. Although he was lost in a fog of anguish, he eventually registered her glistening eyes. The naked fear in them stabbed into his gut, twisting his insides with reproachful self-disgust. He was frightening her, and though he supposed that had been his intent, a wave of shame washed over him. At this moment, he was no better than David Wentworth.

Erik released Melodie in an abrupt motion. He backed away. His hands curled into fists at his sides. "I'm sorry. I'm behaving like a beast. But you must realize that what you ask is an impossibility." Choked with bitterness, he could barely speak. "Leave now. Run. And forget you ever met me."

He expected her to flee, to move as fast as her legs could carry her. Instead, she stood utterly still, the tears receding from her eyes without falling. Her expression shifted to one of troubled sadness as she finally stooped to gather up her cane and reticule.

"I'm sorry, too," Melodie said. "Sorry that you're choosing to run away. I don't know what horrors lie in your past, but you can't let them consume who you are now. You may run as far as you like, but you'll never escape yourself." She inclined her head. "I'll see myself out and wait for the coach outside."

When she had gone, the room seemed cold and devoid of life, as if his own flesh and blood were not warm enough to permeate the space. He marvelled at how someone he had known for a mere few weeks could have become such a presence in his life.

Her parting words haunted him. Nagging doubts began to plague his resolve to leave.

Seething with frustration, Erik tore off the mask and threw it at his feet. He longed to crush it into oblivion with his heel, but he managed to restrain himself. Instead, he kicked the chair before collapsing into it. He closed his eyes and hunched forward, head resting in his hands.

He didn't know what to do.

Such indecisiveness had never ailed him during all his years in the opera house. But now, it drained him of the power and control that he longed to regain in this yet unwritten chapter of his life.

When Erik lifted his head at last, he still had no answers. The mask stared upward with its sightless eye, a blind, empty socket that foretold no visions of the future.

He would have to make that decision himself.

Eight

Although Melodie usually didn't linger at the piano after finishing a lesson with Grace, she found herself doing just that. She ran her fingers over the keys, testing a phrase that was running through her head. She hadn't formally started writing the symphony, but fragments of themes sometimes popped into her mind at random moments.

Tapping out the newly created melody, her thoughts veered in a different direction.

Erik.

It had been three days since Melodie's impromptu visit. She assumed that he had gone to Italy. Whenever she looked back on that day, she wondered if she should have approached the situation differently.

Erik was a tortured man, haunted by a past that still claimed him in its tenacious grip. Melodie had never witnessed such raw emotions in a single person before; a cacophonic blend of anger, sorrow, passion, and desperation seeped from every pore. It was both frightening and fascinating. His eyes had burned with liquid fire so intense, she'd been afraid to breathe.

She was now at a loss as to what to do. Her proposal to live in the man's home had been borne out of desire to work with him, but also out of desperation. With a little over three months to complete the symphony, it would require all of her focus. Though the Annistons treated her well, she couldn't reveal the nature of her composing to them. And it was true that Grace's lessons were suffering because of the distraction.

Melodie required access to a piano, free reign to write, and someone to record the notes – preferably someone who possessed the equivalent of Erik's talent. She truly would need help in the framework of composing such a complex work.

Really, is that so much to ask?

The attempt at lightness did not ease her mood.

Although Erik had never volunteered to share his musical expertise, when she'd asked for his assistance, he'd always delivered beyond her expectations. Their styles were vastly different, but that didn't detract from his uncanny ability to understand what she was trying to accomplish. When she'd stumbled on troublesome areas, he'd been able to guide her toward her goal, or sometimes in new directions she'd never considered.

Melodie's proposition to Erik had been a difficult one to make. She'd had little sleep the previous night, tossing and turning every thought in her mind. The deciding factor had not been his impressive technical ability; it had been that momentous glimpse into the depth of his being, when they'd sat side by side at the piano, sharing pieces of their compositions – pieces of themselves.

Even now, she could hear the enthralling passage, as if Erik sat hunched beside her like a phantom ghost. His music captivated her as nothing else ever had, forming an invisible link between them. She'd tried to convince herself that the bond was imagined, that it wasn't worth the effort to attempt to crack his protective outer shell. But she was only deceiving herself. The connection between them and their music did exist.

It appeared, however, that Erik had decided to sever that connection before the fragile threads had a chance to cohere.

"Melodie?"

Startled by the intrusion, Melodie's fingers slipped. She winced as a discordant chord rang out. Looking toward the voice she recognized as the butler, she said, "Yes?"

"Sorry to disturb you. A young lad is at the door with a message for you. I asked him to leave the note with me, but he insisted on delivering it to you in person."

She rose from the bench. "Thank you. I'll take care of it."

As Melodie maneuvered her way through the room and to the front door, she told herself not to get her hopes up. This might simply be a farewell letter from Erik.

Standing before the door, she straightened her spine and composed her features into a serene expression. She swung the door open. "Peter?" she asked.

"Hello, Melodie," replied the chipper voice. "I brought a letter from Erik."

The textured paper of an envelope was placed into her waiting hand. "Thank you," she said. "Is Erik gone now?"

"No, he's still there. But he looked strange."

Melodie arched a questioning eyebrow. "Strange?" she repeated.

As usual, Peter spoke in an excited rush. "His clothes were all wrinkled, and he had hair on his face, like my dad, but not as thick. I thought he was sick, but he said he wasn't. He says you need to read the letter and then write back to him. Will it take you long?"

It took Melodie a moment to absorb everything the boy had rattled off. "I'm not sure. Could you return in a half hour? I should have something for you by then."

"All right. I'll come back," Peter said.

She heard him hop down the steps. The scurrying sound of his feet faded into the distance.

With the envelope clutched in her hand, Melodie hastened up the stairs and into her chambers. She closed the door behind her. The curtains had already been parted this morning, allowing light to flood the room. After taking a seat at her desk, she tore into the envelope and unfolded a single sheet of paper. She scanned the page:

Dear Melodie,

I apologize for the lengthy time that has passed since our last meeting, but I have had much to consider. I will not bore you with the details of the convoluted means to which I came to a decision. All you need know is that one has been made, and the final decision rests with you.

After my abominable behaviour, you might have reconsidered the wisdom of your proposition. I assure you, I am capable of behaving like a gentleman. However, in the interest of honesty, which seems so important to you, I must warn you that I possess a temper. It has not reared itself often as of late, but when it does, it can be wholly unpleasant – as you have witnessed. It is ingrained within me, so I make no promises that it will never reappear. I do promise that I shall strive to remain the gentleman in your presence.

I would be honoured to work with you in the writing of your symphony. Should you still wish to reside with me, I'll require five days to ready my home. Please make your choice known in a letter and give it to Peter.

Should this be our final correspondence, I wish you well in your endeavours.

Cordially,
Erik

Melodie read the letter three times in succession before her hand dropped to her lap. Her face was flushed with a combination of excitement and anxiety. He had actually accepted. Though she had been hopeful he would, it still shocked her.

Can I really do this?

Reaching down, she slid open the drawer and removed a sheet of paper, ink, and her pen. She sat unmoving for many minutes, one elbow braced on the desk. She gripped the slim writing instrument until her fingers ached. At last, she dipped into the well of ink and began to write:

Dear Erik,

Thank you for your letter and the granting of my request. After considerable thought, I have decided that my proposal is much too forward and foolish. I'm not sure what possessed me to even consider…

The scratching of pen to paper came to a halt. She stared at the fresh wet ink; where the nib jabbed into the grainy surface, a black stain bled outward in a thin trail.

Mellie, you weak-kneed coward.

Melodie yanked open the drawer and withdrew another sheet of paper. As she slammed it shut, her fingers jammed between the edges of wood. Pain shot through the sensitive digits.

"Bloody hell!" Her other hand clawed at the round knob of the drawer until it jerked open.

She jumped to her feet and spun around, cradling her injured hand against her chest. When the sparkling pain subsided to an ache, she flexed her fingers. Thankfully, they all wiggled as they should.

Melodie flounced onto the chair, took pen in hand, and wrote in a frenzy. When she'd finished, her forehead was damp, her cheeks hot. Not even sure of what she'd written, she thought it prudent to read it over:

Dear Erik,

I am pleased that you have granted my request, and would be honoured to take residence with you while we work together. I sense that you are an intensely private person. I know this must have been a difficult decision for you.

I have one request. Please do not feel that you must tread so carefully in my presence. I am aware of your temper, but understand that it is just one facet of your complex nature. I would not wish for you to act anything but yourself in your own home. I believe that we must be true to ourselves in order for our partnership to reach its full potential. I hope you feel the same.

I shall arrive at your door in five days. Should you require additional time, please send word via Peter. I look forward to embarking on this project with you.

Sincerely,
Melodie

Melodie regarded her writing with bemusement; the strokes were spiky, sloppy – most unlike her usual careful penmanship – but the words were honest and spoken from the heart.

As she inserted the letter into an envelope, her hand trembled, betraying the state of her nerves. *I'm really going through with this.*

A shiver rippled through her. She made the final markings on the front of the envelope with a bold flourish: Erik.

The name invoked a myriad of sensations that twirled like a jewelled kaleidoscope in her mind: His deep, lyrical voice. Warm hands that offered comfort and strength. His unique smell of spicy masculinity.

The dizzying fragments finally came to rest on the hypnotic beauty of his eyes, the window into his soul. She had seen them only twice – the first time coldly judgmental, the last time filled with despair.

What had he done to inflict himself with such suffering?

Melodie would undoubtedly come to understand more about Erik, yet she wondered if that answer would ever be revealed.

And perhaps, in the spirit of ultimate honesty, she did not wish to know the answer.

As the carriage lurched along, Henry gazed out the window. Though the countryside was picturesque with its rolling green hills dotted with farmhouses, he saw none of it.

Instead, he reanalysed Melodie's letter in his mind, examining it from every angle like an ancient relic in a historian's hands. How could she move in with a strange man? Not only was it scandalous, but dangerous as well. She couldn't possibly know this man well enough to warrant such trust.

Melodie had led a sheltered life. Her whole world had revolved around the Wentworth home. School had not been an option, so Henry had taught her to read and write. Heading the staff of the household was a full time position, and he'd often left her to her own devices. She had never seemed to mind the solitude, finding refuge in her bountiful imagination and her music.

When David had started receiving lessons from a private tutor, Albert had allowed Melodie to participate as well. Like a thirsty sponge, she'd soaked up knowledge in history, geography, literature, and French. Though none of these subjects were of any practical use, it had pleased Henry to know her horizons were being expanded, if only in the academic sense.

As Melodie grew older, she still remained close to home. She had no social life to speak of, yet she seemed to prefer it that way. So long as she had her music, she claimed never to be lonely.

Henry reached into the inner pocket of his coat and removed her letter. Although he could almost recite it from memory, he perused it once more:

Dearest Henry,

What I am about to write will come as a shock to you. Do find a spot to sit down before you begin. Are you seated? Good.

It has been three days since I moved out of the Anniston's home, under the guise of accepting a teaching position at a boarding school. I did not tell you of my plans in advance because I did not want to worry you. I write this letter from the new home of my temporary residence. I have asked Erik to work with me in the writing of the symphony, and he has accepted. He has also graciously allowed me to reside in his home while we work together. It is the only way we will be able to complete it in time for the grand opening of the theatre.

I am aware of how highly unconventional this must seem to you, but I feel it is a necessity in order for the symphony to be successful. Above all else, that is what is most important to me. Please do not think any less of me. I have always had your support in the past and would find any disapproval on your part a heavy burden to bear.

I hope you will come for a visit sometime. The house is small, more on the scale of a cottage, but it is cozy and I am beginning to feel quite comfortable. Erik has been the perfect gentleman. I only ask that you let us know in advance of your visit, as I have found that Erik is not fond of surprises.

*With love,
Mellie*

Henry clenched his fingers, crumpling a corner of the letter. He stared once more out the window. Whether Erik cared not for surprises was of no concern to Henry. His visit today was unannounced, and intentionally so. In catching the man unaware, Henry thought he might glimpse something suspicious within the home that would otherwise have been hidden. It was an unfair advantage, but considering that Melodie's welfare was at stake, Henry had no qualms about sidestepping polite protocols.

Lost in thought, Henry didn't realize that all motions of the carriage had ceased until the coachman opened the door.

"I think this is it, Mr. Blythe," the young man announced.

After tucking the letter back into his breast pocket, Henry stepped out into the sunny day, squinting against the glare. He held a hand up to his eyes and looked beyond the coachman's shoulder to the house. Its exterior face was comprised of flint grey stone, a wooden door, and a single window. There wasn't a speck of colour to brighten its drab appearance, no bed of flowers in bloom. Even the curtain at the window was plain white.

"I'm not sure how long I'll be, but if you could wait here, Jacob," Henry instructed.

Jacob inclined his head. "Of course, sir."

Pulling his shoulders back, Henry felt the stiffened muscles protesting. He tugged at the lapels of his coat and smoothed away the wrinkles. Once at the front door, he knocked and waited.

The bark of a dog rang out from inside. Several heartbeats later, the door swung inward. Henry had to tilt his head up to regard the homeowner.

The man was dressed in an ivory shirt and black trousers, dark hair combed back with no strand out of place. Half of his forehead was furrowed with lines; the rest was hidden behind a white mask.

Henry mentally kicked aside his shock, hoping he was successful in maintaining a carefree countenance. Melodie had told him about the mask, but he'd forgotten. Henry now also recalled the whispered rumours of a masked man charging away from the Grayson's estate.

Their eyes locked until Erik broke the silence. "Henry," he said, sounding neither pleased nor upset.

Henry drew his eyebrows together. "How do you know who I am? We haven't met before."

Appraising eyes of a striking shade of green continued to regard Henry without so much as a blink. "Melodie has described you accurately. I know she wrote to you, so I expected you would be making a call. I didn't, however, think it would be so soon."

Ignoring the subtle jab at his abrupt appearance, Henry asked, "May I come in?"

Erik stepped back. He made a slight bow and gestured with his hand. "Please do."

Henry crossed the threshold and stood to the side. He swept his gaze around what he could view of the interior. His first impression was identical to a word that Melodie had used in her letter – cozy.

"Shall I take your coat and hat?" Erik offered.

Henry removed his hat and shrugged out of his coat. "Thank you. Is Melodie upstairs?"

"No. She went into town with Peter, a young boy that sometimes assists me," Erik said. "I expect they'll be back soon. Make yourself comfortable, and I'll put on some tea."

Turning on his heel, Erik walked away.

Henry slowly paced about the sitting room before settling on one end of a couch. He pushed aside a blue velvet cushion. His eye was drawn to the upright piano, positioned by a window at the back of the room. Cream-coloured lace curtains were tied back, allowing sunlight to stream through the glass. The rays shone down upon the gleaming piano, as if showcasing this focal point of the home. Fresh cut flowers in a crystal vase adorned the top of the instrument. Beside it was a small table with two chairs. The surface of the table was barely visible beneath the scattered sheets of staff paper.

Henry was surprised that the inside of the home did not match the dreary exterior.

He then noticed the quill set down by the ink well, and surmised that he'd interrupted Erik in the middle of writing; the quill certainly did not belong to Melodie. It seemed the matter of composing was genuine. From his limited observation of things so far, nothing appeared suspect or out of the ordinary.

But he had to admit, he didn't exactly know what he was looking for.

Something entered Henry's vision from the corner of his eye, and he looked down at the newcomer. A border collie regarded him, head cocked to one side.

"Hello there," Henry said, extending his hand.

The dog bowed its head and then lifted it, repeating the movement several times. Intelligent black eyes never strayed from Henry's face. It approached cautiously and sniffed at his fingers. Treated to a scratching behind the ears, the animal seemed to grin, wagging its tail with hearty approval.

"I see Sascha has made a friend," Erik said. He came to stand by the couch.

With the return of her owner, the dog leapt to his side. Erik bent to pat her head.

Henry glanced up at Erik. "She's lovely," he commented. "I noticed the limp. A recent injury?"

Although Henry thought it was an innocent question, something hardened in Erik's eyes, the same steely emotion colouring his voice when he spoke.

"No, it was more than a year ago. If you want to speak to me alone, I suggest we begin. Melodie could literally walk through that door at any moment."

"Then I shall get straight to the point," Henry said. "Perhaps you would care to sit."

Henry watched as Erik made his way to a chair, his movements smooth and graceful for such a large man. It made Henry ever aware of his shorter stature and cursed frailty that advancing age had bestowed upon him. Although his body creakily reminded him that more than sixty years of his life had passed, his mind hadn't yet caught up to that fact; he hoped it never would.

As Henry sat facing Erik, he instinctively felt that he was in formidable company. Even without speaking, the man exuded strength, commanded respect. It was unnerving, but Henry only had to remind himself of why he was here to regain his focus.

"I would like to know what your intentions are with Melodie," Henry said.

Erik's visible eyebrow lifted. "My intentions? I assure you, my intention is to help write this symphony and nothing more."

"And you find nothing wrong with this living arrangement?" Henry pressed.

Erik's tone was frosty. "Perhaps you are not aware of the facts. Melodie requested this arrangement, not me. If you have a problem with it, you should take it up with her."

"I intend to," Henry assured him, "but I wanted to speak with you first. You're telling me you did nothing to encourage this?"

"On the contrary, I tried to discourage it initially, but she can be quite persuasive."

Henry decided to switch tactics. "What can you tell me about yourself? I would like to get to know you better."

For the first time, Erik showed discomfort; he visibly tensed. "What do you want to know?"

"Where are you from? I detect a slight accent. French?" Henry guessed.

Erik sounded wary as he answered. "I've spent most of my life in Paris, yes."

"What made you decide to leave?"

Erik did not reply immediately. He glanced away for a moment before meeting Henry's eyes once more. "Monsieur, I can appreciate what you're trying to do. You obviously care for Melodie. But you must understand that the relationship Melodie and I have is purely professional. We have not discussed our personal lives with each other, so it does not feel right for me to do so with you."

Taken aback, Henry wasn't sure what to say. He didn't like the fact that Erik was being evasive. "I find that hard to believe. Nothing personal at all?"

"It's true," Erik insisted. "We both value our privacy, strange as that may sound." Erik waved a hand in Henry's direction. "For instance, I know that you are an important figure in her life, a paternal figure, but I don't quite understand the relationship. She calls you 'Henry' and has described you as a friend, but I sense there is more to it than that."

This odd situation raised more questions in Henry's mind, but he presumed he would waste his breath in voicing them. Like the mask on his face, Erik seemed to shield himself with an impenetrable wall.

Yet Henry couldn't let this go without expressing one final thought. "Very well. You've made your point, now allow me to make mine. Melodie has mentioned that you've been nothing but a gentleman. I trust that will continue, for if you ever hurt her, there is nowhere in this world that you can hide."

Although Henry spoke in a conversational tone, he kept his expression grave. "I will find you, and the consequence will not be pleasant. Have I made myself clear?"

Erik met his gaze. "Very clear," he said.

Sascha had been reclining at Erik's feet, but now bound upward and trotted toward the door, tail swishing. Erik also stood up. "Impeccable timing," he said. "She's returned."

Seconds later, the door burst open and Melodie appeared. A young boy ran in from behind her. "Henry?" she called out.

The boy and the dog set about rolling around on the floor. Henry tried not to trip over them as he approached Melodie. "How did you know I was here?" he asked, leaning in to kiss her cheek in greeting.

"I just spoke with Jacob," she replied.

Henry glanced down at her basket, filled with fresh vegetables. "You've gone shopping, I see," he said.

Seeming distracted, Melodie tilted her head. "Hmm? Oh, yes, I thought I would pick up some items for dinner. Peter, I would like you to meet a friend of mine. This is Henry."

Peter looked up, one hand in the middle of giving Sascha a belly rub; he waved his other in the air.

The child's toothy grin was engaging, and Henry returned the smile. "Nice to meet you, Peter."

"Is Erik here?" Melodie asked.

Erik had not moved since rising from his chair, choosing to observe from a distance. Though he did not raise his voice, it carried across the room. "I'm here," he said.

Melodie's head swivelled in his direction. "I suppose the two of you have had a chance to chat, then?" She turned to face Henry again. "I do wish you would have given us notice of your visit."

Henry could see that Melodie was flustered, though he wasn't sure if the colour in her cheeks was due to the sun or her emotions. Before Henry had a chance to respond, Erik made his opinion known.

"It's quite all right. We've managed to come to an understanding. Perhaps you would care to stay for dinner?" Erik asked, directing his attention back to Henry.

Henry wondered if the graciousness was an act. "That's very kind, but I must say no. Mellie, I do wish to have a word with you before I leave."

Erik strode to Melodie's side and plucked the basket from her grasp. "You may have your talk in here. Peter, come with me. We'll go out the back door." Without waiting for a reply, Erik began walking away. He threw a last command over his shoulder. "Sascha, come."

After scrambling to her feet, the animal trotted after the retreating man's back. Peter had no choice but to follow along or be left behind.

Henry's gaze returned to Melodie, and he was amused by her demeanour. With arms crossed about her chest and a vague pout of her lips, he was reminded of a much younger girl – one who knew she was about to be chastised.

"Let us sit down," he said, heading toward the couch once more.

In silence, she sat down beside him.

Erik ambled through the expanse of field, green blades of grass rippling to and fro with the spring breeze. Although he still felt most comfortable in the shadowed curtain of night, he'd come to appreciate some of the advantages of daylight. For instance, it would be quite difficult to pick wildflowers while groping blindly in the dark.

Stooping down on one knee, he selected a few bunches of lavender coloured flowers, the petals tiny and delicate in his hands. Up ahead, Peter frolicked with Sascha, the air occasionally punctuated with a bark or high-pitched laughter. The tranquil setting served to put Erik's mind at ease. Unsure of how much time Henry required for his talk with Melodie, Erik decided to sit for a while.

Much had changed over the past week and a half. The last time he had awakened to someone else in his home had been the brief interlude with Christine. There was one significant difference; he had lured Christine, practically abducted her against her will, and brought her to the depths of his lair.

Melodie had requested to reside with him, to work with him, to learn from him. And although Erik had presented her with opportunity to do so, Melodie's hand had never strayed toward his mask, unlike the cruel prying fingers of Christine.

The decision to allow Melodie into his home and his life had been an agonizing one. For two nights and three days, he had tortured himself with the process. While the reasons for accepting her request were varied, there was one of particular significance.

If he decided to assume the identity of Michael Blythe, how wondrous it would be to attend the opening night of the theatre. *What would it be like to stand on the stage, a roar of thunderous applause surrounding you?* It was a ridiculous fantasy, but the possibility of it was tantalizing.

Using a portion of his commission funds, Erik made the interior of the house more liveable by adding furniture and some decorative touches. He was satisfied with the results. Melodie had not commented on the décor, but she had been pleased with her chambers.

The awkwardness of the first day of her arrival had passed, but by no means were they comfortable with the living arrangement yet. Other than discussions regarding the symphony, they remained quiet, treating each other with formal politeness. It felt a little strained, but not unpleasant.

Erik often caught himself staring at her. He would then avert his gaze, rebuking himself for the rudeness.

Henry would not approve of his behaviour.

Erik had been taken by surprise by the visit. In hindsight, he should have expected it. He'd squelched his annoyance at the intrusion, reminding himself that he was capable of behaving like a gentleman. Obviously, Henry cared for Melodie like a father and was equally protective. Erik had been both amused and touched by the unsubtle threat to his well being, should he ever harm Melodie.

She should consider herself lucky to have someone care for her so deeply.

Reduced to feeling ten years of age, Melodie sat with a rigid spine. Henry's opinion was important to her, but she was a grown woman, capable of making her own decisions.

She resisted the urge to fidget as the silence stretched out. At last, she could bear it no longer.

"Henry?" she inquired.

"Sorry," Henry said, "I'm trying to gather my thoughts on how to proceed. I do want to talk with you, yet what I had first intended to say no longer seems suitable."

"Why is that?"

"I don't know." Henry seemed perplexed. "I'm not even sure what I expected to find when I came here. Erik is interesting and charismatic, but how can you put so much faith in a man that you don't know anything about?"

Melodie struggled to come up with an explanation that didn't sound completely illogical. In the end, she spoke honestly. "I have no answer, and I cannot explain it. If you heard his music, you might begin to understand. I believe that someone capable of conjuring such beauty must have a good heart."

"Do you know how naïve that sounds?" Henry accused, sounding exasperated.

She *was* aware of it, but that made her conviction no less true. Never in her wildest dreams would she have imagined herself living with a man, even for the sake of writing a symphony, yet here she was. And although Erik had hinted at a propensity for violence, she felt safe in his home.

"I know," she said. Unable to add anything clever, she shrugged her shoulders in a helpless gesture.

"Are you attracted to this man?" Henry asked.

Melodie's mouth parted. An immediate surge of heat to her face told her that she was blushing. "What? What sort of question is that?" She strove to express indignation but wasn't very convincing.

"When you speak of Erik, you get an odd sort of look in your eyes," Henry advised her. "It was there even when you mentioned him for the first time, but now it's stronger."

"I admire him. That is all," Melodie said firmly.

"He's not an unattractive man," Henry commented.

Melodie refused to respond to that statement.

Henry pressed on. "Even the mask is compelling. Do you know why he wears it?"

"No, I don't."

"Are you not curious?"

"Of course, I am," Melodie snapped. "It's only natural to be curious, but I'm not about to invade his privacy even further."

Henry expelled a breath. "You realize, I hope, that I'm only concerned about you."

Melodie gave a single nod of her head. "I know." A fraction of the flush receded from her cheeks.

Henry patted her clenched hands. "Forgive me. This conversation has taken a turn I didn't intend. I do not have the trust in Erik that you possess, but I do trust you, Mellie. Your instincts have always been better than most. I need you to promise me something."

When Henry paused, Melodie murmured, "What is it?"

"You must promise to keep in contact with me. Should you ever need me, for whatever reason, I want you to come to me right away. You will always have a place with me, even if it means I leave the Wentworths and we venture out on our own."

This time, Henry enclosed her hands with both of his, squeezing lightly. "You are the most important person in my life. Never doubt that," he said.

Melodie blinked back the gathering moisture in her eyes. Her irritation forgotten, she wrapped her arms around Henry and spoke against his ear. "I love you too," she said.

After talking for a while, Melodie accompanied Henry to the door. She hid a smile when he almost set out without his hat and coat, shaking his head at his own absentmindedness. She retrieved the items from the nearby coat rack and gave Henry a kiss on the cheek.

Melodie shut the door, leaned back against it, and closed her eyes.

Henry had not exactly given his blessing, but it appeared she still had his support. For that, she was grateful.

An unbidden thought sprang to mind.

Am I attracted to Erik?

"What are you doing?" asked a childish voice.

Erik glanced up to find Peter looking down at him with curiosity.

"Just thinking," Erik replied.

"Is that for Melodie?"

Following the line of the boy's pointed index finger, Erik regarded the clump of purple wildflowers still clutched and forgotten in his hand. "Yes," he said.

"Can I help?" Peter asked, his voice full of enthusiasm.

At Erik's nod, Peter knelt down on the grass and carefully handpicked each selection. Sascha lay stretched out by her master's side, panting with a lolling tongue.

The boy's face was set with studied concentration as he crawled about, plucking only the worthiest of flowers.

Erik's attention was drawn once more to the faint bruise that darkened the hollow beneath the child's cheekbone. He'd noticed it when Peter had first arrived to accompany Melodie into town.

"How did you get that bruise?" Erik asked.

Peter's head lifted, eyes peeking out from behind a few errant curls, before he dropped his gaze again. "I forgot to close the gate. Some sheep got out, and dad had to chase them around."

"He hit you?"

Thin shoulders shrugged in answer as the boy continued to gather the flowers. The non-verbal response was enough of an admission.

Erik's jaw tightened. Although it had been a long time since anyone had dared to raise a hand against him without facing brute retaliation, he remembered how it felt to be abused as a child, the intermingled feelings of helplessness and shame. Though he would love nothing more than to confront Peter's father, common sense advised him to refrain from such rash measures. He had managed to live here in peace, and now that Melodie had joined him, the last thing he wanted to do was stir up trouble.

But he couldn't turn a blind eye to the situation. "Does this happen often?" Erik asked.

"No," Peter mumbled.

Erik could not judge if the boy was answering truthfully, partly because all he could see was the crown of the child's head.

"Peter, stop and look at me," Erik said. He waited until Peter sat upright, and the child regarded him with a guarded expression. Erik rephrased the question. "Does your father hit you often?"

"No. Only when I do something stupid."

Various platitudes crossed Erik's mind, but none of them would have been helpful. Instead, he found himself saying, "In a few years, you're going to be a lot bigger, a lot stronger, and not such an easy target for your father. But until then, if things ever get out of hand and you need help, I want you to come and find me, day or night. Is that understood?"

With a solemnity beyond his years, Peter nodded.

Melodie's eyes flew open.

I am not attracted to him!

It was a ridiculous notion with no validity. She was attracted to Erik's music and talent, not the man.

But if she stopped to analyse that statement, she had to wonder how one was separated from the other. Those traits came from within Erik and were a part of his being, not isolated entities. How could she claim to be attracted to one and not the other?

Melodie bolted from the door. She tried to remember where she'd left her cane. To stand here and attempt to decipher her feelings was a useless exercise. There was no need to dwell on Henry's misguided inquiries.

Recalling that she had propped the item against the couch, she made her way across the room. Given the simple, uncluttered layout of the house, she had quickly learned her way around. She found the cane and headed for the back door.

Having lived in the city all her life, it still felt strange to walk outside and be enveloped in such serenity. *Strange, but wonderful.* It was as if her favourite bench in the park was at her fingertips, to be enjoyed upon stepping out the door. With such an inspiring setting, the finished symphony was certain to be magnificent.

After several paces, Melodie halted and listened. A bird chirped nearby, but she could not distinguish any sound that gave a clue to the whereabouts of Erik or Peter, not even the bark of a dog. She shuffled onward. She located a few trees on her journey, but no other form of life.

"There's Melodie," came a distant shout, off to the right and slightly behind her.

It was Peter.

Knowing Peter must be watching, Melodie turned and waved. She began walking in that direction, but didn't get far before the same childish voice was right under her nose.

"I picked some flowers for you," Peter said.

She flinched when the proffered flowers almost slapped her in the face. With a chuckle, she accepted the fragrant gift and inhaled the sweet scent.

"Thank you, Peter, they're lovely," she said.

"Erik picked some too, but he said I could give them to you," Peter told her. "I have to go. It's supper time."

Peter left as quickly as he had come, and although Melodie wasn't sure, she thought his absence might have been replaced by the presence of another.

"Hello, Erik," she ventured to say.

She was happy to hear his voice in reply.

"Hello, Melodie."

As usual, Erik had hesitated over the use of her name, but he had finally grown weary of his own mental game. It was a strange stumbling block that he couldn't begin to explain. He hadn't realized that he'd never uttered her name until she'd pointed it out to him.

Erik was rewarded by a smile that illuminated her whole face.

"At last, my name is spoken," Melodie exclaimed. "You may call me Mellie. I actually prefer it."

"All right...Mellie." He tested the sound on his tongue and found it pleasing. "I would advise that in the future, you don't venture out this way unaccompanied."

"Why?"

"When Peter called out to you, you were mere steps away from falling into the river."

Rather than seeming horrified or agreeing with the wisdom of his suggestion, Melodie looked delighted with this news. Her eyes gleamed.

"Really? A river? Odd that I didn't hear the water," she mused. "I usually notice things like that."

"I suppose," Erik conceded, "'river' might be overstating it. It's more of a brook. But there is a steep drop in the bank of a good foot. You could have turned your ankle."

With an airy flick of her hand, Melodie swung around to head back in that direction. "My cane would have informed me of any drop. But I appreciate your concern. A brook sounds charming."

Erik fell into step beside her. He adjusted his long strides to match her pace. Curious as to whether she would find the edge of the embankment on her own, he said nothing to guide her.

She walked for some distance parallel to the water, but after stopping for a few seconds, she veered course, pivoting to the right. With the cane sweeping in a steady motion just beyond her feet, she soon found the drop that he spoke of.

"Shall we sit for a while?" she suggested.

Erik had been doing nothing but sitting for the past twenty minutes. Thinking of the passage that he'd been working on when Henry had made his uninvited visit, he glanced down to reply that they should return.

She was not there.

Erik dropped his gaze lower. Melodie was already sitting on the grassy ledge, legs stretched out, nose buried in the purple petals bunched in one hand.

Stifling a sigh, Erik crouched down and sat beside her, careful to maintain a respectable distance.

"I can hear the water now, though it's not obvious," Melodie said. "I suppose I wasn't listening for it when I first came out here. It's moving slowly, I presume?"

"Yes, it's not deep, nor very fast."

"Since I can't swim, that's probably for the best. I shall strive not to drown myself on your property," she quipped.

"That would be most appreciated," Erik said dryly.

"Where is Sascha? I don't hear her."

Erik glanced back and saw the prone black and white fur of the dog. "She's fallen asleep. I believe Peter wore her out. She'll come to the house on her own."

When Melodie next spoke, her tone was wistful. "It must be beautiful here. I do wish I could see it."

Erik had never heard her lament her lack of vision before. "Were you born with your condition?"

Melodie appeared to take no offense to the personal nature of his inquiry. "No, it's only happened in the last five years or so."

"But your vision is worsening?" he asked.

She mulled over the answer. "It's difficult to judge on a daily basis, but yes, it is getting worse. The deterioration over the last six months has been the most rapid."

"Perhaps you are straining your eyes too much," he suggested.

"I don't know. I don't think so." Her tone changed to one of defiance, and her chin jutted out. "If I'm to lose my vision entirely, why should I deny myself the pleasure of reading a book or writing a letter while I'm still able?"

Erik didn't know what he would do in her position. "I suppose it's your choice to make," he said.

"Exactly," she agreed. "The headaches are a hindrance, but if I limit my time, they're manageable."

Silence settled between them.

Erik closed his eyelids against the light of day, trying to imagine what it would be like to view the world through Melodie's failing eyes. He came to the conclusion that it was impossible to truly understand.

With eyes still shut, Erik realized he was hearing something for the first time – the bubbling water of the brook.

After a few minutes, Melodie said, "I suppose we should head back. Thank you for indulging me."

Erik helped her up and they headed back to the house.

"I'm sorry about Henry," she said, as they walked along. "He's always been rather protective of me."

"Indeed. He made that quite clear."

Melodie's face reflected her dismay. "I hope it wasn't too unpleasant a conversation."

"It was fine," Erik said. "I understand his reasoning, but thinking ahead to future visits, I would appreciate some notice. I trust you will relay this to him."

"Yes, of course," Melodie said.

"And what of your conversation with him?" he countered. "Was it unpleasant?"

When Melodie failed to respond, Erik glanced down and noticed her pink-tinged cheeks. Perhaps she'd been out in the sun too long.

"Not at all," she finally murmured. "He was quite understanding."

She revealed nothing more of their talk, and he did not press for details.

Upon returning to the house, Erik found a shallow bowl in the kitchen for the flowers. He passed it to Melodie to fill with water from the pitcher.

Hearing a rattling sound, he looked toward the kettle. He'd forgotten the water he'd begun to boil for tea when Henry had first arrived.

Erik reached for the brass kettle and somehow managed to get his hand in the way of the billowing steam.

"*Merde!*" He jumped backwards.

Melodie flew to his side, eyes wide with concern. "What is it?"

His hand throbbing with pain, he spoke through gritted teeth. "My hand. I burned it. Stupid."

"Let me see," she said, reaching up to grab hold of his wrist.

Her attempt to inspect his hand was met with resistance, as Erik clutched it against his chest. She spoke sharply. "Erik, don't be a goose. Let me see your hand."

Erik couldn't decide if he was more miffed at her tone of voice or being called a goose.

He allowed Melodie to lead him closer to the window. "The skin is quite red," she observed out loud, "but there are no blisters. It's not too bad." She pulled him back another two steps to the kitchen table, where she dunked the injured appendage into the bowl of water. "How does it feel?" she asked.

"Wet."

"Very funny. Is it painful?"

It was, but he wasn't about to admit it. "I'll live."

Erik knew the burn was minor, but he had never been fussed over before. He found it humourous and rather enjoyable.

He almost snatched his hand back, however, when he became aware of Melodie's next attempt at doctoring. She'd lifted his wrist and was blowing lightly over the reddened skin.

"What are you doing?" he demanded.

She stopped with her lips puckered in mid-breath and began to laugh. "Sorry, it's what Henry used to do when I'd hurt myself as a child. I wasn't even thinking."

For a horrifying moment, Erik thought she was about to kiss his palm. It was torturous enough for his hand to be cradled within hers; he couldn't imagine the feel of her soothing lips against his skin.

Erik reached for a cloth to dry off. Melodie continued to look amused. "I also injured my hand the other day," she said. "Nearly crushed it when I slammed a drawer shut. Considering we're both composers and musicians, we should learn to be more careful. We're quite the pair, are we not?"

Her gaze did not quite meet his eyes, falling in the vicinity of his chin.

In answer to her rhetorical question, Erik regarded Melodie with an expression that rarely graced his features – a genuine smile.

Yes, quite the pair indeed, he agreed.

Nine

Time was fluid and ever changing, sometimes seeming to come to a standstill, but more often racing by with a breathless blur.

Melodie's focus narrowed exclusively to the symphony, and she was hardly aware of the time passing by. Days became warm, the grass lush from the plentiful spring rains, the brook rising higher and flowing faster.

Melodie was amazed to learn they'd entered the month of June. Just over four weeks had gone by since arriving at Erik's home.

They had grown more comfortable with each other, though neither of them were spectacular conversationalists. She knew no more of Erik's past than when she had first come, and since he asked no questions of her, she had not volunteered any information of herself.

Their days had fallen into a routine. Having always been a morning person, Melodie was awake and puttering about early, long before Erik stirred from his bed. She prepared breakfast for the two of them, ate her portion alone, and set aside the rest for him to eat later.

If the weather permitted, she found a suitable spot for her composing and spent the morning outside. Sometimes she sat at the base of a tree, nestled against the rough bark, sheltered by its leafy arms. If she wanted to be lulled by the sound of water, she chose to sit facing the brook, despite Erik's warning not to venture too closely.

Once, not wanting to stray far since the threat of rain seemed imminent, she planted herself just outside the back door. Erik nearly fell on top of her head, cursing as he always did in his native French.

She did not make that error again.

Erik usually rose mid-morning, and he preferred to sit at the piano while writing. In contrast to her early retirement to her chambers, he wrote late into the night, no doubt burning a great many candles down to misshapen stubs.

In the afternoons, they came together, met by the piano and shared their individual works. Those daylight hours were illuminated with flying sparks that ignited the air whenever they argued, equally passionate and stubborn when it came to their own creations. Their musical styles often clashed, making her question whether a blended balance could be reached.

Following a silent brooding dinner, by the time the dishes were put away and the kitchen cleared, they were ready to return to the piano for a session of compromise. Each instance this happened, something unique was added to the developing symphony. The process was arduous yet thrilling. Melodie was happy with the results thus far.

Only one blemish marred her happiness; it was a strange feeling. She had never experienced anything like it before, thus she wasn't quite sure how to classify it. Instinct, however, told her that she was suffering from a malady called *infatuation*.

It had sprung to life so innocently. The object of her attraction and admiration had solely been Erik's music; now that object had grown to include the composer himself. Part of her rational self understood that she was idealizing his persona, much as a pupil might idolize a teacher, but that made the feelings no less real.

She also lamented her weak vision with increased frequency. She longed to see his hands caress the piano keys, his broad shoulders hunched in concentration, his face, his eyes. But ever careful to keep her longings hidden, she remained prim and proper within his company. Even Henry would find no fault with her respectable behaviour.

Henry came for another visit. The two men in her life made polite, albeit halting conversation. Henry informed them the construction of the theatre was on schedule. Opening night was set for the twenty-first of August.

The visit seemed to ease Henry's worries about the living arrangement. Melodie assured him that everything was going well, and she was comfortable. When he left without inquiring about the status of her non-attraction to Erik, she breathed a sigh of relief.

Their only other visitor was Peter. On occasion, Melodie walked in on a reading lesson in progress, and each time, she was surprised by Erik's demeanour. His tone was gentle, his words encouraging, and he exuded a wealth of patience; it was another glimpse into one of his many layers that she was delighted to discover.

Today marked another disagreement, this time over the tempo of the second movement. For reasons she could not understand, Erik insisted on marking it as 'largo', which she argued would be too slow. 'Andante' or even 'adagio' would be more reasonable, in her opinion, but he could not be swayed. Although it was a minor quibble, both of their nerves were rankled.

When Peter's knock sounded at the door, the interruption was almost welcome. Erik invited him to sit for a lesson, and Melodie took a book outside. She found a shady spot and settled down to read, mindful of stopping before any headache could develop. She lost herself in a world of poetry, envious of anyone who could write with such lyrical eloquence. All too soon, her eyes felt grainy and tired, the first signs of straining her vision. She put the book aside with reluctance, closed her eyes, and relaxed against the tree. Her mind began to drift, and with a sudden start, she realized she was no longer alone.

She was also quite horizontal, the smell of grass and earth in her nose.

"Are you asleep?" asked an insistent voice.

Disoriented and groggy, Melodie looked up to find a shadowed blur hovering over her. She recognized Peter's voice. "Hello, Peter," she said.

"I was calling you, but you didn't answer. Erik sent me to find you," the boy said.

Melodie deduced that she must have fallen asleep. She pulled herself to her feet. Before she could ask, Peter handed over her book and cane.

Upon entering the kitchen, she heard the chopping sound of a knife. Erik's voice rumbled from nearby. "Peter, take this basket and go down to the cellar. In the corner, you'll find some plums. Four should suffice. You may take one for yourself."

"But I don't like the cellar," came the whine of protest. "It's dark and scary." Melodie's sleeve was tugged. "Will you come with me?"

"The cellar?" she echoed.

Melodie heard her own voice, as if from a great distance. Perhaps because she'd just awoken from an unintended slumber, she felt caught in a dream, trapped within the confines of an imagined cellar. The walls were caving in on her, suffocating her until she had no breath in her body.

Someone called her name, but she was powerless to answer.

"Erik, something's wrong with Mellie," Peter said.

Erik glanced up to find Melodie strangely frozen in place and Peter regarding her with puzzlement.

Erik put aside the knife and approached her. He called out to her softly. "Mellie?"

She either ignored him or did not hear him. It was the expression in her eyes that caused him the most concern. He'd seen her eyes clouded by that same emotion only once before – the incident in the Empire theatre when she'd trembled in his arms in a full-blown panic.

He raised his voice. "*Melodie*."

When she still failed to respond, Erik took hold of her shoulders and gave them a shake. The book she had been clutching dropped with a thunk to the floor. Her eyes cleared, losing their dazed look.

"What's wrong?" she asked. "I get the distinct feeling everyone is staring at me."

Peter spoke first. "You were in a trance. Or maybe you were sleepwalking. My friend's father does that. Do you sleepwalk, Mellie?"

Fixing the child with a stern gaze, Erik said gruffly, "Peter, that's enough. Never mind the plums. I think it best you go home."

A look of stark disappointment flickered across the boy's features. Erik didn't know if the cause was the loss of the promised fruit or being sent away. In a kinder tone, he added, "Come back tomorrow. I'll have a plum waiting for you."

Seeming mollified, Peter retrieved the fallen book and set it on the kitchen table before scampering off.

"You may release me," Melodie said. She held herself stiffly. "I'm fine. I was simply distracted."

Erik studied her face, noted the smattering of freckles in vivid contrast against the pale skin, as if she'd been drained of her life's blood. "Distracted?

You looked as if you were about to faint." Worry tinged his voice with harshness, making the statement sound like an accusation.

Judging by the rosy hue that began to invade her cheeks, she took offense to his remark. "I've never fainted in my life," she scoffed. "You're overreacting. And I believe I asked you to release me."

With her shoulders still captured in his firm grip, Erik led her over to a chair. "Not until you sit down."

Melodie could have jerked out of his grasp, but she allowed him to guide her. Once she was seated, Erik pulled out a chair for himself and sat down beside her. "Would you like some water?" he asked.

"No thank you. I told you I'm – "

"Yes," he interrupted, "it's obvious that you're fine now, but a minute ago, you looked ready to collapse. I want to know why."

Melodie turned her head away. "Why does it matter? I promise, it won't happen again."

"Why? I don't ever want to see that look in your eyes again, that's why. And you're right, it won't happen again because I won't allow it." Aware of the severity of his tone, Erik smoothed its rough edge. "You have to trust me enough to be honest with me. Haven't you always insisted on honesty between us?"

Shifting in her seat, Melodie said, "Yes, I suppose I have." She cleared her throat, sat back in the chair, and folded her hands in her lap. "It's childish, but I can't seem to control my reaction. I have a fear of small, enclosed spaces, particularly when they are coupled with darkness. A prime example would be the room that we were forced to hide in at the Empire."

The connection between that incident and what had just occurred was obvious to Erik now.

"Or a cellar," he said.

Melodie's eyes fluttered closed for a moment, as if blocking out the sight of something hideous. "Yes, a cellar. That is the root of this ridiculous fear of mine, and it stems from a singular episode from my childhood. I suppose you want to hear about that too."

A warning flag waved in Erik's mind; he was crossing into personal territory. He swept the intruding thought aside. "I do," he said, "but the choice is yours to make."

"I've come this far. I may as well relay the whole story. I was young, about six or seven. There was a wine cellar in the Wentworth's home. David, the son of the family, is two years older than me, and we used to play together. One day, he thought it would be amusing to lock me in the cellar. I remember it was completely black. I stumbled around for a while, crying out for help, but no one came. All I could do was sit and wait." Her voice faltered. "I felt...*things*...spiders, perhaps, crawling across my arms."

Melodie shuddered. "I was trapped for almost an entire day. Henry would have noticed my absence, but he was away on an errand since morning. Only upon his return did anyone realize I was missing. That's when David confessed, claiming that he hadn't meant for the prank to extend for so long, and he'd simply forgotten about me."

"That's difficult to believe," Erik muttered. He knew firsthand that children were capable of cruelty. David likely knew exactly what he was doing.

Melodie shrugged one shoulder in a careless gesture, though her expression was pained. "Everyone seemed to believe it, including Henry. It happened so long ago. I should have outgrown this childish fear, but it still exists."

Melodie's words had painted a vivid picture. Erik could see a terrified little girl, screaming for help in the nightmarish darkness, only to find herself abandoned and alone. *She had been locked in that hell for a whole day?* It was inconceivable.

Even as a child, David Wentworth was worthy of contempt.

Another series of unbidden images filtered into Erik's mind, this time in recollection of what he'd witnessed on the terrace of the Grayson's estate: David's leering gaze. Melodie's discomfort. The bastard's hand poised to strike her face.

A sudden suspicion came upon Erik. "Why did you leave the Wentworths?" he asked, his voice deceptively quiet. "It was your home. You had Henry there, a man who adores you like a father. Something happened to make you leave, and my gut tells me that David Wentworth was involved."

"Why would you think that?" Melodie questioned.

"The night of 'Celebration's' debut. I was there, remember? I saw your reaction to him, and the way he looked at you."

Melodie appeared stricken. Her mouth opened and closed twice, yet no sound emerged.

Erik noticed her hands curled in her lap, clenched so fiercely the nails were digging into her palms. "Stop that," he chided. "You'll draw blood." He plucked at her fingers until they unfurled. "Did he hurt you? Tell me," he urged.

When Melodie finally responded, her voice was monotone. "Your perceptiveness continually amazes me, Erik. Yes, David caught me alone one day. I tried to run away, but he tripped me. I fell, and then he was on top of me, his mouth on mine." She grimaced. "I refuse to call it a kiss. I managed to free one of my hands and stabbed him. Then I escaped."

"Stabbed him? With a knife?" The thought of a wounded, bleeding David pleased Erik.

"No, unfortunately a knife wasn't available," Melodie said wryly. "I used my trusty pen."

Erik gripped the edge of the table. Melodie had provided few details, but he was more than capable of filling in the gaps. He was flooded with disturbing images yet again.

A rush of hot blood raced through his veins. Equal portions of his fury were directed at David and himself.

I should have killed the bastard while I had the chance.

Erik leapt to his feet. The chair nearly overturned beneath him before he caught it with one hand. He knew he was a hair width away from exploding.

Melodie glanced upward with a quizzical look.

Erik's gaze flitted around the room and landed on a nearby glass. He swiped it from the table. As soon as his fingers closed around the smooth surface, he realized that no amount of water would cool the rage that threatened to spiral out of control.

The glass flew from his fingertips. It struck the stone wall in a far corner, and shattered with a sharp burst of sound.

Erik blinked, watching the glittering fragments sprinkle to the floor. He unclenched his fists. The tension in his muscles eased.

It was odd, but he couldn't recall throwing the glass.

"Erik?" Melodie was standing, her eyes wide.

"I dropped a glass," he intoned, his voice raspy.

Although she gave no indication of whether she believed that dubious statement, she didn't question it. "You're upset," she said. "With me?"

"No, ma chère, not with you."

"With David, then. Perhaps I shouldn't have told you. He's not worth getting upset over."

Erik felt drained, as if all his energy had disintegrated with the shards of glass littering the floor. But he had to say or do something.

He stepped forward and cupped Melodie's elbow. "Come with me and wait by the hearth," he directed. "I have something to show you."

"The glass – " she started to say.

"I'll clean it up later," Erik cut in. "You're not to touch it."

He led her to the couch in the sitting room and then went upstairs, taking the steps two at a time before he could change his mind.

Melodie waited on the cushioned seat.

After everything she had revealed, she had no idea what Erik was thinking. Her only clue was a broken glass. And the fact that it had been thrown, not dropped as he had claimed; the startling smash had been too far away.

She heard Sascha emit a whine; the sound seemed sympathetic. Melodie smiled, holding out her hand. Soft fur soon met her fingers, and she stroked the dog's head. She'd never had a pet, but had always been fond of animals. Sascha, in particular, was easy to love – gentle, good natured, and a fine companion.

Melodie didn't have much time to mull over her thoughts. Erik returned quickly and placed something beside her.

"Down, Sascha," Erik said. "Mellie, this is for you. It's large, so it may take you a while to peruse it."

Intrigued, Melodie leaned in for a closer look. Her lips parted with astonishment.

"I'm sorry it's not framed," Erik went on. "I intended to make one, but haven't had the time. Considering all the unpleasantness, I thought you might appreciate this now."

Melodie barely comprehended what he was prattling on about. "You did this? For me?"

"Yes," he replied.

Melodie stared at her gift. It was a watercolour painting of a place that she resided in, but could only picture in her imagination – until now.

In the foreground stood Erik's home. Beyond it lay the green fields and running brook. The opposite side of the water held rolling hills and clumps of trees.

Melodie's eyes roamed eagerly, trying to take in everything at once. The detail was exquisite, from the stones of the house to the purple wildflowers scattered amongst the grass.

She drew back at last, nearly moved to tears, not only by the sheer beauty of the painting, but the thoughtfulness behind it.

Erik sounded concerned as he asked, "Do you not like it?"

Melodie swallowed the lump in her throat before she could speak. "Forgive me, I'm overwhelmed. It's beautiful, Erik, more so than I can express in words. Thank you."

Her response seemed to satisfy him. "Good," he said.

Erik sank down beside her on the couch, not so close that they touched, yet she could feel the warmth radiating from him. An intake of breath preceded his speech. "I want to make one thing very clear to you. You are completely safe here. Consider David Wentworth to be nothing more than an unpleasant memory. Nothing will harm you while you're here with me. Is that understood?"

Although his means of comforting her resembled more of an order, Melodie nodded.

And with a twinge, she realized her infatuation had grown a little deeper.

Ten

Erik stood at the counter, contemplating whether he should buy some eggs. He realized that the woman had asked him a question. "Pardon?" he had to ask.

"I said I haven't seen you in a while," she repeated. She continued to wrap the round of cheese in paper. "How is your lovely niece?"

"She's fine," he replied. Deciding he had everything he needed, he paid for his purchase. The store clerk's cheerful goodbye called out to him from behind.

Erik secured the package in the saddlebag of his horse, yanking at the ties. Ever since his 'niece' had started residing with him, she had apparently charmed more than half the shopkeepers in town. Erik had never experienced so many people attempting to speak with him before. It was disconcerting, and frankly, he wasn't sure if he liked it. Engaging in small talk and conversational pleasantries were skills he sorely lacked, but he supposed those were the expectations in society.

Isn't that what you want? To become a part of society?

Snorting with derision, Erik hoisted himself onto the saddle, and they were off with a jolt. He slowed the animal down after a brief sprint. In response, the horse tossed its head, and the reins jerked in Erik's hands. He had allowed the spirited stallion to race at top speed for almost the entire distance into town. To do so again now wouldn't be healthy, like a child indulging in too much candy.

Erik patted the animal's neck. "Sorry, but you've had your fun. I promise we'll go riding more often."

Another month had passed by in the blink of an eye, with good progress being made on the symphony. Erik was pleased with the advancement of the work and Melodie's technical abilities. With the combination of her intelligence and intuition, she was a quick learner.

The last three days had been especially productive, the notes streaming onto the page. Instead of spending their mornings apart, they had hardly left each other's side, and barely taken the time to eat or sleep; music had been their sustenance.

This afternoon, the whirlwind of activity began to wind down. Since Melodie had not gone into town recently, provisions were slim. Erik had decided it would be best to go on horseback before the shops closed for the evening.

Their meal tonight would be simple: bread, cheese, and wine. He had even purchased dessert, shortbread dipped in chocolate.

Though he didn't know if Melodie possessed a sweet tooth, he hoped she would enjoy the treat.

Melodie gave way to a yawn. She was bone-tired after the rigors of the last few days. The intense session of writing had been extraordinary. In all her years of composing, she had never experienced anything like it.

Feeling the heaviness in her eyelids, she imagined the couch would be soft and inviting. She rose from the piano bench.

A sudden banging noise made her jump; it had come from the kitchen, presumably the door. After a pause, the pounding resumed. She then heard the door creak open.

"Erik? Mellie?" Peter called out.

Melodie hurried to the kitchen, able to weave her way around the house now without her cane. "Peter, what is it?" she asked.

"Is Erik here?"

"No, he's gone into town. What's wrong? You sound upset."

Melodie's hand was grabbed, and she was pulled along.

"You have to come with me," Peter said, his voice filled with urgency. "He's hurting her. He won't listen to me."

Melodie went as far as the door and then stopped in her tracks, literally digging her heels in. "Peter, wait," she said.

His hand continued to tug on hers. Melodie bent down to his level until she could see the boy's face. She spoke in a calm, firm tone. "Tell me what's happening. I can't help you if I don't understand what is going on."

Peter's eyes swam with tears. "It's my father. He found out that Sascha is here, and he wants her back. She tried to bite him, and then he kicked her. I told him to stop, but he won't listen." Peter gave her a beseeching look. "Please, Mellie, maybe he'll listen to you."

Melodie tried to piece together some facts. She recalled Peter telling her that Sascha used to belong to his father. She knew the dog had been badly beaten when Erik had found her. It wouldn't be a far stretch to presume that Mr. Bain had caused those injuries. Though she doubted such a man would listen to anything she had to say, she couldn't stand idly by and do nothing.

"All right," Melodie relented. "Let's go."

Peter took off like a shot. Still connected with his hand, Melodie ran headlong in his tracks. She was strangely terrified and exhilarated to be out in the fields without her cane.

As she became short of breath, she also lost all sense of time and direction. "Do you see them? How much farther?" she asked.

"I see my dad," Peter told her. "We're almost there."

Melodie stumbled several times, but managed to stay upright. A series of ferocious barks peeled through the air, making the hairs on the back of her neck stand on end. She had never heard Sascha issue such threatening sounds before. Intermingled with the noise coming from Sascha was male cursing.

"Dad, stop it!" Peter shouted.

"I told you to go home. Who the hell is this?" demanded the surly voice of Mr. Bain.

Melodie let go of Peter's hand, trying to orient herself with the man's voice. "My name is Melodie. I'm Erik's niece, and this is his dog."

"The hell it is," Bain said. "She was mine before this Erik stole her. The best damn sheep herder I ever had. Now he's been stealing my boy's time too. I need him on the farm, not wasting his time here with his head in the clouds."

"If she was so valuable, why would you have beaten her to within an inch of her life?" Melodie countered. "If it wasn't for Erik, she wouldn't be alive."

Bain sounded hesitant for the first time. "I didn't mean to. It was an accident."

"You were drunk," piped up a childish voice.

"Shut up," his father growled.

"So you admit to beating her," Melodie said. "You may as well admit that Erik didn't steal her. She showed up at his door close to death, and he nursed her back to health. You have no right now to claim this dog as your own."

When he did not respond to her speech, she was hopeful he might be capable of reason after all. She knelt down and held out one hand, crooning softly. "Sascha, come here." A cold wet nose grazed her fingertips. "That's it. You're all right now," Melodie soothed. "We're going home."

It seemed Bain didn't appreciate that declaration. "Stop your meddling, girl," he ordered.

The shove to Melodie's shoulder surprised her. She reeled backwards until she fell on her behind. She wasn't hurt, but the immediate reaction from Sascha made her flinch.

The dog went wild in a frenzied, ear-splitting din of snarling and barking. Added to the commotion were the screams of father and son. A human howl of agony rang out, and Melodie assumed Sascha's teeth had found their mark.

"Sascha, stop it," Melodie cried. Hearing the growling nearby, she crawled a short distance and found the warm fur within reach.

"Goddamn dog bit me," Bain exclaimed.

More barking ensued. Melodie tried to grab on to Sascha before the dog could lunge again.

When the burst of pain exploded in her chest, Melodie didn't know what was happening. She slumped to the ground.

Erik let himself in the front door, juggling the packages in his arms. All was quiet and still. He guessed that Melodie was indulging in a nap.

After depositing everything onto the kitchen table, he went upstairs. As he passed by Melodie's room, he halted at the sight of her bed; it was empty. She wasn't in the house.

Perhaps she went for a walk.

Erik spun around and retraced his steps. Something was amiss, but he couldn't connect the pieces of the puzzle yet. His uneasiness deepened when he spied Melodie's cane by the piano. Not once could he remember her venturing outdoors without it.

He strode once more to the kitchen, his footsteps falling rapidly. The back door was open. He had thought nothing of it earlier; when the afternoons grew stuffy, the door was often left open to allow a breeze to flow in.

Erik stepped outside and looked around. Surely, she wouldn't have wandered too great a distance.

"Mellie," he called.

Erik walked a bit farther. His eyes darted about. He expected to see her sitting somewhere with a book in hand. Nothing but waves of green grass and lone trees met his gaze. He looked toward the water, his sightline following along the bank.

He could see something there in the distance – one figure, possibly two. But Melodie would not have ventured that far without her cane.

Erik almost turned away, but something drew his gaze back again. He squinted against the late afternoon sun.

A faint sound carried on the wind. He recognized it instantly. Sascha's bark.

Erik broke into a run.

As Melodie lay there, fighting for breath, she was aware of the grass tickling her nose. It almost made her laugh, except she felt like crying. Sascha continued her incessant, crazed barking. Peter was yelling at the top of his lungs.

Melodie closed her eyes. She wished she could dig a hole into the earth, bury her head in it, and block out the horrendous noise.

Peter called her name.

She groaned and squeezed her eyelids even tighter. *Please, just leave me alone.*

But the child was persistent, his voice laced with panic. "Mellie, I think I killed him. He's not moving."

That got her attention. "What?" she croaked.

"I pushed him, and Sascha jumped on him." Peter stumbled over his words, nearly incoherent. "He fell…in the water…hit his head on a…a rock. I think he's dead. I killed him."

His shaky voice dissolved into sobs.

Melodie tried to think. *Maybe the man is merely unconscious. However, considering he fell into the brook…*

"Peter, is he facedown in the water?" she asked.

The only response from the boy was weeping. It took effort, but Melodie forced some authority into her voice. "Peter! This is important. Look at your father and tell me if he is facedown in the water."

Peter's crying came to a choking halt. "Yes," he said. "What does that mean?"

If he's not dead already, he soon will be.

Melodie attempted to push herself up; her body refused to cooperate. Lifting an arm, she motioned to Peter. "You have to help me. I can't stand on my own."

With his assistance, she was able to rise. "Take me to your father," she said.

Erik raced through the field.

He couldn't tear his eyes away from the tableau in the distance. He could now discern that the large figure was a man. Next to him was a smaller silhouette, a boy, possibly Peter. Although he did not see Sascha, he could hear her fierce barking.

If Erik had blinked, he would have missed what happened next. He saw the boy and the dog – a flash of black and white – leaping at the man, almost simultaneously. The man fell out of sight into the water.

Each second brought Erik closer to the scene. He spotted a lump of grey, crumpled on the ground.

Isn't Melodie wearing a grey dress today?

Dread knotted inside of him. He found himself doing something he hadn't done in thirty-plus years.

He prayed.

Dear God, let her be all right.

Melodie floundered into the brook. She gasped at the shock of cold water. In contrast, her face felt fiery from exertion.

She bent forward, soaking the front of her dress. Reaching out, she found the man's prone form. His face was submerged under water. She shoved at the body.

"Peter, help me," she said.

"I'm trying," the child replied. "He won't move."

Melodie tried again, willing the man to roll over. It was hopeless. Even if she wasn't injured, she doubted their combined strength would be enough to budge him an inch. It wasn't in her nature to admit defeat, but she was at a loss.

Peter started to cry again. Melodie's heart ached for him. She needed to assure him he was not at fault.

"What the devil is going on here?" boomed an unexpected, blessed voice.

Erik stared down at them, relieved that Melodie seemed to be all right. Though he had been worried to see her collapsed on the ground, he'd then seen her stagger into the water. He assumed she was relatively unhurt, though she looked a fine mess. Her silvery-grey dress was sopping, darkened almost to black. Wet clumps of hair half obscured her face, the rest tangled down her back.

Peter and Melodie burst out talking at once, forming an unintelligible babble.

Erik held up a hand. Before he could speak, Melodie laid her hand on Peter's forearm. "Darling, hush for a moment," she said. She then tilted her head up. "Erik, you must get Mr. Bain out of the water. He's hit his head and is unconscious. I've tried, but I can't move him."

"Of course you can't," Erik said. "He's more than twice your size. Peter, move aside."

They both scrambled out of the way. Erik crouched down and threw the man's arm across his shoulder, hoisting him up. Grunting with the effort, he dragged the limp body up onto the bank and laid him on his back. The round face was pasty white, mouth slack. Water dripped everywhere. But the most important observation was the lack of rise and fall in the chest.

"He's not breathing," Erik said. A memory stirred within him.

Erik rolled the man onto his generously endowed stomach. Starting at the small of the back, Erik ran his hands up along either side of the spine, pressing down hard. He repeated the motion, muttering, "Breathe, damnit."

"What are you doing?" Peter asked.

"He's taken water into his lungs," Erik explained. "I've seen someone revived by this method once. But he has to – "

Erik cut himself off in mid-speech when the body convulsed beneath his hands. Choking and sputtering, Bain spat out a gush of water. He gulped in air with heaving breaths, and then groaned.

Peter escaped from Melodie's grasp and jumped to his father's side. "You're alive! I'm sorry, I didn't mean to do it."

Moaning once more, Bain pulled himself into a sitting position. He touched the side of his head with tentative fingers and winced. "You damn near killed me, boy," he rasped.

"Someone had better tell me what's been happening here," Erik advised.

When Bain looked at him, he recoiled at the sight of Erik's half-masked face. Gesturing for Peter to help him, he teetered to his feet.

The men locked gazes until Bain said, "You're Erik?"

"That's right."

"I came to get my dog. I'm her rightful owner," Bain said, his bearing full of self-righteous anger.

Erik glanced at Sascha. The dog was motionless at Melodie's side, growling from deep in her throat.

"Let us strike a bargain," Erik said. "If the dog goes to you willingly, you may take her."

Bain cast a wary eye at the animal. He stiffened at the sound of more audible growling. "I don't have to bargain with you. I'm within my rights." Though he attempted to put on a show of bravado, nervousness oozed from every pore.

"What good is owning an animal that is more likely to tear off your head than obey any directive from you?" Erik questioned. "She isn't fit for herding sheep any longer. You made sure of that."

A flush of red crept up Bain's neck until it stained his entire face. Erik was surprised when the man did not deny the accusation.

"Fine, you can have the damn dog. But stay away from my boy."

"Dad," Peter protested, his voice small.

Bain threw a withering glance at his son. "Shut up, Peter."

Erik jabbed his index finger into the man's chest and drove him a step back. "You should learn to be more respectful. He is your child, not your property. What is the harm in having him learn to read and write? He's a smart lad with a future ahead of him."

Bain knocked away his hand. "Don't tell me how to raise my son. *My* son, not yours. His life is here on the farm, and that is where he'll stay."

Erik swallowed a stinging retort. One hand clenched into a fist, but he restrained himself from lashing out. Unfortunately, he had no say in this matter.

When Sascha emitted a whine, Erik swivelled around in time to see Melodie keel over. She sprawled onto the grass in a heap.

Erik leapt to her side and drew his arms around her. "What's wrong?" he asked.

"I can't…breathe…my chest…it hurts," she whispered.

Erik raked his gaze across the front of her dress. He could see no bleeding or sign of injury.

Melodie's doe eyes were murky, her face wrenched with pain. "Erik?"

"You're all right," he said, laying her back down. "I'll take you home soon. You're fine, Mellie, don't worry."

Erik stood up. He fixed Bain with a hardened stare that had been known to reduce men to blubbering pools of jelly. "What did you do to her?" he demanded.

The man's mouth opened and closed like a gaping fish, as he stuttered, "I…I didn't do…do anything."

Erik advanced on him in two strides, using his greater height to loom over the man. Baring his teeth, he snarled, "If you value your life, you will tell me what put Melodie into this state, or I swear that I will tear you limb from limb."

Bain goggled at him through bulging eyes, his lips quivering and rendered incapable of speech.

"Speak!" Erik ordered.

Flinching, the cork popped from Bain's mouth, and a torrent of words flowed out. "It was an accident, I swear. The dog bit me, went crazy, I don't know why – "

"Because you pushed Mellie," Peter cut in, scowling at his father.

A pulse ticked beneath Erik's right eye. "You pushed her." His tone was cold and flat.

Bain attempted an explanation, his hands held outward as if warding off an expected blow. "It was barely a push. I didn't hurt her. But then, like I said, the dog came at me. I was just defending myself."

Bain paused. His tongue darted out to lick his lips. "I meant to kick the dog. I knew she was going to jump at me again. She was eyeing my throat, aiming to tear me apart." Pointing at Melodie with a shaky finger, he blurted out, "She got in the way. I didn't mean to kick her. I swear I didn't. Peter, tell him!" He ended the speech on an imploring note.

Peter said nothing.

And Erik heard nothing beyond the boiling blood and fury that roared through him; the force of it obliterated everything from his senses – everything except the snivelling man that cowered before him.

When Bain seemed to comprehend that he was in the direct path of danger, he turned to run.

Erik grabbed hold of the man's shoulder and yanked him back around. At that first contact with the coward's flesh, warm beneath the dampness of his shirt, Erik knew the descent into blind raging fire had begun. And once that slide began, there was no turning back.

The terrified man tripped over his own feet. His clumsy missteps made it all the more easy for Erik. Bain tumbled down in a tangle of limbs. Erik reached out and wrapped his fingers around the man's throat.

As Erik squeezed, Bain's crimson face shifted to form other visages from Erik's past: his father, the gypsy who imprisoned him, country folk who tormented him, and even David Wentworth. Their mouths were cavernous holes that split across their faces in silent screams, their eyes red and streaming with a mixture of tears and blood, begging for a mercy that did not exist.

The nightmarish images twirled from one to another, tossed in a turbulent storm.

Erik gnashed his teeth. Sweat snaked down his temples. His jaw ached with a pounding throb. At last, the whirling visions began to recede, leaving only the face of Bain in its wake – the man who dared to inflict pain on Sascha, Peter, and now Melodie. Erik's stranglehold remained, crushing the life from the body trapped beneath him.

"Erik, stop it. Mellie, make him stop," came a childish cry.

Erik was dimly aware of Peter's plea, but took no heed. Peter was better off without his father.

I'm better off without my father. He sold me to the gypsies. How could he do that? My own father.

Erik frowned. His grip on the throat relaxed slightly. Whose life – whose father – was he trying to extinguish? He did not know the answer.

A pity it isn't David Wentworth's neck between my fingers.

Erik shuddered through another wave of icy sweat. His hands trembled. He stared at them, transfixed; they seemed to be a separate entity, as if he had no control over their impulse to kill.

"Erik, please stop," said a feminine voice. "Listen to me, Erik. You must stop this."

The words cut through the fog of his delirium. Somehow, Erik recognized that it was the voice of reason and sanity. Focusing on the calm tone, the other whisperings in his head ceased their torment.

He let Bain go.

Erik fell back and sat on the grass, his mind reeling. Bain coughed and wheezed. The colour of his face gradually returned to a semblance of normality. With his son's help, he pulled himself into a sitting position. He regarded Erik with a blank expression, his voice hoarse as he said, "You're insane."

Erik threw his head back and laughed. "You have no idea. Ironic, isn't it, that I first saved your life. But remember this – if you ever come near Sascha or Melodie again, if I ever see another bruise on your son, I will kill you."

Erik spoke in a matter-of-fact tone. "And if you think this is an idle threat, you would be mistaken. You have no idea what I'm capable of. Consider yourself lucky today."

As Erik stood up, he avoided Peter's gaze, afraid of what he would find in the boy's eyes. Bain was a pathetic excuse for a father, but he was the only parent the child had. Peter should not have witnessed the attempted murder of his own father.

Instead, Erik's eyes sought out Melodie. She was struggling to take in each breath, her face white.

"Erik, are you all right?" she asked.

"I'm fine," he said brusquely.

"Is Mellie going to d-die?" Peter asked, his voice cracking.

Erik answered without looking at him. "Of course not."

"I, um, could fetch a doctor," came Bain's raspy suggestion.

Erik pivoted around. Bain appeared to regard Melodie with actual concern. "I didn't mean to harm her," he said. "There's a doctor in town who could – "

"No doctor," Erik interrupted. "She's…"

She's mine.

"…my responsibility," he finished.

Erik stepped forward and then halted. "Peter." He waited until the boy looked up at him. Tears shimmered in the bright eyes. "I'm sorry," Erik said.

Without waiting for a reaction, Erik turned his back on father and son. As he scooped the injured woman into his arms, she moaned and bit her lip.

Erik walked as fast as he dared, trying his best not to jostle her. The house looked impossibly far in the distance. Sascha trotted along beside them.

"Erik?"

"Yes, ma chère?"

He glanced down and saw a ghost of a smile hover on Melodie's lips. "I like it when you call me that," she murmured. "Remember...when I said...that I've never fainted...in my life? I think I..."

The sentence was never completed. She slipped into unconsciousness, her head lolling against his shoulder.

Erik increased his pace, awash with déjà vu. It beckoned a memory of the other woman he had once cradled so closely:

Christine.

He had not thought of her in many months. To his amazement, he could think of her now without wincing from the stab of loss that used to plague him at the very breath of her name.

"Christine," he said aloud, testing the name upon his tongue. When he felt no clawing at his heart, no longing in his soul, a sense of freedom overcame him, as if the chains that bound him to the past had been severed.

While Melodie had initially felt as light as a feather, by the time Erik reached the house, his shoulders and arms ached with the strain of supporting her. Sascha sought out her water bowl in the kitchen, and Erik headed upstairs.

He entered Melodie's room and laid her on the bed. The hem of her sodden dress had stopped dripping, but it was still heavy with wetness. He found some blankets in the storage chest. Though it took some maneuvering, he managed to settle her atop the blankets.

As Erik swept a stray tendril of hair from her cheek, he faced a sudden doubt. He had acted out of impulse when he'd refused Bain's offer to find a doctor. In his experience, so-called men of medicine were inept, arrogant fools who killed more patients than they saved.

Erik was no stranger to bruised ribs. Although terribly painful, they healed on their own. He assumed that Melodie suffered from the same ailment; however, he realized he couldn't be certain. If she were to die because he hadn't allowed Bain to summon a doctor...

She's not going to die. She's had her ribs bruised. That's all.

He would have to examine her. And that would entail the removal of her clothing. Had Melodie been conscious, he wasn't sure which of them would be more mortified.

Erik's mouth clamped down into a thin line. He regarded her face once more, taking in the dark, curved lashes, pale skin, and tangled tresses.

"Mellie," he said.

There was no reaction from the unconscious woman.

Dropping his gaze to the high neckline of her dress, he began unbuttoning it. The tiny pearl buttons were too dainty for his large hands, making the task awkward. He finally parted the material to reveal the next layer.

Erik's lips tightened further at the sight of the complex-looking corset. He had not anticipated this endeavour would be so difficult. His eyes travelled upward to rest on the swell of her breasts, hidden beneath the plain white chemise.

A bolt of liquid arousal shot through him, coursing with such intensity that his hands shook.

Erik averted his gaze. But that didn't halt the flood of heat from spreading like wildfire, burning a path through every nerve ending. His breath became harsh and uneven.

He was disgusted by his lack of self-control. Melodie deserved better than this – better than him.

A restless moan caught his ear, and his eyes shifted back to her face. While she had previously looked peaceful, her eyebrows were now drawn together. Her head tossed from side to side. Another sound escaped her throat, more resembling a whimper this time.

Erik wasn't sure if she was in pain or in the throes of a nightmare.

If she focuses on the simple art of breathing, she'll survive.

Erik and Mr. Bain are arguing, their voices raised, but she can't waste her energy in trying to interpret what's happening.

In and out. That's it, Mellie. Breathe in and out. Keep going.

"Erik, stop it. Mellie, make him stop."

Peter's voice severs her concentration, steering her attention away from the overwhelming pain in her chest. She can hear the distressed gagging noises of a life being smothered. It must be Mr. Bain. Whatever Erik is doing to him, he must come to his senses and stop.

She calls out to Erik.

When he laughs, the anguished sound sends a shiver down her spine. What tragedies has he endured to make him behave this way? Without knowing a single detail, she knows the answer must be horrific. It's enough to break her heart.

"Mellie," says a low voice.

Though Erik hides his emotions, every so often a crack emerges, giving her the tiniest glimpse into his soul. He once told her that she would run screaming into the night if he truly revealed himself to her.

Is he right? Is that what she would do?

"Mellie, if you can hear me, wake up," says the persistent voice.

Is she that much of a coward?

"I'm not a coward," Melodie mumbled.

"What?"

"I'm not a coward!"

Good Lord, why is she shouting?

"Shhh, of course you're not, ma chère," the voice soothed. "Far from it."

Melodie's eyelids fluttered and then remained open, her eyes seeing a curtain of nothingness. It took a moment to regain her bearing. Breathing seemed easier, alleviating her earlier panic, and the pain had somewhat subsided.

She was probably in her chambers, though the rough woollen surface beneath her hands was unfamiliar. She guessed it was a blanket, placed underneath her so as not to dampen the bed. Her wet feet and legs trapped under the soaked folds of her dress were uncomfortable.

The room was silent, but she knew he was there.

"Erik?"

"I'm right here," he said.

"How long have I been…?"

"Not very long. Just a few minutes."

She angled her head toward him, reassured by his presence and yet, it wasn't enough. "Would you please come closer, so I may see your face?" she asked.

Seconds ticked by, and Melodie began to regret her impulsive request. He must be offended. Just as she was about to utter an apology, the face from her dreams filtered into view, the edges softened and blurred by her vision.

Erik's eyes were the intriguing green that she remembered; they pierced through to her very core. Her hand strayed to the unmasked side of his face. Erik flinched, but didn't draw back, his eyes narrowing.

Melodie's fingertips connected with his skin, surprisingly smooth to the touch. As she caressed his cheek, his eyelids closed, allowing her gaze to wander. She drank in every detail, from the crinkles adorning the corner of his eye to the full curve of his mouth.

"Thank you," she whispered. And all too soon, she was returned to her sightless world as he faded into a memory.

"How do you feel?" Erik asked.

"Better. The pain is more manageable now."

"Good. You should get out of your wet clothes. Once you've changed into another chemise, get into bed and wait for me," he instructed.

Melodie's jaw dropped. "Pardon me?"

"Forgive me, that didn't come out as I intended," Erik said, wry humour in his tone. "What I mean to say is that I need to examine you. I'm fairly certain that your ribs have been bruised, but I want to rule out any other possibilities."

Heat rose in Melodie's cheeks. "I hardly think that's necessary. I told you I feel – "

"This is not a request, Mellie," Erik cut in abruptly. "I need to change into dry clothes myself. I shall return in fifteen minutes. I trust that will be sufficient time for you."

He exited the room and shut the door behind him. Melodie wondered what he would do if he returned to find she had disobeyed his direct order.

He'll probably undress you himself. You better get moving.

With a sigh, Melodie tried to pull herself into a sitting position. She fell back at the flare of pain. Panting, she slid her legs over the side of the bed. She managed to stand upright with a lesser amount of discomfort.

When she lifted her hands to where the top button of her dress should have been, she discovered that the removal of her clothing had already been started.

Bloody hell.

Melodie continued disrobing, her face hot. Even the tips of her ears were burning.

She moved slowly and carefully, taking the full fifteen minutes to change into a shift. No doubt prompt to the second, a knock resounded on the door just as she tied the sash of her dressing gown about her waist.

"Come in," she said.

After propping up the pillows on the bed, she sat back against them, entwined her hands in her lap, and waited.

Erik approached her, clearing his throat. "I believe you'll have to lower the neckline."

Melodie hesitated. She would have to loosen the drawstring and slip her arms out. "Turn around, please," she said.

"I'm turned," he informed her.

"How do I know you're...never mind."

"You have my word," Erik said, "as a gentleman."

Though his voice gave nothing away, Melodie was certain he was laughing at her.

Ignoring the protests of her ribs, she slipped her arms out of the shift and lay back down. She retained her modesty by covering her bosom with the blanket.

Melodie announced she was ready, and Erik pulled up a chair. When his fingers found their target, she sucked in a breath, unable to hide her wince.

"Sorry," he said, "I know how painful this is. The area is red and swollen, but the skin hasn't broken. It appears the last two ribs of your right side are affected. I'll make a compress with cold water. That should help ease some of the pain and swelling."

The examination was quick and efficient. Melodie rearranged her clothing and sat against the pillows once more. Getting up was more of an ordeal than lying down; she was slightly winded from the exertion.

"What happened to me?" she asked. "I have an idea, of course. I know you were arguing with Peter's father about it."

"He claims he was defending himself against Sascha by trying to kick her," Erik said. "And you got in the way of his boot."

Melodie's guess had been correct. She supposed it was a consolation that the man hadn't deliberately tried to hurt her, but his abuse of Sascha was inexcusable.

"I'm sorry," Erik said.

He spoke so quietly, she barely heard him. "Sorry for what?" she asked.

"I promised that nothing would harm you here, that I would keep you safe. I've failed you."

Melodie couldn't believe he felt responsible for what happened. "Erik, this isn't your fault. That's ridiculous for you to even think that."

"Is it?" He didn't sound convinced.

"Yes, but..." She trailed off, uncertain whether to continue.

"But?" Erik prompted.

Melodie plunged ahead with her thoughts. "Erik, I want you to know that I've come to admire and care for you a great deal. You are the most complex person I've ever met. You can be so kind and gentle, yet I know you have a temper. I knew that when I came here."

Her fingers picked at the edge of the blanket. "I can't ignore what happened today. You tried to kill that man. What if I had been unconscious or more severely injured? I may not have been able to stop you. There is such a well of anger and violence in you. It frightens me, I admit, but I'm more afraid *for* you."

Melodie could hear Erik breathing, though he said nothing. "I'm afraid that one day you'll be swallowed whole by this darkness, that I won't recognize you anymore. And that *does* frighten me," she said emphatically.

She had no way of gauging Erik's reaction. Forcing herself to continue, she said, "We've had an unspoken agreement not to delve into each other's personal affairs, but I'm asking you to trust me. To share your burdens with me. You need to let them out. That's the only way you'll ever be free of those demons."

"And you think talking about them is going to help?" Erik asked, obviously in disbelief.

"It would be a start," Melodie said. "Please, Erik, don't push me away. Just tell me you'll think about it."

Never did a silence seem to fill a room as loudly as it did now.

Melodie focused on keeping her hands still in her lap. She felt a slight pressure against her hair; the touch was so light she might have imagined it.

"Your hair is tangled, and it will be difficult for you to brush it," Erik said. "Would you allow me?"

Nonplussed, Melodie murmured, "Certainly."

Erik returned momentarily with the brush. She closed her eyes, weariness settling over her limbs. The bristles stroked through her hair.

Just when Melodie thought she would drift off to sleep right where she sat, Erik's voice spoke softly.

"I'll think about it."

Eleven

For the next week, Erik kept himself busy. He centered his attention on Melodie and tried to accommodate every possible need. Each time her breathing seemed laboured or her face creased with pain, the sting of guilt propelled him to her side.

His efforts were received with appreciation the day following the incident. On the second day, she grumbled that she was not an invalid. By the third morning, she informed him that his smothering was irritating her nerves. Understanding that she took pride in her independence, he granted her the space she desired.

They continued to work on the symphony. Although Erik suggested putting it aside while Melodie recovered, she wouldn't hear of it. They simply took a break whenever she grew weary.

Erik filled the remainder of his time with physical activities – horseback riding, walks with Sascha, repairing things around the home that had been neglected. As long as he kept himself occupied, he didn't have to reflect on the foolish statement he had uttered.

I'll think about it.

When Erik could no longer avoid turning in for the night, he lay in bed with open eyes, his mind succumbing to thoughts he'd eluded during the day. The countryside was dormant, but he remained alert, torn with uncertainty.

Madame Giry was the only person to whom he had opened up to about his past, yet even she did not know every detail of the horrors he longed to forget. There were some secrets that would stay with him to the grave.

When Melodie had regained consciousness and asked to see his face, he'd stiffened with suspicion. And when her hand lifted, he imagined her fingers like talons, extending out to snatch away the protective mask. The coolness of her fingertips met his unmarred cheek, stroking with such gentleness that his eyes closed of their own volition. It was a moment of surrender, of making himself vulnerable to her feminine whim. His breath stopped, time itself stopped, and his heart thudded painfully in anticipation.

There was no unmasking, no exposure of his deformity, only a whispered 'thank you'. The brief contact between them, from hand to cheek, had meant reassurance to both of them in very different ways.

Twice now, Melodie – or the mere thought of her – had pulled him back from the alluring call of madness. The root of the power she seemed to hold over him was baffling. No one had ever affected him this way before. That was almost reason enough to grant her wish.

Erik was certain of one thing: the devastation of losing Christine had nearly driven him insane with rage and despair; to lose Melodie would be a sentence to death, for the next time insanity lured him to the edge, there would be no one to stop him from tumbling into the abyss.

Evening arrived with darkened stormy skies. Charcoal grey clouds had been threatening rain all day. At last, the first drops spattered onto the wooden floorboards.

Erik hastened to shut the door, just as the downpour began. He placed the last of the dishes away in the cupboard, and listened to the music that wafted from the other room. Melodie had been playing the piano for the last while, not any one piece, but snippets of works from various sources. Some he recognized, but many were unfamiliar. He wondered if they were her own compositions. The current melody was unlike any of the others, and curiosity drew him out of the kitchen.

Dressed in a simple beige housedress with her hair tied back in a ribbon, Melodie appeared rather childlike. The plucking of the notes ceased when she noticed his presence.

"Don't stop on my account," Erik said.

"I'm just playing at random. It's of no import." Her head slanted toward the window. "The rain has come. I hope it will cool things down."

Erik leaned against the piano. "I'm curious about the last piece you were playing. It was charming."

Melodie chuckled. "That's kind of you to say. It's part of the first composition I ever wrote. Very simplistic, naturally."

His interest deepened with this disclosure. "How old were you?" he asked.

"I was eight."

Erik's tongue loosened unexpectedly. "I was six when I composed my first work. When my father discovered my gift, which he was sure had been bestowed upon me by the devil, it was the final straw. He sold me to a band of gypsies the next day."

"Sold you? How could he...but your mother...?"

"I believe my mother loved me, but she was a weak, submissive woman." Erik strove to keep the bitterness from his tone. "The weight of my father's fists and the garbage that spewed from his mouth were constant, unrelenting. She couldn't fight for herself, let alone her child."

Erik contemplated Melodie's upturned face, the eyes that brimmed with sorrow. After the days and nights of indecision, it had come to this.

"Are you sure, Mellie, that you want to hear the tale of a monster?" he asked. "Once I begin, I will reveal it all to you, for you deserve the absolute truth. There is a strong chance that you will never think of me the same way again. The man that you admire may crumble before you, and what is left will be my true self. Someone you might despise." He asked her one last time. "Are you certain you are ready, mademoiselle?"

If Melodie had answered without hesitation, he would have known she was lying or deceiving herself.

She replied after a drawn out moment. "Yes, I am ready."

"Then let us be seated more comfortably. We have a long night ahead of us," he advised. He led Melodie to the couch, lit a candle, and settled down beside her.

He decided to begin at the very beginning.

~~~~~

I've been told that my birth was a difficult one, and that my mother nearly died from the copious loss of blood. I was born prematurely, a tiny, scrawny thing, perfectly formed save for half my face. My father took one look at me and saw not his son, but a repulsive creature that God had cursed him with. He blamed my mother for having spawned me, for surely it was punishment for her wickedness. Had he not been a devout Catholic, he would have put me out of my misery, but both my mother and I miraculously lived.

Until my mother recovered, I had not even a name. She called me Erik, after her father. I have no surname, for while my father allowed me shelter in his home for the first part of my childhood, he refused to acknowledge that I shared his lineage.

My mother created a mask for me. I learned very early on to never allow my father to see me without it. We had a nightly bedtime ritual, he and I. I would kneel on the cold, hard floor by my bed, while he thrust a mirror at me. With my mask removed, I stared at my hated reflection and prayed to God to forgive me for my sins. While I had no idea what sins I had committed, I must have done something to deserve my deformity and my father's contempt. Only once had I carelessly stepped into his view without my mask. He beat me to a bloody pulp for the insolent act, and my mother suffered the same blows for having allowed it to happen.

Although I had no knowledge of the outside world, I had an odd sense of self-awareness. I knew that something other than my face set me apart from others. My mother was my only companion, and she introduced me to music. We had a piano and violin in our home, passed on by my grandfather. From the age of four, I played both instruments flawlessly. I also learned I could sing, often making my mother weep from the purity of my voice.

These abilities were kept secret from my father, but I suppose it was inevitable that he would one day stumble upon them. I can still recall the expression on his face when he heard me playing the piano, singing one of my own compositions; it was one of rapt awe. When I saw him standing there, gaping at me as if in a trance, I was terrified, certain that I was about to receive a thorough beating – or worse, that he would smash the piano to pieces. Rather than being relieved, I should have known something was terribly wrong when he stalked away without saying a word.

The next morning, I was hauled from my bed and marched downstairs. Upon exclaiming that I did not have my mask, he muttered that it was not required. I knew then that I was doomed. My mother cried, begged, threw herself at his feet, but he only kicked her aside and stated that he was about to do something that should have been done long ago.

We walked forever down a country path through the woods. I did not attempt to flee, only covered the right side of my face with both hands, riddled with shame. When we entered what I now know to be a gypsy camp, I was frightened and confused.

My father spoke to large man with black hair and obsidian eyes, his aged face obscured by a beard. The man threw aside the shield of my hands and grinned with sheer fascination at the nightmare of my face. Tinkling silver coins were exchanged. I still did not comprehend what was happening – not until my father turned and strode away, leaving me in the clutches of the stranger. He had always forbidden me to address him as 'Father', but at that moment of abandonment, I screamed it over and over again, hoping to stir some wisp of compassion in his heart.

He never looked back.

As my tears dried, I instinctively knew that I had been condemned to a fate worse than death. While part of me wanted to collapse with defeat, another part of me, stronger and more demanding, rose up to take over my being. It was the same will to survive that had sustained me as an infant. I had no need of God, my father, or even my mother; I could only look to myself.

Approximately five years passed as I travelled with the gypsies from town to town, throughout France and other parts of Europe. I was chained like a dog and put on display for anyone who desired to gawk at "Satan's Son". Since I was treated like an animal, I behaved like one, for I didn't want to disappoint my paying customers. I did not speak, preferring to snarl and bite. There was an occasion where a man's hand strayed too close, and I foolishly tore a chunk out of his flesh. I never saw the fist of my keeper that slammed into my ear, rendering me unconscious for two days.

Only one bloom of a rare sort of happiness was permitted to flourish on the odd day that my keeper was in good spirits, usually when there was an unexpected volume of coins showered at my feet. The gypsies were great lovers of music. I often heard them singing and carousing with a detached kind of longing. I once meekly asked for the violin, and though my keeper roared with laughter, he tossed it to me. When I started playing, he stood stock still with a dazed expression of wonder. Without any false arrogance, I knew my skills far exceeded the best fiddler in the camp. From that day on, I lived for those fleeting moments of pleasure when he would wordlessly hand me the violin. As I touched bow to string, coaxing magnificent melodies out of the instrument, the gypsies all hovered round, like bees gathering to nectar. Music flowed over me, washed away the stench and filth of the hell that had become my life, if only for those few minutes. And for the first time in my bleak existence, I felt powerful.

After two years of being away from France, we returned to my homeland. I took some small pleasure in hearing French being spoken again.

The night of my escape was unremarkable. I endured a beating like any other day, the blows raining down on bruises that never had a chance to heal. When I was released from my chain – a monthly treat that allowed me to roam an enclosed area while under the watchful eye of my keeper – something inside me snapped. To this day, I don't know what made me act in that moment.

Somehow, the chain was in my hands and then around his neck. With the strength of years of hatred in my thin arms, I strangled him until he was dead. How can I explain to you the wild joy that I felt as I regarded his bulging, lifeless eyes? I wanted to howl with laughter and scream with triumph, though I didn't dare make a sound.

Keeping to the shadows, I made my escape through the countryside and by morning, I reached Paris. I survived on the streets for several days, sleeping in alleyways and stealing food from the market. But one afternoon, an observant vendor caught me in the act. He began to chase me and soon, a police constable joined the hunt.

They were relentless in pursuing me. I couldn't seem to dodge them. As I sped around another corner, nearly on my last breath, I ran headlong into a young girl just as she was exiting a building. Before I could pick myself up and continue running, she asked if I needed help.

I was flabbergasted. No one had ever asked me such a question. I'm not sure what response I gave, but she grabbed my hand and took me inside the sanctuary of the Paris opera house.

Her name is Thérèse Giry, and she saved my life. We grew up together in the theatre – she as a ballerina in the dormitories and I, five levels down in the bowels below. She became my contact with the exterior world, giving me everything I could possibly need, including food, clothing, and most importantly, books. I read voraciously on every subject matter, from music and architecture to mathematics and magic. There was nothing that didn't interest me.

Years went by, and as I crossed the threshold from boy to man, books were no longer enough to sustain me. I wanted to conquer the real world. Fearing for my safety, Thérèse tried to dissuade me, but I was determined. I assured her that I would return one day.

My travels took me across Europe and to exotic lands such as Persia. I learned many arts, not from the written page, but from darkly mysterious men who first viewed me as an amusing companion, yet soon came to fear me. Not only did I become highly proficient with a sword and Punjab lasso, but my alluring voice could also hypnotize a man into practically handing over his weapon. Many attempts were made on my life during that perilous phase of my journey and I killed without compunction, though always in self-defence. Well, that is not entirely true, and I did promise you the absolute truth. There was a singular time I accepted money to assassinate a man. I did it only once, as I found it quite distasteful, even knowing that the victim was an unjust and brutal man. Income was found in other ways, such as picking the pockets of the wealthy.

There came a time when I grew weary of it all – the foreign lands and the innate cruelty of people. Just as I had reassured Thérèse, I returned home to Paris. I found that while much had remained the same at the opera house, some things had changed. For instance, Thérèse was recently widowed and had a young daughter. I couldn't impose upon her time and good will to the extent I once had. Besides, I was much more resourceful and independent now. And having experienced a taste of society, I was content to live in peace and solitude in the comfortable lair that I created.

That is, until *she* came along.

~~~~~~

The muted candlelit glow of the room flashed for a split second with white light before fading away. Melodie heard the answering rumble of thunder in the distance.

She detected a change in Erik's tone as he talked about *her*. Until now, he'd spoken without any emotion, as if the monumental events of his life had happened to someone else. But as he told her about Christine Daaé, there were subtle nuances in his voice, a tenderness that made her wonder how this particular tale would end.

Melodie's head was bloated with all that had been exposed. She couldn't stop to think. All she could do was try to absorb the details as they poured out of Erik's mouth. She learned of how Christine had come to live in the dormitories as a young woman; how Erik had become obsessed with her voice, and then his desperate need to possess her body and soul; his contempt and hatred of Raoul, the Vicomte de Chagny. He told her of yet another killing, a stagehand named Joseph Buquet who perished for simply being in the wrong place at the wrong time.

Erik next described the night of the opera house disaster. He sent the chandelier crashing down in the middle of a performance, and amidst the ensuing panic, brought Christine to his lair. When the Vicomte entered his domain, Erik took him prisoner.

Melodie's ribs were aching again, her head pounding, stomach churning, but she dared not ask Erik to stop. He had yet to reveal the Vicomte's fate. Melodie didn't know if she could find it in her heart to excuse another senseless murder. Perhaps Erik was right; there was a possibility that at the end of this night, she would no longer think of him the same way again.

"…so I let him go," Erik was saying. "I let them both go."

For the first time since Erik had begun this tale, Melodie's attention had wavered. "What did you say?" she asked. "You let Christine and the Vicomte go?"

"Yes. Christine didn't love me. Couldn't possibly love me. She loved the boy. I'd had enough of the violence and madness, so I let them go. I'm sure they're living happily ever after," he added sardonically. "I avoided the mob by using the underground tunnels. After hiding for two days, I returned to my lair. It was ransacked and many valuables were gone, but I had my savings well hidden. The ruin of the theatre and rumours of the Phantom made it too dangerous for me to stay in Paris. I came here to England, bought this home, and led a quiet life for two years. Then we met. And I'm very glad we did."

They had come full circle to the present. Melodie was relieved that Erik had not succumbed to killing the Vicomte after all. It gave her hope that he could emerge from this history of bloodlust without drowning in its depths.

Erik's voice had grown hoarse from the continuous talking. "I have a question to ask you."

Melodie tried to pull together her scattered wits. "Yes?"

"You have never inquired about my mask. Why?"

She considered the matter. "I suppose I didn't want to be rude. And perhaps, because of my lack of sight, I don't think about people's appearance as much as I may have in the past."

Erik fell silent for a long moment, and then said, "Mellie, there is one more step in this promise to reveal everything to you. This..." His voice faltered. "This is very difficult for me. The last time my mask was removed was, shall we say, an unpleasant experience. Are you ready, ma chère?"

Not trusting herself to speak, Melodie resorted to nodding. She attempted to steel herself against whatever was coming next. She had assumed he must be hiding a disfigurement of some sort beneath the mask. Now she knew he had been born with it. And suffered greatly because of it.

Erik's face swam into bleary focus. A strangled gasp almost made it past Melodie's throat. She managed to swallow it just in time.

If she was not seeing this face before her eyes, she would not have believed it possible; the left side was so perfect, so strikingly handsome, and the right, God help her, could only be described as monstrous.

The skin was a sickly yellow, mottled with queer lumps in some places and concavities in others. Its texture was a mishmash of thick, almost scaly patches, with areas so thin the skin appeared translucent. The flesh and blood underneath were visible, the skin atop it appearing entirely too fragile; she feared a single touch would make it burst. His cheek was twisted, distorted, as if the bone beneath had shattered and frozen in place, rendering its surface with jagged peaks and valleys.

Melodie's gaze next regarded the right side of his nose, which was simply not there. It extended down normally from his face, but where the tip or nostril should have been was a gaping void. She looked up to see how his right eye was slightly sunken into his face, sitting a fraction lower than the other eye. The ghastly skin puckered around it, extending up through the forehead into the hairline. She now realized that he had been wearing a wig. His real hair was a light shade of brown, seemingly full on the normal side, but straggly and sparse on the right.

Melodie had viewed it all. Now she had to react, not just sit here blankly. Her eyes met his. Though the exposure of Erik's entire face almost made him unrecognizable, the beauty within his eyes remained the same.

Melodie's tone was matter-of-fact. "It certainly isn't pretty."

Erik's gaze flickered with surprise at her statement. Even Melodie was shocked by her quip; it seemed to come out of nowhere.

As they faced each other on the couch, she exhaled a breath and hesitantly raised her hand, not sure of how he would react. When he didn't pull back, she gently pressed her palm against the ravages of his cheek. It felt rough, warm, and possibly not as fragile as it appeared. "Does it hurt?" she asked.

His eyes grew large. "No one has ever asked me that before. No, it's never been painful. You can bear to look at me? To touch me?"

Melodie spoke slowly. "Yes, I can bear it. You are still Erik, and you are still a man. There is no monster here, unless you believe yourself to be one in your heart."

Erik struggled with his words, sounding sluggish as he glanced away from her. "I want…to be a man but…the things I've done…can you forgive me?"

"You have been nothing but kind and good to me. I have nothing to forgive. It is you who must forgive yourself."

Melodie touched his cheek again, waiting until Erik's eyes found hers once more. "If you had killed the Vicomte, who sounds like a noble and decent man who truly loved Christine, you would have been right. I would not have been able to look upon you again without seeing a murderer and nothing else. But you let him go. You let Mr. Bain go. It's not too late for you, Erik. You've already started a new life. It's time to let go of the past."

"And will you be a part of my new life?"

Unsure of the entirety of what he was asking, Melodie hesitated, yet answered truthfully. "I'm not going anywhere."

Erik squeezed his eyes shut. His face crumpled and he fell out of sight.

Melodie felt a tug on her dress. Reaching out with her hands, she found the top of his head. Erik had dropped to the floor and buried his face, just above her knees. A faint sound reached her ears; he was crying.

Melodie froze. She had never expected to witness the towering strength of this man reduced to clutching and weeping into the folds of her dress. The reason came to her with sudden clarity; she wasn't leaving him. At the very heart of it, that is what had frightened him the most.

Melodie bent forward, ignoring the strain on her ribs. She entwined one of her hands within the soft strands of his hair, the other rubbed at his back. A delayed reaction to everything Erik had told her tonight hit her with an invisible force, knocking the breath from her.

Like every human being in this world, Erik had been born pure and innocent. Perhaps God had blessed him with extraordinary genius to compensate for the deformity. He should have been sheltered and nurtured. Instead, he'd been cast out of his home, out of society, and had suffered unimaginable abuse.

Melodie's eyes welled with tears as she thought about the cruelties he'd endured at the hands of his father, the gypsy, and even his mother – a woman who, above anyone else, should have fought with every fiber of her being to protect him.

Erik had been rejected by everyone in his life. Melodie understood that had she turned away in disgust from his face, proclaiming that she could no longer remain in his presence, it would have killed him.

The lump in her throat grew painful, choking her. Tears spilled down her cheeks as she rubbed circles against his back. Beneath her hand, his muscles trembled. She murmured wordless soothing sounds.

And while the thunderstorm raged outside, rain pelting against the window, they held each other until their tears ran dry.

The storm passed, and in the space of that single night, something shifted in their relationship; a friendship had developed.

After the initial shock waned, Melodie was besieged by questions. She longed to know so much more, but was afraid to ask. She did not wish to shatter the fragile bond that had formed.

Melodie did make one point clear. She told Erik that his mask was not necessary – not in her presence, and not in his own house. He replied that he usually wore it even when he was alone, unless it grew uncomfortable after a long day. It had been so ingrained in him, he confessed to feeling naked without it.

Melodie asked to see the mask, admitting she was curious as to how it remained so impeccably in place. Though she wasn't sure if Erik would object, he placed the mask into her hands. She marvelled at its simplistic yet ingenious design. Made of white leather, there was a wire loop that attached to its side. A small spring and a clasp allowed it to snugly fit over the ear. Erik told her that a leather craftsman cut the mask to custom-fit his face, but he designed the critical wire attachment himself. After much trial and error, he found the perfect balance so it sat properly.

Work on the symphony fell back into its usual routine after Melodie recovered from her injury. Although progress had been slowed, they were still in good shape. The completed work was expected to be submitted in two weeks. That would allow the orchestra enough rehearsal time before opening night.

Melodie sat at the piano now, trying out a variation of a theme from the first movement. For the last twenty minutes, she'd been stuck on this frustrating little thorn. She altered it slightly, but remained displeased.

Erik was seated at the adjacent table and noticed her mood. "What is it?" he inquired.

"I don't like this." She played it for him and waited for his reaction.

"It is a bit awkward," he agreed. As he slid next to her on the bench, she shifted over to make room. "Is this for the woodwinds?"

"Yes, for the clarinet."

Erik hummed under his breath before saying, "How about this?" He tapped out another version of the original theme, but also changed the key.

"Much better," Melodie said. "How do you *do* that?"

"Musical brilliance. It comes with the territory," Erik said drolly.

"Indeed?" Turning to him with mock indignation, she asked, "And how about arrogant conceit?"

His laughing eyes came into focus. "I have that in spades too," he replied.

A knock on the front door prevented Melodie's retort.

"He's early," Erik muttered, sounding annoyed.

The warmth of Erik's body left Melodie's side. Henry was coming by for a visit, but wasn't expected until early evening.

"Peter, is something wrong?" Erik's startled question floated from across the room.

"No," Peter said.

"Does your father know you're here?"

"He knows."

Peter's voice came closer, and Melodie swung around on the bench. "Mellie, you're all right," the boy exclaimed, throwing his arms around her.

"Be mindful of her injury," Erik scolded.

Melodie waved off his concern. "It's fine. What a nice surprise. It's good to see you too." She returned the hug and patted the child's back.

Peter chattered away. "I wanted to come before, but my father wouldn't let me. Not until today. He wanted to know if you're all right."

"I'm doing fine, as you can see," Melodie said.

"He feels awful about what happened," Peter advised them.

"Does he, now," Erik interjected dryly.

"He says that I can have my lessons with you, but not as often."

Although this was good news, Melodie didn't hear the expected excitement in Peter's tone. "You don't sound very happy. Is it because of what happened with Erik and your father?" she asked.

Peter did not reply.

Erik cleared his throat and said, "I'm sorry about what happened that day. I know I frightened you. I let my anger get the better of me. It won't happen again."

"But you said if you ever saw another bruise on me, you would..." Unable to finish the sentence, Peter trailed off, sounding shaky.

It took Erik a few seconds to respond. "It was just a threat. I wanted him to know how strongly I felt about him hurting you. Has he hit you since that day?"

"No."

"Good. You need not worry, Peter," Erik said. "I have a temper, but I'm learning to control it. I won't harm your father again."

"Promise?" Peter asked.

"Yes, I promise."

Apparently satisfied, Peter asked if he could stay for a lesson. Erik told him that he would be busy for the next while, but to come again after a fortnight.

When the child had gone, Erik commented, "I don't know if I handled that very well."

"You handled it just fine," Melodie assured him.

"It's hard to believe Bain has had such a change of heart."

She tried to remain optimistic. "Perhaps you got through to him."

"Perhaps," he said, though he didn't seem convinced.

Melodie knew she might be risking Erik's ire, but she asked the question. "Did you make that promise to Peter just to placate him?"

"No, I meant what I said. But if Bain does return to his old ways, there are other means of making him see the light. Don't look so alarmed, Mellie. I have no intention of raising a hand against him again. I have other ways of being persuasive." Erik changed topic with ease. "Where were we? Ah yes, the variation. I assume you want to insert it before the coda?"

Melodie nodded, still musing over his strange answer. She had no idea how to interpret what he meant by 'persuasive'.

It was another mystery that was part of Erik's dubious charm.

Staring at the run of notes in front of him, Erik blinked, realizing he was going over the same phrase and getting nowhere. He tossed aside the quill and leaned back in the chair, stretching out his arms.

Henry and Melodie were in the kitchen, talking over a pot of tea. He had arrived over an hour late. There had been some drama at the Wentworths that he needed to deal with; one of the valets had been accused of stealing.

Other than the delayed start, the meal and conversation had been pleasant. Most of the awkwardness between Erik and Henry had eased over the past few months. Despite his initial reservations, Erik was becoming fond of the man.

Henry had an easy nature and a quick laugh. His relationship with Melodie was a loving one, and Erik often watched the two of them, enjoying their rapport. That kind of closeness was something foreign to him. Even with Madame Giry, there had always been a formality between them that had prevented them from becoming overly familiar with each other. He had preferred it that way.

It was best to keep people at bay. At least, that had always been his philosophy until a certain doe-eyed female composer had crept her way under his skin.

Each morning, Erik held his breath until he was sure that she hadn't fled during the night. The fact that she remained after seeing his face and looking into his past was miraculous to him.

I'm not going anywhere.

After hearing those words, Erik had wanted to kiss her hands, her feet, every inch of her. Instead, he'd wept, clinging to her like a distraught child. In her arms, a sweet calmness had washed over him. It was a feeling he'd never experienced before, and one that he hadn't been able to name until days later.

Peace.

Erik glanced at the clock on the mantel. It was growing late. As if on cue, Henry emerged into view with Melodie on his arm. Erik pushed to his feet.

"I didn't realize the time," Henry said.

Melodie turned her head to stifle a yawn. "I'm ready for bed." She patted Henry's arm. "Shall I walk out with you?"

"No, that's all right," Henry replied. "If Erik doesn't mind, I hoped to speak with him for a few minutes."

Surprised, Erik saw the same look mirrored on Melodie's face.

"Oh. I shall just say goodnight, then," she said. After giving Henry a hug and kiss on the cheek, Melodie wound her way across the room. "Goodnight, Erik."

Even though the motion would be lost on her, Erik inclined his head. "Goodnight."

Erik took a seat across from Henry. With his face half hidden by the mask, he was confident that his discomfiture wasn't obvious. "I hope I've done nothing to warrant another warning from you," he said, recalling the last time they had faced each other like this.

"On the contrary, I wanted to thank you for taking care of Mellie when she was injured," Henry said. "She told me what happened."

Erik wondered how detailed Melodie had been in relaying the story. "No trouble at all. She seems to have recovered well."

"Yes. She speaks very highly of you."

Erik didn't know how to respond to that, but Henry was eyeing him and seemed to expect some sort of reaction. "That's kind of you to say," Erik said cautiously. "I have the utmost respect for her as well."

"Both personally and professionally?"

Erik was certain now that he was being baited. He said nothing, waiting for whatever was coming next.

At last, Henry resumed speaking. "It's quite all right, Erik. Mellie also tells me that the two of you have moved beyond that ridiculous rule of knowing each other on strictly professional terms. She didn't go into any detail, other than to say that you've overcome many obstacles in your life."

Henry paused and then said, "I'm sure you're wondering where I'm going with all of this. It's not like me to ramble, but it has been a long day. I get like this when I'm tired. I know how independent Mellie is, but I can't help worrying about her."

His tone grew wistful. "She was like a gift to me, that child. To this day, I shudder to think what would have befallen her had circumstances been different. Did you know she's originally from France as well?"

Erik raised an eyebrow at that revelation. "No, I didn't."

"I was in Paris, visiting my sister. On one of my walks, I heard the cry of an infant, just as I passed between two buildings. I discovered a baby, wrapped in a blanket, and left to die in that alley. Although I knocked on a few doors in the vicinity, no one knew the child. My sister had her own life and didn't want the burden of a baby."

Henry sank back deeper on the couch. "I could have gone to the authorities, but I couldn't bear the thought of her being relegated to an orphanage. So I brought her back with me. Raised her on my own. Do you think me a foolish man?"

"No," Erik said. "Most men would have ignored her cries or handed her over to an institution. You've raised her with love, supporting her in every way. I think you are a most admirable man."

Erik swayed between compassion and anger at the tragic beginnings of Melodie's life. It seemed they shared another similarity from their childhood. He couldn't decide which was worse – being sold off like some trinket or being thrown into the street with the sewage. "Does Mellie know…?"

Henry expelled a sigh. "Yes, she knows. As she grew older and started asking questions, I considered making up a pretty fairy tale. But in the end, I told her the honest truth."

Henry's voice hardened with an unexpected edge. "And if you wonder why she calls me Henry when I would dearly love to hear her call me Father, I have Mrs. Wentworth to thank for that. She thought it improper for an unwed man such as myself to rear a child on my own. The only way she allowed it was for me to assume the role of a caregiver, not a father."

The coldness in that logic flayed Erik's nerves. "Regardless of what she calls you, you are her father in every way," Erik stated. "I understand that now."

Henry briefly rubbed at his temple. He then leaned forward and gave Erik another direct look. "You've patiently endured my ramblings. Thank you. Now to get to the heart of the matter, have you decided whether to make an appearance on opening night?"

"I've decided not to attend. I'm not fond of public appearances. I'm sure you understand."

"Yes, of course I do," Henry said, his expression pensive.

Erik sensed the older man was holding something back. "What's on your mind, Henry?" he asked.

"I'm sure I'm worrying over nothing, but if you were to attend that night, I was going to ask you to keep an eye on Mellie for me."

"Why?"

Henry spoke slowly, as if choosing his words with care. "It has to do with the son of the family I work for, David Wentworth."

Erik bristled at the name, rasping, "*Him*, that *fils de...*" Before the endearment could be completed, he swallowed hard and snapped, "What about him? Don't tell me he plans to be there."

"I'm afraid he does," Henry said ruefully. "He's been pestering me about information on Mellie. I tell him nothing, of course, but the opening of the theatre and the new symphony are public knowledge. He knows she wouldn't miss it. I assume you know about his harassment of her?"

Erik gave a curt nod of his head as he considered this newest development. He wasn't ready to step into the role of Michael Blythe, the non-existent phantom composer. But neither would he allow Melodie to attend the gala alone with that predator stalking her.

Erik realized that Henry was continuing to drone on. "...known David all his life. He's not a bad young man, just a misguided one. I don't think he would actually harm her, but – "

Erik cut him off. Although they weren't related by blood, it was quite clear from whom Melodie inherited her naiveté. "Stop making excuses for him. You wouldn't have brought this up if you weren't concerned, and from what I know of him, you're right to be worried. However, I give you my word that I'll find a way to watch over her."

Henry angled his head, his brow wrinkling. "I don't understand. How is that possible if you don't attend?"

As Erik answered that perfectly reasonable question, he knew his smile did not reach his eyes.

"I have my ways."

Twelve

Melodie's excitement grew with each day that brought her closer to the symphony's premiere. On the evening that the work was declared complete, she and Erik indulged in a celebratory dinner, complete with a fine bottle of wine and chocolate for dessert. Even Sascha received a treat in the form of a large bone.

Melodie met Henry in front of the newly constructed Skylon theatre, and together, they went in to speak with the managers. Henry had kept in contact with them, but this was the first time she was introduced to the gentlemen – James Wallace and Craig Rosenberg. They presented her with the payment for the symphony. The commission was far greater than what she had received for 'Celebration'. Melodie requested to attend rehearsals so she could make adjustments to the score. She had to assure them she was more than capable of this task on behalf of the composer. When they seemed skeptical of her claim, Henry rose to her defence. They finally relented.

The managers inquired whether the elusive Mr. Blythe would attend on opening night. Melodie regretfully informed them that he would not. Obviously disappointed, they urged her to change his mind, reminding her of the generous bonus that was at stake.

At the rehearsals, Melodie initially relegated herself to a corner, quietly taking notes. The first time she approached the conductor with an alteration, he looked down his nose at her with disdain. Having been warned by the managers that this was precisely why she was there, however, he didn't shoo her away. When she pressed for his opinion later, he admitted that the change was for the better.

Melodie kept Erik informed of all that went on during the sessions. When she asked how he felt about her making these decisions on her own, he stated that he trusted her judgment. She considered that to be high praise coming from him.

The much-anticipated day arrived at last. Melodie was restless and unable to concentrate on anything, much to Erik's amusement. Dinner was a half-hearted attempt to nibble on fruit and cheese. Although Erik persuaded her to have some bread, the dryness snagged at her throat, almost making her choke.

Excusing herself, she pushed away from the table. "I should get ready," she said.

There was a muted thunk as Erik put down his glass. "Be sure to take a look on your bed. I left something for you."

"What is it?" she asked.

"Something you may find useful tonight."

The cryptic words swam round Melodie's head as she proceeded upstairs. Once in her chambers, she shut the door. With hands outstretched, she gingerly inspected the surface of the bed. Her fingers connected with what felt like ripples of silk, cool to the touch. Gathering it more closely to her, she gasped. "Oh my," she breathed.

It was a gown of the loveliest shade of midnight blue she had ever seen. The rich colour reminded her of twilight skies. And like sparkling stars in their midst, she noticed something bejewelled that was attached to the neckline. She removed it and discovered that it was a pale blue crystal hairclip, charmingly shaped like a ribbon tied into a bow. When she touched one finger to the ends of the 'ribbon' hanging down, they gently swung to and fro.

Melodie snapped out of her shock and began rushing about, impatient to try on the dress. After all the necessary layers were in place, she slipped into her new gown. She skimmed her hands down her hips, noting with amazement that the garment fit perfectly.

Melodie sat down and brushed her hair. She then gathered up the sides of her hair and attached the clip, high on the back of her head. Looking into the mirror, she could see there was no need to pinch her cheeks; they exuded a healthy glow on their own.

Her gaze moved lower to look at the bodice, but her eyes couldn't focus. Giving up, she ran her palm along the edge of the neckline, feeling the delicate ruffling. The sleeves were short and off the shoulder, exposing more skin than she was accustomed to. With a final pat to her hair, she was ready.

Melodie floated downstairs, eager to thank the man behind this surprise. "Erik?" she called out.

He was not there. Venturing to the kitchen, she called his name, but her voice only echoed back to her. She returned to the sitting room to check the time on the mantel clock.

"Mellie," came Erik's voice from the direction of the stairs.

Melodie turned toward him. "Erik, I don't know what to say except thank you. Thank you so much. It's so beautiful, and the hairclip, I adore it. Do I look all right?"

During her awkward speech, Erik had closed the distance between them. "You look exquisite," he murmured. "I knew this colour would be most becoming on you."

Melodie flushed with pleasure at the compliment. "Turn around for me," Erik requested. When she obliged, he said, "Everything is perfect, except for the hairclip. It's already sliding out of place. Your hair is so damned silky, I wasn't sure if it would work. Let me try something."

Melodie felt a tugging at the crown of her head as he made an adjustment. "There," Erik said, sounding satisfied. "Is that uncomfortable?"

"No, it's fine," Melodie replied. She pivoted to face him. "I wish you would reconsider, Erik. It saddens me that we won't be sharing the premiere together. You deserve recognition for your work."

"As do you," Erik said. "Does it truly not bother you that the fictional Michael Blythe will receive all the credit?"

Melodie compressed her lips. "I suppose it bothers me a little. But as long as people appreciate the work, then it's enough satisfaction for me."

Several beats of silence went by. "What are you thinking?" Melodie asked.

"There is something I must tell you. I've waited until now because there was no need to upset you in advance," Erik said.

She couldn't begin to guess what was coming next. "Go on."

"David Wentworth plans to be there tonight. And so do I."

Melodie sucked in a breath. "What? I don't understand. How do you know he'll be there?"

"Henry told me. He asked that I watch over you, which I intend to do."

Erik launched into an explanation. "The two of us have probably spent an equal amount of time at the theatre these last few weeks. I've learned the layout, and made some minor adjustments. I should be able to keep an eye on everything that's going on without being observed. I have a good view of all areas inside except the backstage hallways." Erik's tone changed to one of warning. "Whatever you do, Mellie, do not let Wentworth lure you backstage alone."

Melodie almost jumped at the sudden grip of his hand on her bare shoulder. Erik's face came partially into her view. "Is that clear?" he said.

Her head nodded in a jerky movement. His voice softened as he said, "Don't worry. I won't allow him to hurt you again."

Though it didn't help her vision to squint, Melodie regarded Erik through narrowed eyes. "You're wearing a different mask. It's black."

His barely discernible visage disappeared again, along with the warmth of his hand. "Yes. I don't wear it often, but it's less visible than the white one," Erik said.

"So you'll at least be able to hear the symphony," Melodie mused out loud.

"Yes."

Melodie reached out until her hand connected with the glossy finish of Erik's black dresscoat. Now only inches away, she had a direct view of his crisp white shirt. She wished she could see him from head to foot; no doubt he cut a commanding yet elegant figure.

Erik was a man of thoughtful actions more than words. She was touched that he would go to such great lengths to protect her.

Tilting her head back, she stood up on her toes and brought her right hand up to his face. Erik lowered his head until she could see his questioning eyes. She pressed her lips against that smooth cheek, lingering a few seconds longer than she'd intended. "Thank you...for everything," she whispered, breathing in his scent.

Before she completely lost her senses, Melodie pulled away and retreated upstairs.

Erik jumped down from the saddle. He took hold of the rein and led his horse to one of the stable boys. As the lad took the offered bag of coins, he seemed impressed by the weight of it.

Erik had drawn the hood of his cloak over his head before approaching the boy. Combined with the black mask and the darkening of evening, he knew his face was lost in obscure shadow. "I trust you'll take good care of him," Erik said.

Pocketing the generous wage, the boy nodded. "Yes, sir."

Erik crossed through the stable, his strides swift, heels kicking up dust and straw in his wake. As long as he moved with purposeful intent, he was confident that no one would question his presence.

The corridors backstage were buzzing with activity and crammed with people: members of the orchestra, theatre employees, invited guests, and patrons. Wading through the crowd, Erik looked for Melodie but did not see her.

He ducked around a corner and ascended a series of stairs that led up to the flies, high above the stage. The layout of the catwalks suited his needs; they travelled in a 'U' shape, from one wing of the stage, around the rear of the theatre, and down to the opposite wing. It was meant for ease of maintenance on these upper levels, and he admired the architect for this clever design. Hidden doorways were situated at key points to allow access to certain areas.

Erik had spent the last three weeks going over every inch of this building until he knew it as intimately as the Empire or the Paris opera house. He had roamed at night, leaving after Melodie had gone to bed, returning home before sunrise. The Skylon housed no dormitories, and staff kept regular business hours, thus it was empty after the last worker left for the day.

Erik had created three windows, one on each side of the theatre, the third overlooking the front lobby. The panels could easily be removed and then put back in place. Unless someone was searching for them, they would never be found. He'd chosen the locations for the windows carefully; each one was situated behind gilded statues. His viewing area was large enough that he could see over and to either side of the obstruction. There was a risk that someone might catch a glimpse of him, but the statues were high enough in the air that he wasn't concerned.

Erik strode down the walkway now, his cloak fluttering at his back. The path was dingy, narrow, and cramped, but it didn't bother him. In fact, he felt comfortable, as though he had returned home to familiar territory. Perhaps life in the idyllic countryside hadn't completely tamed the phantom that resided within.

Erik halted, realizing he had reached the midpoint of his travels. On one side of the catwalk lay the rear section of the theatre, and on the other, the grand hall of the lobby. He pulled open the hidden panel of his window and took in the view below.

People milled about, their overlapping voices and laughter rising to meet his ears. Everything was polished and sparkling, from the marble floor and columns to the rainbow hue of the women's gowns and jewels.

Erik swept his gaze over the crowd, searching for a particular shade of blue. He finally found the one he was seeking, standing alone on the perimeter of the activity. With her cane clutched in hand, Melodie looked forlorn, as if unsure what to do. Other than her expression, she appeared refined and graceful in her new dress. Erik would not have permitted her to make another appearance in that frilly concoction she'd worn at her last public reception. He congratulated himself on making a splendid choice in this simple yet sophisticated gown.

A rotund and balding middle-aged man approached Melodie. She instantly became animated, smiling and chatting. After a few minutes, the man left, and Henry soon joined her side.

Erik shifted to the right and glanced around to the opposite side of the hall. He knew it would be more difficult to pinpoint Wentworth in the sea of black trousers and dresscoats. Erik's eyes flickered from one gentleman to the next. He then noticed that people were moving inward, flowing toward the theatre entrance directly below him. As he began to turn away, he caught sight of two men coming into the hall; one of them was Wentworth.

Erik glared at the handsomely cut figure. After replacing the panel, he made his way to the next vantage point. Though it was unlikely his footsteps would echo loudly enough to be heard, he tread lightly out of pure habit. This time, he took his position above the box seats, close to the stage. Melodie had her arm linked through Henry's as he led her down the carpeted aisle to the front row. They settled into the red velvet seats.

The programme began with an array of speeches from several people, including the two managers. Bored, Erik gave way to a yawn. The past few weeks of little sleep were catching up to him.

When the first strains of music began, he snapped awake. He recognized the overture to Mozart's 'The Abduction from the Seraglio'. Next, a woman in a bright pink gown with ridiculous feathers in her hair sang two arias. Her voice was average, at best; better than Carlotta's screeching, but nowhere near the bell-like purity of Christine's divine tone.

The showcase piece saved for the finale was the debut of Michael Blythe's 'Symphony No. 1 in E minor'. Erik listened with a critical ear, noting some of the adjustments Melodie had made and finding most of them agreeable.

As the orchestra swelled to the dramatic conclusion, a satisfied smile spread across Erik's face. Melodie had been right; together, they'd created something extraordinary.

The audience failed to react immediately. Then a roar of applause rang out, thunderous in its approval. In a rippling wave, everyone rose to their feet for a standing ovation.

The managers, Wallace and Rosenberg, took to the stage. Wallace was the portly man that Erik had seen speaking to Melodie earlier, while Rosenberg was younger and more dashing. Both men raised their arms in a silent request that they be heard.

"Thank you, ladies and gentlemen," Rosenberg said. "That was a remarkable performance, and we are proud to have debuted this symphony in our theatre. Unfortunately, the composer, Mr. Michael Blythe, was unable to attend tonight. We are, however, pleased to have his lovely assistant here on his behalf, who is a splendid musician in her own right. Please help me in welcoming her to the stage. Melodie, if you would kindly join us."

Clapping began anew. Erik watched as Melodie turned to Henry. Though she was shaking her head, Henry encouraged her to her feet and took hold of her elbow. He led her to the foot of the side stairs that ascended to the stage. Wallace met her at the top step and guided her to the centre.

At first, she was frozen in place. But as the polite applause grew in volume, even encompassing a few cheers, she broke into a beguiling smile and dropped a curtsey. Lifting his arms once more, Rosenberg brought his speech to a close. "Ladies and gentlemen, thank you. And now the night continues in the front hall with more music and celebration. Please enjoy yourselves."

Although most of the guests returned to the hall for the party, some mingled in their seats and along the aisles. Erik held his position, continuing to observe as his 'assistant' made the rounds on stage, having a word with the managers, the conductor, and some of the musicians.

At last, Melodie headed toward the reception area. Erik closed off his view with the panel and retraced his steps along the catwalk. Opening up the middle view port once more, he looked down upon the party in progress.

The denser press of bodies made it difficult to locate Melodie again. After several minutes, Erik finally spotted her making her way toward the far wall. Only then did it dawn on him that she wasn't fond of crowds. Melodie conversed with a few people who approached her, but did not budge from her spot. Erik fidgeted as the time passed.

A familiar looking young man stopped to chat with Melodie. When she accepted his arm and disappeared with him through a side door, Erik's eyes bulged.

What the hell?

He searched his memory, certain he had seen that face before. The answer came to him at last with an accompanying chill.

The man was here with Wentworth. They had come in together.

"*Merde!*"

Erik almost dropped the panel as he fumbled to replace it. He then ran down the walkway and down the steep staircase, practically flying through the air.

Had he not made it clear that she was not to be lured to the backstage hallways?

Erik kept the anger close to his heart to avoid acknowledging that other emotion that was extending its spidery tendrils:

Fear.

David gulped at his drink as he ambled along, surveying the crowd around him. There was no sign of Melodie. He knew he should have tracked her movements after she'd taken her bows onstage, but the lure of drinks in the grand hall had been too delicious to resist.

"I don't see her on that side either," reported the voice of Ramsey Farr.

David turned to face his friend. Ramsey continued in a bored tone, saying, "Really, David, is she worth all this trouble? Granted, she's pretty enough, I suppose, but there are far greater beauties here." He jutted his chin outward. "Like that curvy blonde bird over there. I've seen her trying to catch your eye more than once tonight."

Following Ramsey's sightline, David regarded the woman who was indeed, a ravishing creature – creamy, flawless skin, golden ringlets of hair, and an enchanting figure encased in red satin. As David met her gaze, she smiled coyly at him. He inclined his head in acknowledgment. Then he turned his back on her and brought the glass of champagne to his lips.

"Later," David murmured, savouring the refreshing liquid. "This is twice now that I've suffered through a mind numbing concert for her, and I won't let it be for naught. I'm not leaving until I've had the satisfaction of speaking with her."

Ramsey's dark eyes danced with amusement, and his moustache twitched. "At least I enjoyed the concert," he said. "The symphony was quite good. Your reason for being here is rather sad, my friend."

David glared at him. "If I want your opinion, I'll ask for it," he snapped. "Did you see her up on that stage, soaking in all that glory? How could this have happened? She's a servant girl, an orphan, who should be relegated to a meaningless life of obscurity. Yet she's up there, having the time of her life, while I'm down here and hating every minute of mine."

Aware that his jealousy was too apparent, David bit his tongue and stemmed the bitter flow of words. As he downed the remaining champagne in his glass, he grimaced. His spite had soured the smoothness of the drink, leaving a rancid aftertaste.

Ramsey chortled under his breath. "Now the truth emerges. I thought you simply viewed her as a conquest since she's rejected your advances. But you're actually jealous of her."

"So what?" David muttered. He fingered his empty glass, already thirsty for another. "I'm jealous of you too. You're a barrister. Important. You love your work."

"Most of the time, yes, but sometimes I hate it too. That's life. I'm sorry to sound like your father, but you need to find some direction. Why not give in and work at his company?" Ramsey suggested. "It might not be as terrible as you think."

David rolled his eyes. "Thread and yarn. That's what he produces. Could anything possibly be less interesting?"

"He's made his fortune from it. I wouldn't dismiss it so easily."

David waved a hand. "He's been threatening to disown me for years. If he really meant it, he would have done it by now. Why don't you stop acting like my father, and start acting like a friend."

"Very well." Ramsey exhaled a sigh. "It's my duty, then, to point out that she's right over there."

David swivelled around to once again follow the other man's gaze. He squinted. "Where?" he asked.

"There, almost hidden behind that pillar. Move to the right and you'll see her."

Taking Ramsey's suggestion, David saw Melodie at last. She was standing alone with her back to the wall. He moved forward and then stopped. Past experience enlightened him to the fact that she wouldn't talk to him. Having her escape from him again was not an option, so he had to entice her away from this crowd. He required a private location for their conversation.

"Ramsey, I have a plan," David said.

Melodie had lost track of how many people had shaken her hand, patted her shoulder, and offered their congratulations. Although the glow of the evening seemed to be wearing off, she held on to its warm sheen for as long as possible. It wrapped around her like a soothing blanket, helping to ward off the jittery anxiety she felt in the midst of this cloying press of bodies.

Melodie wondered how Erik had reacted to hearing the symphony for the first time with the full richness of the orchestra. She hoped he'd found it pleasing. Perhaps he was watching her even at this moment; the thought was disturbing and comforting at the same time.

"Excuse me, Melodie?"

She turned her attention to the unfamiliar voice. "Yes?"

"My name is Ramsey. I work here at the theatre. Though we haven't been formally introduced, I've seen you about. Mr. Wallace wanted to speak to you privately and asked that I find you. Would you mind accompanying me?"

"Oh. Certainly," Melodie replied. As she extended her cane, she felt his hand on her arm.

"Perhaps you would allow me? It would be my pleasure," he said.

"All right."

She accepted the proffered arm, and he guided her through a door. As they walked, he chatted amiably. "I must tell you how much I enjoyed the symphony. There was both drama and beauty, and some passages sounded remarkably exotic."

Melodie listened intently as Ramsey continued his commentary. Thus distracted, she realized they were in the backstage corridors, but had lost her sense of direction. "Haven't we passed Mr. Wallace's office?" she asked.

"Yes, but there is another meeting in there right now. He asked that you wait for him in one of the spare rooms a little further down. Ah, here we are," Ramsey said. He led her into the room. "Just a moment, and I'll turn up the lamp."

The glow of the gas lamp brightened the haze of her vision. Ramsey was already edging out of the room. "I'll let Mr. Wallace know that you're here. He was most anxious to speak with you, so it shouldn't be long."

Left alone, Melodie heard his footsteps fade down the hallway. Her thumb flicked at the top of her cane in a repetitive motion. Even with sufficient light, she remained on edge. When she remembered Erik's warning to not enter the backstage areas alone, her uneasiness grew.

Convinced that lingering any longer wasn't wise, she hurried forward. Before she could get far, a different set of footsteps fast approaching made her hesitate. "Mr. Wallace?" she called out.

In reply, she heard the door close, accompanied by a voice that made her scalp prickle.

"Hello, Melodie."

Those innocuous two words were filled with mocking laughter and a ring of triumph.

Melodie's voice was brittle when she spoke. "David, what an unpleasant surprise. Was this elaborate ruse really necessary?"

"You wouldn't have spoken to me otherwise."

"That's true. Now that your mission is accomplished, what do you want?"

Aware that David had ventured closer to her, she fought the urge to back away. She had no intention of revealing the fact that he intimidated her.

"Just a casual conversation. Seeing you here reminded me of when we were children, and we used to hide behind those curtains to watch the dancing. Remember?"

Melodie nodded. Her guard dropped a fraction as she recalled the fond memory. "I remember," she said.

Parties at the Wentworth home had been frequent when they were children. Their presence had been strictly forbidden, but David had discovered a hiding place in a back corner. They had often spied on the elegant proceedings by peeking between the green and gold velvet curtains. Melodie had been enamoured with the glamorous attire of the guests, and longed for the day when she could be dressed in a fancy gown. David had amused himself by poking fun at people. His observations had always made her giggle.

David's voice interrupted her reverie. "We had such fun," he said. "Not everything that involves me is unpleasant. You've come a long way since childhood. Who would have imagined that years later, you would be the shining star with everyone applauding you."

Melodie was firmly back in the present and wary once more. "They were applauding the symphony and Mr. Blythe, not me. Is there a point to all this?"

"I'm curious about your arrangement with Blythe. How exactly do you assist him?"

"That's none of your affair," Melodie said, "but you know my love of music, and that I have the theoretical ability to write. Mr. Blythe is the composer, and I assist him." She kept her answer deliberately vague.

"But how?" David pressed.

Melodie wasn't about to reveal any details. "You've wasted enough of my time," she said, her voice clipped. "I'm not obligated to answer to you. Goodbye, David."

Making as wide a berth as possible, she started toward the door. Her arm was pinched in a hurtful grasp.

"Don't walk away from me." His tone shifted from charming to cold in a mere blink.

Despite the pounding of her heart, Melodie kept her voice even. "I'm not a servant in your household any longer. I won't take orders from you. Let go of me."

Rather than being released, she was wrenched forward and collided with the solidness of his body. She winced when he entangled a fist within her hair, forcing her head back.

David's face came into view. "I know you're hiding something. Be a good girl and tell me what it is. Or perhaps I should kiss it out of you?"

Melodie's skin crawled at the very suggestion. Her right hand, the one still clutching her cane, was free. Her first impulse was to jab him in the eye, but as much as she despised David, she couldn't bring herself to possibly blind him. She jammed the end of the cane against his throat.

David made a strangled gurgling sound. Freed of his grip, Melodie dropped the cane and whirled around. She ran for the door with arms outstretched. Her palms slapped against wood, but she lost precious seconds as her hands flailed about, searching for the handle. When her fingers closed around it, she almost cried out with relief. She threw open the door and took one step into the corridor.

Melodie squeaked with dismay as she was jerked back into the room. The door was shut so quickly, it almost snagged her hair. Hands clenched around her shoulders, and she was knocked backwards against the wall. The clip in her hair dug painfully into her scalp. She gritted her teeth.

"We've been playing this game for far too long," David snarled, "and I'm tired of being the injured party. You won't get the better of me this time."

As his face started to come into focus again, she opened her mouth to scream.

It was deserted backstage. Everyone had either joined the party or gone home. Erik had already searched half of the maze of hallways to no avail.

Erik heard a sound behind him. He spun around and glimpsed the hem of a blue dress swishing into the corridor before vanishing again. A faint cry reached his ears, followed by a door slamming shut.

He bolted forward and then stopped short as he was faced with a series of doors. Lowering his eyes, he found one with a horizontal shaft of light beaming from below. The lamp was on in this room.

Erik burst through the door. The sight of David with his hands on Melodie filled Erik with fury.

David recoiled, but it was too late. Erik grabbed him by the shoulders. He half dragged, half lifted him off his feet, propelled him through the doorway, and battered him against the opposite wall, face first. Flesh and bone crunched against wood. The resounding yelp of pain was like music to Erik's ears. He hauled the man around. One of his hands wrapped around David's throat; the other flattened against his chest. Erik shoved him backwards into the wall, pinning him there and inspecting him like an insect.

Blood trickled from David's nose. His face began to flush red from a lack of air, and blue eyes brimmed with frightened confusion. "Who…are…you?" David gasped.

Erik tightened his grip. "Since you strut around like Don Giovanni, preying on innocent women, I'm the Commendatore. And I'm sending you straight to hell," he rasped. His icy smile sent David into a paroxysm of struggling against the vice-like grip on his throat.

"What is going on here?" demanded a new voice.

Erik jerked his head around. "This is none of your…" The heated words died on his lips as he recognized Rosenberg, the younger manager.

"Unhand him at once, sir," Rosenberg barked, his tone full of misplaced outrage.

Erik reacted with unhurried reluctance. He issued a final, vicious squeeze on the windpipe and then drew back his hands. As Erik stepped aside, David collapsed in a heap on the ground, wheezing, "He…tried to…kill me."

Rosenberg seemed uncertain of what to do next. "Shall I summon the authorities?"

David pulled himself up, one hand braced on the wall. He swayed on his feet, nose dripping with blood. "No, no," he muttered huskily. "I just need to clean myself up. I'm fine."

Erik couldn't allow the man to slink away. When he took a step toward David, Rosenberg blocked his path.

"I'll ask you to stay put, sir," the manager said. "I think you've done enough." His gaze veered to the side. "Melodie, there you are. I've been looking for...I say, are you all right?"

Erik turned to see Melodie framed in the doorway, pale and dishevelled. He waged a silent war between wanting to shake her or enfold her into his arms.

"Mr. Rosenberg?" she said. "Yes, I'm all right."

As Rosenberg walked away to speak to her, Erik whipped around, only to find the corridor deserted. David was gone. Erik mentally uttered a few choice curses and debated whether to give chase.

"...then I must have misunderstood," Rosenberg was saying. "Sir, my apologies. I didn't realize you were coming to Melodie's aid."

Erik said nothing, regarding the man with a frosty gaze. Rosenberg held out his hand. "Craig Rosenberg. I'm one of the managers of the Skylon. And you are?"

Erik heard Melodie draw in a breath. As if his mouth belonged to someone else, he said, "Michael Blythe."

Erik grasped the extended hand. Rosenberg was so astonished, the appendage lay there like a limp fish. His expression bordered on comical, eyes rounded and jaw unhinged.

At last, Erik's hand was pumped up and down, as Rosenberg stammered, "My God, my *God*, of course. The mask. Those rumours. Mr. Blythe, it's an honour. Thank you so much for coming."

"Could I trouble you for my hand back?" Erik said dryly.

"Of course, terribly sorry. I'm just so excited that you're here. You will join the party, won't you?"

Erik had not thought that far ahead. "I don't know," he replied. "Give me a minute."

He reached out to Melodie, fingers splayed on the small of her back. He guided her back into the room to allow them some privacy. "Are you truly all right? Did he hurt you?" he asked, his voice low.

Melodie grimaced. "When I was about to scream, he knocked my head against the wall. I think it stunned me a little. That's why it took me a while to come out of the room. Is he gone?"

Erik didn't hide his irritation. "Yes, he slipped away."

Closing her eyes briefly, she asked, "Would you remove my hairclip? It's become painful."

Erik moved around her and frowned at the sight of her mussed hair. The thought of that bastard's hands within her hair, on her skin, made him sick with renewed rage. Trying to control the tremors that ran through him, he managed to detach the clip.

He parted the dark strands and found a red welt on her scalp. "The edge of the clip must have dug into your skin," he said. "It's a shallow cut."

"Is it broken?" she asked, sounding anxious.

Erik wasn't sure what she was referring to. "The skin?"

"No, the hairclip."

Her concern over the newly acquired gift almost made him smile. "The clip is fine."

"Good. Please keep it safe for me and put it in your pocket."

Erik slipped the jewelled ribbon into his breast pocket and then retrieved Melodie's cane from the floor. He considered rejecting Rosenberg's suggestion and exiting through the back of the theatre, but he'd already claimed Blythe's identity. Why not carry on the charade?

The party was in full swing in the grand hall. Rosenberg led the way, and Erik entered with Melodie at his side. The manager leapt onto the small stage that was set up for the string quartet. He halted the music and called out for attention. As people became aware of him, the conversations gradually quieted.

"Ladies and gentlemen, I have a special announcement to make," Rosenberg said. "Tonight, we heard Michael Blythe's symphony, and I know we are all impressed. No doubt that it will be performed and equally enjoyed a century down the road." He flashed a grin and raised an arm. "I'm pleased to inform you that Mr. Blythe has been able to join us after all. There he is, off to my left, the gentleman in the black mask. Let us show him our appreciation of his work."

As Erik stood there, a surging tide of applause rolled over him like an ocean wave. For this one moment, he permitted himself to revel in the approval. It all seemed surreal, as if he'd just stumbled into a living fantasy. He made a deep bow.

The applause faded. Erik turned to Melodie and noted the glazed look in her eyes. "Ready to go home?" he asked. She nodded, as if too weary to speak.

They shuffled through the throng. Erik held himself stiffly, ignoring the many eyes upon him. Several people shook his hand as he went by, and although it was obvious they wanted to converse with him, he kept moving.

Henry stepped forth from the crowd. "Mr. Blythe, it looks like you've gone public."

"I suppose I have," Erik said. "It's good to see you, Henry."

"Likewise. Mellie, where have you been?" Henry asked. "I was getting worried, so I asked Mr. Rosenberg to find you."

Melodie was overly cheery when she replied. "Oh, you know how I hate crowded places. I wanted to be alone for a while. I'm sorry to have worried you."

Looking unconvinced, Henry's gaze slid to Erik. "Is that true?"

"I'm standing right here," Melodie snapped. "You asked me a question, and I answered it. Don't ask for verification from someone else. Goodnight, Henry." She pulled on Erik's arm. "Let's go, Er…Mr. Blythe."

Erik held his position. "Mellie – " he started to say.

"Fine, I'll see my own way out." She ripped her arm from his and marched away.

Erik was baffled by Melodie's abrupt display of temper. It was a side of her he'd never witnessed before.

Henry's face was creased with a similarly perturbed expression.

"Sorry, Henry," Erik said. "Could you order her carriage? We'll wait below."

Henry nodded. He fixed Erik with a look that spoke volumes. "Take care of her."

Erik inclined his head. "I will."

Erik chased after the retreating figure. Rather bemused, he watched as Melodie's cane swung back and forth. Most people saw her drawing near and moved out of her way, but those who didn't found their ankles clipped. Judging by their pained expressions, it wasn't a gentle tap. Melodie swept by them with an insincere sounding 'sorry'. Once past the lobby, she located the handrail and glided down the stairs.

Erik tried again. "Mellie, would you slow down?" His attempt to take her arm was thwarted as she shook off his hand.

"I'm perfectly fine," she said.

Though she struggled with the large, heavy main door, she pushed it open. Erik followed her outside. He eyed the next flight of steps that led down to the street. There was no handrail here, just a steep descent of solid grey stone. Melodie used her cane to find the edge of the top stair. She managed three steps before tripping on the hem of her dress.

As Melodie teetered there precariously, Erik had a nightmarish vision of her tumbling down to the cobblestone street and lying in a broken pile of bones. He was at her side in an instant, even as she regained her balance.

"Good God, woman, are you determined to break your neck?" he growled, grabbing hold of her upper arm.

"I told you I'm fine. I can do this on my own," she insisted.

"Either you allow me to assist you, or I swear I will throw you over my shoulder and carry you down."

Her eyes widened and glittered with outrage. "You wouldn't dare."

"Wouldn't I? Do not test me, Mellie," Erik warned, his tone sharp.

Pursing her lips, she averted her head and transferred the cane to her left hand. They traversed down the steps together in silence. The skies were overcast, and despite the glow of the lamps, the street was shadowed in misty darkness.

"Why did you lie to Henry?" Erik asked.

"I didn't want to worry him."

"He's worried anyway, and with good reason. Why on earth would you permit a strange man to lead you away?"

"He told me that he worked here," Melodie said, "that Mr. Wallace wanted to talk to me."

Erik had to admit that Wentworth's plan had been clever. "And of course you believed him. You have always been too trusting."

Melodie gaped at him. "Are you saying this was my fault?"

"Not entirely, but – "

She cut him off, glaring in his direction with reproachful eyes. "How dare you! Yes, that man tricked me, but I could not have foreseen his intentions."

"I specifically told you not to be lured to the backstage hallways. If you weren't so naïve, this never would have happened." His brusque voice lashed out at her.

"Stop shouting at me."

"I'm not shouting," he said, though his fiery breath burned his throat.

"Yes, you are! Your arrogance is beyond belief. Giving me orders, assuming you know what's best for me, an appalling temper." Each phrase was hurled like well-aimed stones. "You're just as bad as *he* is," she finished. Her accusing voice stabbed the air.

Erik flinched as if he'd been struck in the face. The sound of creaky wheels and clip clop of hooves signalled the carriage's approach from behind the theatre. "Your carriage is here," he said coldly, his mouth so rigid he could barely form the words.

The driver opened the side door, and Melodie clambered inside.

"Take her home," Erik said. He sounded as tired as he felt.

"Yes, sir." The driver tipped his hat before scrambling onto the high seat. With a flick of the reins, the carriage lurched forward.

As Erik watched them recede from sight, he fingered the crystal pin tucked into his pocket. Turning at last, he headed for the stable.

David observed the scene unfolding before him. He was hidden behind one of the enormous pillars just outside the theatre doors. While he would have enjoyed booting the couple down the stairs, he simply watched as they continued their discussion on the street.

His nose had stopped bleeding, but not before a few crimson drops had ruined his favourite shirt. He was still seething from the humiliation.

The door nearest him swung open, and Ramsey poked his head out. David beckoned to him.

"Lover's quarrel?" Ramsey asked jokingly.

"Interesting choice of words," David mused. "Do you think it's possible?"

"Anything is possible."

The couple were clearly arguing, but David could only make out snippets of what they were saying. Before long, the carriage arrived, and Melodie got in alone. The masked man spun away and disappeared behind the theatre.

"What do you think is behind that mask?" David asked. He had heard the manager's speech about the composer, but no mention had been made about why the mask was worn. Perhaps it was a means of generating publicity through an aura of mystery.

Ramsey looked thoughtful. "Funny you should ask. I could be wrong, but I am almost certain I've seen him before."

"Go on," David urged.

"Did you ever hear about the disaster at the Paris opera house?"

David shook his head, and Ramsey went on. "It happened about two years ago. I was there."

David listened as his friend's tale unfolded. Ramsey had been romancing a woman who was in the chorus of the opera. That night, during a performance of 'Faust', he had been backstage with her. When he heard an explosion, he ran back through the corridor, intent on investigating. A hideously deformed man knocked past him, dragging the beautiful star of the show in his wake. Ramsey turned to yell out, but in the space of a second, they had inexplicably vanished. Although shocked, he continued toward the stage and took in the chaos. The chandelier had crashed upon the heads of the audience, and fire was roaring its way through the theatre.

David leaned against the pillar, mulling over the story. "And you think these two men are one and the same?" he asked.

"There's no way of knowing unless the mask is removed. That will be your answer." Ramsey shuddered. "That face, it's like looking at Satan himself."

"Michael Blythe," David murmured. "Man or devil? I'll make it my duty to find out."

Thirteen

As the carriage rolled along, Melodie slumped lower in the seat. Her emotions were so jumbled, she didn't know what she felt anymore. This evening should have been wonderful. It *had* been wonderful, until David had ruined everything.

But she admitted that the sour note upon which she'd parted from Erik had been her own doing. Just thinking about the last words she'd thrown at him made her wince. He hadn't deserved that. She hadn't even thanked him for leaping to her defence when David had her cornered.

The ride home seemed long. Usually, she would have nodded off, but tonight, she couldn't sleep a wink; her nerves were too taut. And though she hadn't done anything to strain her eyes, they felt irritated. She couldn't help rubbing at them. No doubt they were red and swollen by now.

Home at last, the driver took her hand and helped her down from the cab. Melodie dipped into her reticule to give him a generous tip. He was a good natured, older man who had been taking her to and from the theatre these past few weeks.

"Did you enjoy the evening, miss?" he asked.

"Yes, it was lovely." She managed a wan smile. "Goodnight."

Melodie entered the house and was greeted by Sascha, a bundle of warm, welcoming fur. Sascha chuffed with contentment as she received a scratch behind the ears and the promise of a belly rub.

In her chambers, Melodie disrobed, saddened to slip out of the beautiful dress. After hanging it in the wardrobe, she trailed her fingers down the material before shutting it away. She stripped off the rest of her layers, breathing easier when the corset was removed. Once changed into her nightgown, she ran a brush through her hair. She hissed with pain when the bristles found the cut on the back of her head. As she stood there, she could feel David's hands entwining through her hair, snaking across her shoulders, his breath hot on her face.

Shuddering, Melodie flung the brush across the room. It rattled and skidded along the wooden floorboards. She hated feeling afraid. She hated feeling helpless. And damn him for making her feel this way.

Where is Erik? He should have been home by now.

She inhaled deeply until she stopped shaking. She then braided her hair as she usually did before bedtime. The mundane task helped calm her. Feeling chilly, she pulled on her dressing gown and then went downstairs.

Melodie approached the mantel to view the clock. It was almost one in the morning. Surely Erik wouldn't have stopped somewhere along the way.

Biting her lip, she fretted that perhaps he had decided not to come home at all.

Melodie curled up on the couch. She soon had company in the form of Sascha. As if sensing her mood, the dog issued a sympathetic whine and licked her face. The unexpected wetness against Melodie's cheek made her chuckle. Sascha sank down beside her and she patted the silky head.

All she could do was wait.

Rather than taking the direct route, Erik chose the most roundabout path to return home. It gave him a chance to cool his head. Barrelling down the near-empty streets atop the stallion's back, his thoughts raced. His anger scattered in all directions, encompassing Wentworth and his companion, Rosenberg, Melodie, and even himself. Despite his best intentions, Melodie had still been hurt, and Wentworth had received only a minor thrashing – far less than what he deserved.

How dare Mellie lump me in the same category as Wentworth.

He rode recklessly toward the outskirts of London. At one point, he rounded a corner and narrowly missed trampling a man who screamed with fright. Erik slowed the horse to a more reasonable pace. As he reached the peaceful country roads, the blanket of night served its comforting purpose. By the time he arrived home and dismounted in front of the gate, his emotions were in check and under control.

Erik ensured the horse was settled in for the night and then let himself in the front door. He lit a candle, illuminating a wavering flame of light. Sascha ambled over to him for a few strokes on the head before retreating to her corner to resume sleeping.

Erik assumed that Melodie had gone to bed. He would have passed by her had she not expelled a sigh. He held the candle outward and saw her stretched out on the couch, nestled on her side. The thin, ruffled dressing gown clung to her body. Within the flicker of candlelight, she appeared to cast an ethereal glow. One hand was tucked under her chin, the fingers curled into a loose fist.

A surge of tenderness rose within him. He couldn't remain angry with her for long. Erik set down the candle. He removed his cloak and covered her with it, the impromptu blanket enveloping her altogether.

Melodie shifted, burying deeper beneath the cloak before her eyes opened. "Erik?" she mumbled.

"I didn't mean to wake you," he said.

Rubbing at eyes still heavy with sleep, she blinked and then sat up. "I was waiting for you. I was afraid that you might not return home."

Although Erik found that particular fear ironic, he dismissed her words. "It doesn't matter."

"It *does* matter. Please, would you sit down?"

He hesitated, but granted her request. As they angled toward each other, Erik was reminded of the night he had made his confessions to her, revealing the secrets of his past.

"I don't think you're anything like David," Melodie said. "I'm sorry I said such a thing. I was upset about everything that happened. I didn't even thank you for finding me when you did. I'm sorry," she repeated.

"I also spoke out of anger," Erik admitted. "Anger and concern for you."

"I know." A visible tremor ran through Melodie, her voice almost inaudible. "I hate admitting this, but I was really frightened."

Erik could see the glint of tears in her eyes. He said nothing, reaching out to cup her cheek with the palm of his hand. Leaning into it, she closed her eyes, then scooted forward and embraced him. She buried her face into his chest. The feel of her feminine curves moulded against him caused an old, familiar hunger to stir. If he had any sense, he would push her away now. Instead, his arms locked around her, holding her close.

Melodie nuzzled at the crook of his neck. "Erik, please, kiss me," she breathed.

Erik hadn't realized he'd closed his eyes until they flew open. "What?" he croaked.

"I don't want this night to end remembering his hands, his lips. I want you. Please."

Melodie's voice held a note of pleading. Drawn by an invisible force, he couldn't resist. He didn't want to resist.

Erik swallowed past the knot in his throat and raised one hand to the nape of her slender neck. As his mouth came down upon hers, his heart thudded erratically, a dizzying rush of excitement and desire making his head spin. Though her lips were soft and pliable beneath his, he sensed her shyness, her mouth merely accepting the kiss. He considered pulling away. He then heard her moan in the back of her throat. Her arms tightened around him. When she began to return the kiss, her lips meeting his with a sweet urgency, he felt a thrill of pleasure.

Her hand brushed upward, tracing along his jaw line. He froze when her fingers came to rest against his mask. He released her mouth and stared down at her.

"I want the real you," Melodie said softly. "You don't have to hide behind your mask. Not with me. If you trust me."

Wariness battled with longing until he finally surrendered, removing the mask and the wig. She first caressed the tortured flesh of his cheek with soothing fingers, and then bestowed feathery kisses upon it. Erik shut his eyes, on the verge of weeping. This couldn't be real. He expected to open his eyes and emerge from a dream. What other explanation could there be for having this passionate woman in his arms, kissing him in all his repulsive glory?

Erik opened his eyes. Melodie was still here, mouth rosy and swollen, cheeks flushed, and a mirrored desire in her eyes. With a strangled groan, he reclaimed her lips and deepened the kiss. When her mouth parted, he pressed his advantage, exploring the moist, inner recesses with his tongue. She stiffened for a moment at the unexpected invasion, but then relaxed. The hesitant touch of her tongue upon his lips ignited liquid heat through his veins. He shivered. He dragged his mouth away to trail kisses down her neck and explore the intriguing hollow of her throat. "God, you're intoxicating," he said, his voice husky. "Your hair. I want it loose and flowing. May I?"

At her nod, he found the tie and loosened it. He thrust one hand through the glossy strands until they spilled over her shoulders. Without thinking, he had gradually nudged her backwards until he was lying atop her. He was careful not to crush her, but the weight of him settled over her small frame.

Melodie's hand pushed up against his chest.

"Erik?"

The tremulous sound of his name cut through the haze of desire. And his rather blatant arousal. Erik sat upright, breathing raggedly as he fought to regain control of himself.

Melodie also pulled herself up. "I'm sorry, I didn't mean – " she started to say.

"It's all right," he cut in, sounding strained. His teeth were clenched so hard his jaw ached. "You asked me to kiss you, not maul you. My apologies."

"No, don't you dare apologize," she said, her voice fierce. She crept closer again and clutched his shoulder. "You showed me how wonderful a kiss could be. I never imagined it could be like that. I'm not very experienced at this."

Erik uttered a curt, humourless laugh. "Neither am I."

"I only stopped you because I could feel…that is, I knew you were…oh dear…." Melodie trailed off helplessly.

"You were right to stop me. At least one of us needs to keep our wits intact. I think it best that we say goodnight."

He held the candle aloft and they went upstairs. He stopped in front of her room. Grasping her hand, he pressed his lips against her fingers. "Sleep well, ma chère."

Once shut in his chambers, Erik fell into a chair. The physical ache of unfulfilled longing was fading, but the exhaustion he had continually batted aside began to invade his muscles and bones. Moving with the speed of someone twice his age, he cast aside his jacket, waistcoat, and cravat. He kicked off his shoes and started unbuttoning his shirt when a knock sounded at the door.

He opened the door and leaned against the frame, waiting for Melodie to speak.

"I don't want to be alone tonight," she stated.

"Mellie..."

"Could we not just hold each other?" she asked, her guileless eyes making the request seem innocent. "Sleep side by side? I know it's a scandalous thing to ask of you, but that doesn't seem to have stopped me before."

Erik rubbed at his temples. "You're determined to test me in every way tonight, aren't you. Do you really think this is wise?"

"I trust you."

"Come in," he grumbled. As he took her elbow and led her to the bed, he noted that she was still wrapped in her dressing gown. What a chaste couple they made.

The bed was barely large enough for the two of them. Erik lay flat on his back while Melodie turned on her side to face him. "Do you make it a habit of sleeping in your clothes?" she asked, her tone teasing.

"Only when there's a beautiful woman in my bed that I'm intent on not ravishing."

"What did you think of the symphony?"

He withheld a sigh. "I'm not in the mood to discuss this right now."

"But did you like it?"

"Yes, I liked it," he said tersely. "Goodnight, Mellie."

"Goodnight," she said.

Erik blew out the candle on the adjacent table and settled his head on the pillow. He was painfully conscious of the enticing figure mere inches away. He had never slept with someone at his side.

Once his eyes closed, enveloping his world to black, he was asleep before he finished the next thought.

In a twist of irony that was both wonderful and cruel, Melodie was never sightless in her dreams. Everything was viewed through perfect vision with rich, saturated colours and vibrant clarity. Awakening to her blurry reality was always a disappointment – unless she was having a nightmare.

Melodie awoke with her heart pounding, mouth dry, feeling as if she'd been fleeing for her life. The details were already receding, yet the feeling of being hunted remained.

She was lying on her side. When she attempted to roll forward, she couldn't move. A heavy weight was draped over her midriff. Another obstruction was across her legs. Panicked at finding herself trapped, the burst of fear in her chest lasted only until she remembered where she was – in Erik's bed.

Melodie extended a hand and felt the outline of his forearm possessively flung atop her from behind. As she regained her senses, she realized just how close he really was. The heat of his body seeped through her shift and gown, warming her skin from her shoulders, down her back. She could only assume that was one of his legs thrown atop hers, the material of his trousers scratchy against her bare legs. The resulting mental picture was vividly clear, making her blush hotly.

Her request had been reasonable enough last night, when she'd been in such a vulnerable state. In the light of morning, however, her fears seemed silly and unwarranted.

Melodie curled her toes at the memory of Erik's mouth on hers. The pulse-quickening sensation of desire was entirely new to her. And now that she'd had a taste of it, she could understand its addiction.

Rhythmic puffs of Erik's warm breath tickled the nape of her neck. As much as she was enjoying his nearness, it was time to get up. She attempted to lift his arm and struggled with the weight of it. He grunted at the jostling movement. She was still trapped, her legs entangled with his.

"Erik?"

She shook his arm and repeated his name louder. Another muffled snort reached her ears. The pressure about her midriff tightened. Then, with an abruptness that startled her, she was released.

She knew he had risen from the bed. He had moved so fast, he must have sprung to his feet.

"Sorry," Erik mumbled thickly.

"It's all right. Did you sleep well?" Despite feeling tongue-tied, Melodie tried to sound nonchalant.

"Yes, I did."

Melodie sat up, adjusted the neckline of her gown, and finally stood to face him. "Sorry to have woken you. Why don't you go back to sleep?" she suggested.

"I'm awake now," he said, though his voice still rumbled in his throat.

She could think of nothing clever to say. "I'll see you downstairs, then."

Melodie hastened to her room. After pouring water into the basin, she washed her face and completed the rest of her morning routine. She then changed into a fresh blouse and skirt. When she reached for her hairbrush, she remembered her fit of temper. Annoyed with herself, she dropped to her hands and knees and made sweeping motions across the floor. She found several hairpins, but that was all.

Melodie jumped up and threw open the door. She tilted her head at the sound of approaching footsteps.

"Is something wrong?" Erik asked.

"I can't find my hairbrush."

She allowed him to enter, then took a few steps and swirled her arm around. "I dropped it here somewhere."

Ten seconds later, Erik placed the elusive item into her hand. "Amazing how you managed to drop it so far beneath the bed," he observed, his tone wry. "Hold still for me. I want to take a look at your wound."

After a moment, he said, "It appears fine. I thought to clean it this morning, but it doesn't seem necessary. It's not painful, I presume?"

"As long as I don't jab it with the brush," Melodie replied.

"Ahh, I think I understand. I wanted to return this to you as well."

She pivoted around to accept the next object, which she recognized as her hairclip. "Oh yes, thank you."

As she looked up, she noticed that Erik had inclined his head just enough for her to discern a bleary view of his face. She blinked twice. "You're not wearing your mask." Her voice was hitched with surprise.

"It does chafe against my skin sometimes," Erik said, his manner hesitant. "Physically, it would be more comfortable not to wear it. That is, if you find it acceptable."

"I've already told you that I do," Melodie said, "and I meant it."

Erik's hand flashed across her vision. He briefly caressed her hair and then tucked the stray strands behind her ear. "Mellie, now that our work is complete, what do you intend to do?"

She had managed to avoid asking herself this question until now. "I don't know."

"Could I convince you to stay?"

The thought of leaving was unbearable, but Melodie had no ready answers. "I don't see how it's possible," she said.

Silence stretched between them until Erik spoke briskly. "Nothing needs to be decided now. Perhaps our next decision should simply be what to have for breakfast."

Melodie wished all of life's decisions could be that simple.

Fourteen

Henry shrugged into his coat and strode down the carpeted hallway toward the front door.

"Henry," called a voice from behind.

Stopping in his tracks, he turned to face the man. "Yes, David?"

"I wish to speak with you," David said.

Despite his irritation at the order, Henry managed to keep his face neutral. "As you can see, I'm just heading out."

"This won't take long."

David disappeared into the drawing room. As much as Henry wished to ignore the directive, he had no choice but to follow. He entered the warmly decorated room, coloured mainly in forest green. As he stood among the comfortable chaises and chairs, his gaze slid to the piano. The instrument gleamed from regular polishes by the housemaids.

Henry tended to avoid this room; it reminded him of Melodie. He supposed it was inevitable that she would have left him one day, but the moment had come too soon. And this man standing before him had been the cause.

"What is this about?" Henry asked.

"That was quite the spectacle the other night," David said. "Everyone I know is still twittering over the mysterious Michael Blythe. According to Father, you're the one who arranged it all. Is that true?"

Henry met the younger man's penetrating gaze. "That is true."

"Fascinating."

David stepped closer. Henry was unnerved by the intensity radiating from him. Usually, David was ducking out of the way of his father's scrutiny or laughing on the arm of a lovely female companion, looking as if he didn't have a care in the world. This focused, serious David was new and somehow dangerous.

"I find it interesting," David continued, "that you share the same surname of 'Blythe'. That could hardly be coincidence."

Not for the first time, Henry cursed his uninspired imagination. When he had conjured up the name of the composer, he'd said the first thing that popped to mind. 'Blythe' was not an uncommon name, yet to claim coincidence at this point would likely be suspicious.

"You're right," Henry said. "We are related, far down the family line in France. He's a distant cousin of mine."

David's eyes appeared to alight with an inner flame at this revelation. "So he *is* from France."

Henry wondered why that particular fact was so interesting. "Yes. Surely you noticed his accent. And you know I have relatives there."

David nodded, looking thoughtful. "Yes, I had forgotten. Since he is family, I assume you know him well?"

Henry answered the question with one of his own. "Why the sudden interest? You've never cared to inquire about my private life before."

"Let's just say my curiosity has been aroused. For instance, what lies behind that mask of his?"

Henry shifted his weight from one foot to the other. "He has his reasons," he said.

"A horrific deformity, perhaps?" David probed.

Henry narrowed his eyes and said, "This is a pointless conversation and becoming insulting. If you'll excuse me, I really must go."

Intending to turn on his heel, he was stayed by David's upheld hand. "Wait, I do have a point," David said. "You don't know your cousin as well as you think. He's a wanted criminal."

"That's preposterous," Henry scoffed, with as much indignation as he could muster.

"It's the truth. Consider that the source is Ramsey Farr, my good friend and barrister."

As Henry listened to David's tale, he wavered between disbelief and a disturbing fear that this outlandish claim could be true. There seemed to be some plausible elements – Paris, an opera house, a composer half hidden behind a mask.

However, Henry was determined to give Erik the benefit of the doubt. The man had come to Melodie's aid several times and seemed to care for her well being.

"A remarkable story," Henry said.

David smiled, but it held no warmth. "No story. It's a fact. You can check your own sources, since you have ties to Paris. I'm surprised at your lack of concern, considering this man is Melodie's employer."

"Leave Mellie out of this." Not bothering to excuse himself this time, Henry turned his back on David and left the room.

David called out to him. "Ask him yourself if you don't believe me!"

Henry kept marching ahead. He closed the front door with more force than necessary, and the glass pane rattled. Jacob was waiting for him by the carriage. After flinging a set of directions to the young man, Henry climbed into the cab.

His thoughts swirled round his brain. As much as he wanted to confront Erik about this news, he reasoned it might be best to approach Melodie first. Henry reminded himself that the bearer of this information was David, regardless of his claim that Ramsey had been a witness to the disaster at the opera house. While he did not know it with any certainty, Henry guessed that David's interest in the fictitious Michael Blythe was somehow related to Melodie.

When the carriage rolled to a stop in front of the iron gate, Henry did not wait for Jacob to assist him. He stepped down to the dirt road and tilted his head back. "Might I have a word with you, Jacob?"

"Yes, sir."

Jacob descended from his post. He held his thin frame with a rigid tenseness, as if expecting to be reprimanded. He regarded Henry through unkempt hair that had fallen across his eyes.

"Has David ever inquired whom you're taking me to visit or where I'm going?" Henry asked.

Jacob looked surprised. "Young Mr. Wentworth? No, sir, he's never asked me that."

"Has anyone else?"

Jacob paused to consider the question. "Mrs. Wentworth asked me once. I told her you were going to the doctor."

"Good, just as we discussed. Now, if David – young Mr. Wentworth – ever asks you this question, you are to recite the same story. I'm visiting the doctor."

With a pointed index finger, Henry extended his arm toward the stone cottage. "You are never to reveal this location under any circumstance, nor the fact that Melodie resides here. I'm sorry to sound harsh, but remember that I am your employer and I expect you to follow my directions. I hope I've made myself clear."

"Yes, sir, very clear."

Henry softened his tone. "I'm sure this is bewildering to you, but I appreciate your discretion. Thank you, Jacob, that is all."

Henry walked up the short path that led to the house. He took a deep breath before rapping on the door.

"Is this better?"

"Yes, Peter, much improved. Go on to the next page," Erik instructed.

Melodie smiled to herself at this exchange, continuing to play the piano. In conjunction with reading lessons, Peter was also learning to write. He had proudly shown her samples of his work, and she was impressed by how rapidly he was progressing. With his keen intelligence, it was a shame he was not enrolled in school. She hoped his future would one day expand beyond the horizon of his father's farm.

Almost a full week had passed since the night of the symphony, yet Melodie remained in Erik's home. He had not asked her again what she intended to do, and she had not brought up the subject herself. She was still in the process of pondering her limited options.

After the considerable closeness she and Erik had shared, they'd spent the last few days avoiding each other. Her bold requests that night had stemmed from the desperate need to erase David's touch from her memory. While she had expected comfort or perhaps a simple pleasantness in Erik's kiss, the acute spark of desire that had ignited within her had left her shocked, thrilled, and shamed. It was safest to keep her distance from him and apparently, he felt the same way.

Melodie's fingers stilled at the knock on the door. Rising to her feet, she heard Erik's familiar footsteps cross the room and then Henry's voice. They had received a note from Henry yesterday, informing them of his plan to visit.

"Do I have to go?" Peter asked with obvious disappointment.

"I'm afraid so," Melodie replied. "Perhaps you can ask Erik which section to work on for your next lesson."

The boy raced away to clamor for his teacher's attention.

"Mellie," Henry said.

Melodie turned to him and accepted a kiss on the cheek. "Hello, Henry. Would you like some tea? I can start the – "

He interrupted her. "No, not tonight. I must speak with you privately."

Sensing his urgency, her brow furrowed. "Privately? I thought you had news for both me and Erik."

"Yes, I shall talk to you together later. But for now, we need to converse in private."

"All right. We can go out back," Melodie suggested.

She let Erik know where they were going and led Henry toward the kitchen. Once outside, she shut the door. "What is this about?" she asked. "You're starting to worry me."

"I don't quite know how to approach the subject, so I'll just come out with it," Henry said. "David made some disturbing accusations against Erik today, connecting him to a tragedy at the Paris opera house two years ago. It's a tale that is almost too fantastical to believe, but I couldn't just ignore it."

Melodie pressed a hand to her roiling stomach. Her heart began to thud faster. *How could David possibly have found out about this?*

"I know you've talked with Erik about his past," Henry went on. "Did he mention the opera house at all?"

Melodie pivoted away from Henry's gaze, her fingers continuing to dig into her stomach. "I'm not sure," she said weakly.

"Mellie, what is it?" Henry asked, sounding concerned.

"I'm just surprised."

She gasped when Henry clamped down on her shoulder. "No," he stated with sudden surety, "you're not surprised. You're worried. I see it in your eyes. My God, so it's true."

Melodie willed herself to deny it, to lie, to protect Erik as he had striven to protect her. But she couldn't do it. *Forgive me, Erik.*

"It's true," she whispered.

She was released from his grasp. Henry began pacing, shuffling back and forth. In her mind, she could visualize the scowl on his face, the creases of age deepening into lines of anxiety.

"How long have you known about this?" he demanded.

"For a while."

"And yet you continue to live with this man. Have you lost all sense of reason? He's dangerous." Henry spoke so rapidly, his words jumbled into each other. "This ends tonight. Gather your things together. You're leaving."

"Henry, I need to know exactly what David told you," Melodie said.

"Why? You've already admitted it's the truth."

"Yes, from the little you've told me. But you know David can't be trusted. He may have added his own embellishments and lies."

Though Henry uttered an impatient sigh, he repeated David's version of what happened that fateful night in Paris. Melodie's heart sank as she realized that all the details in the story were true. While all suspicions and fingers had pointed to the rumoured 'Phantom' of the theatre, it seemed that David's friend Ramsey had been an actual witness, able to place Erik at the scene.

"Well?" Henry questioned. "Are there any inaccuracies?"

"No," she admitted.

"Then let's go."

At the touch of Henry's hand on her arm, Melodie spun away. "No, I can't leave. Not like this," she exclaimed. "I'm sorry to defy you, but I'm not a child. I won't leave as if I'm running away in fear. Yes, I know what Erik has done, but it's in the past and he is a changed man. He would never hurt me," she declared. "The night of the gala, David conspired with his friend to lure me away from the party. If Erik hadn't shown up when he did, David would have…"

Melodie hesitated and then lifted her chin. "Thankfully Erik came to my aid, and he bloodied David's nose. That's why David has come to you with this. He's intent on hurting me in any way possible. Now he's included Erik in his sights."

"This isn't about David," Henry argued. "It's about Erik, and nothing that you've told me convinces me that he's a changed man. People were killed that night, Mellie! Both from the chandelier and the fire. He *is* dangerous, whether you choose to acknowledge it or not."

Henry seemed perplexed. "Your judgment is usually sound, but something is blinding you to Erik's faults." After a lengthy pause, he issued a quiet statement. "You're in love with him, aren't you."

Melodie emitted a strained laugh. "Of course not. That's absurd." She had no control over the blood that surged to her cheeks, flooding her face with heat.

"I've observed the two of you together. The signs are there, whether you realize it or not. I should never have permitted this arrangement," Henry muttered.

Melodie's spine stiffened. "I did not ask for your permission. You're not my…"

She caught herself in time, dismayed at what had been about to fall from her lips.

"I'm not your father. Is that what you were going to say?" Henry's voice was hardened by fury and hurt, almost unrecognizable in its coldness.

"I'm sorry, Henry, I didn't mean it." Melodie reached out to him; her hands found nothing but air.

She heard the creak of the door opening and flinched as Henry bellowed Erik's name. With her heart in her throat, she followed Henry inside.

After seeing Peter out, Erik circled the room before sitting down on his chair by the hearth. He was puzzled by Henry's odd demeanour. Yesterday's letter had intimated at good news, but clearly, something was troubling the man.

Erik shifted in the chair, restless. It had been several days since he had asked Melodie to stay. He'd done so out of pure selfishness, never considering the consequences. He imagined Henry would have an objection if he knew the situation. While Erik couldn't bring himself to retract his request, neither did he mention it again. Being near Melodie, inhaling her scent, caressing her mouth with his eyes – all amounted to sheer torture, so he kept his distance.

"Erik!" came Henry's shout.

Mellie must have told him. Erik braced himself for a father's wrath as he stood and turned around.

Henry strode forth, his normally placid face set with tight-lipped outrage. Melodie rushed in from behind, looking positively ill.

Henry spoke first. "When I first met you, I asked what your intentions were toward Mellie. You lied to me." His glare was hostile.

"I never lied to you," Erik protested.

"I don't believe you. You first tried to lure Christine Daaé into your web, and now you've moved on to Mellie."

Erik almost reeled backwards, assaulted by a wave of shock. His gaze slid to Melodie. Her betrayal of his confidence left him numb with icy rage.

"I trusted you," he spat.

"No, Erik, it wasn't me. It was David," Melodie informed him.

"What?" Erik was jolted by yet another surprise.

"Henry, tell him," she implored.

Erik's eyes returned to the older man, who gave a terse nod of his head.

"Yes, it was David. He stopped me today, just as I was heading out the door," Henry said. "A friend of his was a witness to what happened at the Paris opera house, the way you dragged Miss Daaé away and disappeared. It seems that no one actually saw you tamper with the chandelier, but the belief is that you also sent it hurtling down. Do you deny it?"

For the first time in a long while, Erik felt like an animal, backed into a corner. His past would forever haunt him. "It's true," he said.

Something flickered across Henry's features, as if he hadn't expected Erik's admission. "Now I know why you first refused to answer my questions about your past. What do you have to say for yourself now?"

"I'm not proud of what I did," Erik said, "but it's in the past. I'm trying to forge a new life."

"Mellie thinks you're a changed man. Are you?"

Erik knew that Henry's questions were justified, but the interrogation strained his nerves. His tension mounted. "I'm trying."

"That's not good enough. I think this has been your plan all along. What you failed to do with Christine, you're now attempting with Mellie."

Hearing *her* name once more was the breaking point. "Do not speak to me about Christine!" Erik exploded. "You know nothing of her or of my life, so do not presume to pass judgment on me."

Erik struggled to rein in his temper. "Whether or not you believe me, I have no ulterior motive where Mellie is concerned. I have committed terrible deeds. I don't deny it. And while I'm trying to move on, people like you and Wentworth continue to throw my past in my face."

Henry would not back down. "You committed a deliberate act of destruction that cost people their lives. Shouldn't you face the consequences of your actions?"

"If I return to Paris, I'll be executed. Would that please you, Henry?" Erik asked grimly.

Silence descended between them as they regarded each other.

When Henry responded at last, he sounded weary. "No. I would find no pleasure in yet another death." He rubbed at the nape of his neck and turned his attention to Melodie. "Mellie, what can I say to convince you to leave?"

"I'm sorry. I've made my decision." Though her voice was soft, it was firm in her resolve.

Henry reached into his coat pocket. He withdrew a bag and a sealed envelope, and handed both items to Erik. "This is the original reason for my visit," Henry said. "I had a meeting with Mr. Wallace and Mr. Rosenberg. They've honoured their promise of a bonus for Michael Blythe's appearance at the gala. In that note, you'll find their request for another commission."

Erik raised an eyebrow. "You have no objection to Mellie and me continuing to work together?"

"It seems that neither my opinions nor my concerns are of any import. Mellie has made it clear that she's capable of making her own decisions and doesn't need my permission."

Henry's tone was coolly rigid. "I think it best that I not visit for a while. I'm not sure why David came to me with all of this, but obviously he has some ulterior motive. I don't want to risk being followed." He gave a slight nod of his head. "No need to see me to the door. I'll let myself out."

As Henry marched away, Melodie looked toward his retreating figure. Her mouth had opened, as if she meant to call after him, but she said nothing.

Erik tossed the bag onto his chair, flicked open the envelope, and scanned the note. "They want a concerto next," he said. He glanced up to find Melodie standing like a statue, as if immobilized by shock. "Mellie, are you all right?"

When her head swung back to face him, he realized she was fighting against tears. "Not really." Her voice cracked and she blinked rapidly.

Erik began to approach her. She backed away, saying, "Please, don't."

The rejection stung. "So he's turned you against me then," he said.

"I'm not going. Not tonight."

In a voice tinged with bitterness, Erik stated, "But you are going."

Melodie's mouth trembled. "I can't talk about this right now."

She fled upstairs. The distinct slamming of a door reached Erik's ears.

He crumpled the paper still clutched in his hand and flung it to the floor. News of the next commission should have been a celebratory one; however, in the aftermath of tonight's confrontation, it hardly seemed to matter.

The time had come. She was leaving him.

He knew it had been unavoidable, yet that didn't make this any easier. If David and Henry hadn't interfered, things could have been different.

Erik's fingers twitched. He launched himself at the mantel and pounded one fist against the jagged stone edge. Blood dripped from the split skin, seeped into the cuff of his shirt. He didn't notice, didn't feel anything, continuing to beat a driving, punishing rhythm.

I have no one to blame but myself.

The note from Wallace and Rosenberg had requested a meeting with Michael Blythe, so the following day, Melodie accompanied her 'employer' to the theatre. The managers wished his next work to be a violin concerto, and if possible, wanted it completed by mid-November. The schedule was aggressive but not impossible. Mr. Blythe agreed to the terms.

When they returned home, Erik suggested that Melodie could compose the concerto herself. He reasoned that she now had the technical ability to do so.

Surprised by the offer, Melodie considered it. She was torn. The independent side of her wanted to accept the challenge of writing the music on her own. Since their relationship had become strained, it would almost be easier. But another part of her – the one that melted within Erik's presence, all logic fleeing from her mind – couldn't stop thinking about Henry's accusation.

You're in love with him.

She had never been in love before. After much pondering, she feared it must be true; despite Henry's anger and her own sense of propriety, she didn't want to leave Erik. And yet she knew she must.

On her next trip into town, Melodie spoke with some shopkeepers about possible accommodations. One woman brightened at the inquiry, as she had a room above the shop that had been vacant for the last year. Melodie explained that while she adored her 'uncle', he'd become increasingly difficult to live with, leaving her no choice but to move out on her own.

With this housing arrangement, Melodie felt she could continue to work with Erik, even justifying it with the fact that he was more of an expert on the violin. The simple truth was she didn't want their partnership to end.

When Melodie announced her plans to Erik, he took the news well; he displayed no emotion. His reaction, or lack thereof, left her both disappointed and relieved. This revelation of being in love was still fresh, fragile, and quite honestly, she didn't know what to do with it yet.

Tonight was her final night in Erik's home. Melodie sat on one end of the couch, attempting to read a book. Erik was in his chair, doing his own reading.

She was finding it difficult to concentrate. Although several candles were lit, it probably wasn't the best idea for her to read in the dim light. She set the book aside and rubbed her eyes.

"Stop that," Erik chided. "You've been rubbing at your eyes for the past twenty minutes."

"Have I?"

"Yes. Actually, I've noticed you doing so for the last few weeks. Have they been bothering you lately?"

"A little," she lied, choosing not to reveal how much they had been irritating her. To speak of her fears aloud would be too akin to sealing her fate.

"You should stop straining your eyes," he said.

Erik's advice was predictable; he had issued it from the day they had met. Melodie didn't respond. She sank down against the cushions and closed her eyes.

After several moments, Erik spoke again. "Have you written to Henry?"

"No, not yet," she replied. "I will."

Recollection of that night stabbed her with guilt. Her words had been so heartless, so cruel. Henry was her father in every way, regardless of their lack of shared blood. She owed him a letter of apology.

Melodie's thoughts flickered to another nagging concern. "Why would David go to Henry about your past?" she asked aloud. "What could possibly be his intent?"

"Something malicious, I'm sure," Erik grumbled, "but I wouldn't want to hazard a guess."

Melodie found it infuriating that they could do nothing but wait for David to make his next move, like an opponent in some crazed game of chess. She worried that he might start spreading rumours. There was nothing society loved more than scandalous gossip. If anyone were able to corroborate Ramsey's story, Erik would be doomed.

Melodie's hand strayed to her eyes again before her wrist was caught in Erik's gentle grip. Her skin seemed to tingle at the contact. With a sheepish half-smile, she drew back her hand to the safety of her lap.

"I could read to you," he offered.

"I would like that."

Lulled by his soothing voice, Melodie's body relaxed until it was limp and pliant, and all thoughts of David were swept into the furthest corner of her mind.

Fifteen

"And here we are," Lauralee said. After unlocking the door, the woman held it open for her new tenant.

Melodie stepped past her, cane in one hand and a large carpetbag in the other. Erik carried her wooden trunk. He dropped it to the floor with a thud.

"It can get stifling in the summer," Lauralee advised, "but now that we're in to September, it's quite comfortable. I've left the window open to bring in some air, and the room has been freshly scrubbed. I'll let you get settled. You know where to find me if you need anything."

"Thank you," Melodie said, setting down her bag. She swung around to address Erik once they were alone. "So, what do you think? I confess that when Lauralee first showed me the room, I didn't inspect it thoroughly. It's not horrible, is it?"

Erik walked about. "No, it's certainly not horrible. The space is small but clean. While I have use of the cart, I'll return to the house and bring some more items."

"Oh? Such as?"

"A small table, a more comfortable chair, perhaps a cushion or two."

"That's really not necessary," Melodie protested. But when he failed to respond, she murmured, "Thank you."

Melodie began to explore her surroundings. With the aid of her cane, she found the bed and then maneuvered around it to the next piece of furniture. Skimming its surface with her hand, she surmised it was the dresser. She pulled open the top drawer.

An undistinguished blur of grey flashed before her eyes. As she stumbled backwards, she felt the scamper of tiny feet scurrying across her collarbone. She shrieked. With arms flailing, she landed squarely on her behind. The impact was jarring, clacking her teeth together.

Melodie sat dazed for several seconds before swiping at the neckline of her bodice with both hands. "Is it gone?" she asked, her voice at least one octave above normal.

"I think it may have run under your skirts," Erik said.

Melodie issued another strangled scream, and bolted to her feet. She shook the heavy cotton of her skirts furiously.

When the distinct sound of male guffawing reached her ears, Melodie froze.

"I'm sorry, Mellie, I couldn't resist teasing," Erik said, choked with laughter.

She stomped toward him and slapped at his chest; the blows landed in time with each word. "That…is…not…funny!"

"Forgive me," he apologized again, though his attempt to inject a seriousness to his tone failed miserably. "Are you hurt?" he asked.

"Only my pride." Melodie bit on her lower lip to prevent a smile. She wasn't about to give him the satisfaction. But she did have a favour to ask. "Would you please check the other drawers? I don't wish to find another surprise."

"It's the least I can do," Erik said.

He completed his search and stated that all was clear.

Before he left, Melodie said, "Just for the record, mice don't usually frighten me. Only when they lunge for my throat."

As Erik's chuckles faded into the distance, she finally succumbed to helpless laughter.

Considering the extent of the recent upheavals, Erik marvelled at the ease in which he and Melodie returned to their routine of composing together. She usually came by in the afternoon and departed by early evening. At his insistence, he accompanied her back into town, still wary of Wentworth making an appearance.

Their relationship reverted to one of strict professionalism. Erik had come to accept it, telling himself he should be grateful she remained in his life at all. He suspected that most women would have bowed under Henry's pressure and fled, never to be seen again.

During their last days of residing together, he'd hovered on the edge of asking her to reconsider her decision and stay, but he'd held his tongue. The former Opera Ghost would not have relinquished her so easily; however, he was trying to set a new path as a man of civilized society. He was determined to respect her wishes.

When not in her presence, Erik had Sascha for company, and occasionally Peter. For someone who had spent years in self-imposed solitude, it was a disturbing revelation to find himself lonely within his own home. Erik anticipated Melodie's arrival each day with ridiculous eagerness, and after seeing her safely to the shop door, he loathed to bid her goodnight.

The concerto had progressed nicely over the past month; they were now in the midst of the second movement. While the symphony had been boldly dramatic, they decided to make the concerto lush and romantic. What better instrument than the violin to evoke an emotional response from the audience. If Erik had his way, there wouldn't be a dry eye in the theatre.

This morning, Erik began the day by starting to work on a theme he'd been developing since yesterday. Following a quick bite of lunch, he returned to the piano. He came to the conclusion that the theme would be better suited for the final movement and made a mental note to confer with Melodie about it. As he hummed to himself, another fragment of a lyrical phrase started to take shape. He experimented with it for a while before putting quill to paper.

Satisfied with the result, he consulted the clock and was surprised by the hour. Melodie should have been here by now.

Erik wasn't the only one waiting for her; Sascha lay by the front door, eyes watchful for it to spring open. He ventured outside with the dog at his heels, going as far as the gate. He peered down the empty road.

"Perhaps she's ill," he muttered out loud.

Sascha issued a throaty whine, as if in agreement. After taking the dog back into the house, Erik readied Midnight, his newly christened horse. Melodie had named the stallion several weeks ago, stating it was long overdue.

Erik hoisted himself onto the saddle, and he realized he'd forgotten his coat. Dressed casually in a cream-coloured shirt and black trousers, he felt he was presentable enough. With a jab into the flanks of his mount, they were off. It had been a few days since he'd taken Midnight for a good hard run. He could literally feel the powerful animal chomping at the bit. He allowed Midnight his head until they reached the outskirts of town.

Once in front of the shop, Erik dismounted and tethered the animal. He pushed open the door, his arrival announced by a tinkling bell. The shop was crowded, stacked high with goods, and the pungent aroma of cheese permeated the air. Several ladies' heads swivelled round to regard him. Erik took no notice, heading straight for the counter. Two more women who were being served at the front clutched their shawls and scowled at him as he barged his way forward.

"Have you seen Melodie today?" he asked, his tone brusque.

Annoyance flared in Lauralee's eyes, yet her softly rounded features remained composed as she addressed him. "As you can see, I'm with some customers right now. Could you wait a moment?"

No, I can't.

Erik bit back the impatient retort, and said, "Very well. But have you seen her?"

"No, I haven't, but it's been busy today. Just give me a few minutes."

Lauralee returned her attention to her precious customers. Erik spun away and headed for the stairs at the rear of the store, nearly knocking over a precarious display of preserves. At the top of the stairs, he rapped his knuckles on the door. He called Melodie's name. The handle rattled under his hand, but it was locked. He cursed his lack of foresight in bringing his trusty lock-picking tool with him.

Forming a fist, he pounded on the thick wood. "Mellie, it's Erik. Are you all right? If you can't come to the door, call out to me so I can hear you."

The only response was silence.

Erik bounded back down the narrow stairwell and entered the shop once more. He placed himself in front of the counter. The two older ladies were still there; one of them ignored him while the other openly goggled, apparently never having clapped eyes on a masked man before.

Erik pierced the woman with a scalding gaze. "Is there something in particular about me that interests you, Madame?" he asked.

Spindly fingers fluttered to the base of her throat, her winged eyebrows arching so high on her forehead, they appeared poised to take flight. She snatched her wrapped parcels from the countertop, and said, "I'll wait for you outside." The cheery bell and the slamming of the door marked her dramatic exit.

Lauralee ignored them, working efficiently to finish wrapping her remaining customer's goods. She passed them to the woman with an overly exuberant smile. "Thank you. See you next week."

The woman hurried away without a glance in Erik's direction.

Lauralee brushed her hands together. "You were asking about Melodie?"

"Yes, I'm concerned about her," Erik said. "She might be ill. I tried knocking on her door, but she's not answering."

"Perhaps she's gone out. It's been so busy, I might not have noticed."

Lauralee's reasonable tone of voice only heightened Erik's frustration.

He slapped his palms onto the counter. "We've been working together on a daily basis. I expected her hours ago. Something must be wrong. Either you unlock her door, or I will gladly kick it down. The choice is yours."

Lauralee pursed her lips and glared at him. "There's no need to get nasty," she retorted. "I'll open it."

As she brushed past him, she withdrew a ring of keys from the pocket of her apron. Erik followed her plump figure up the stairs, trailing closely behind. Even standing a step below, he felt as if he were towering over her in the cramped quarters.

Lauralee knocked on the door. "Hello, Melodie, are you in there?" she called out. "Your uncle is here to see you."

Erik clenched his jaw. He managed to restrain himself from yanking the keys out of her hands. "I told you she's not answering," he growled.

"I just want to be certain before we go barging in there."

At last, he heard the snick of the lock turning and the creaking of the door. The next sound was Lauralee's gasp and a distressed, "Oh my."

Erik practically pushed her aside to make his way in. "What is...?" The question died on his lips as he surveyed the room.

It was a mess; sheets of staff paper littered the floor, a chair was overturned, a shattered mirror lay fragmented at the foot of the dresser. Erik's gaze flitted over the destruction, and like a moth to a flame, he was drawn to the jagged shards of the reflective silver; they were smeared with dark red, the violent image all too familiar. Blood.

Erik followed the splotchy trail across the wooden floorboards with his eyes until he saw her sprawled in the far corner, unmoving.

"Christ," he swore, and in the ensuing breath, he was kneeling by her prone form. A pulsing knot formed in his stomach.

Melodie lay curled on her side, clad only in her nightgown. Gashes crisscrossed the soft pads of her feet, but the cuts had long crusted over. From a cursory visual inspection, they appeared to be her only wounds.

Erik swept her hair back from her face. The sight of her open eyes that stared into nothingness jolted him. Fear sang a sharp tune, slicing into his heart, stealing air from his lungs. He forced trembling fingers to the side of her throat. Though her skin seemed unnaturally cold, beneath the fragile surface, he felt a slow and rhythmic pulse.

Intense relief rolled over him, weakening his knees so he had to catch himself from keeling over.

"Is...she...?" quavered a feminine voice.

Erik had forgotten that Lauralee was here. He glanced back over his shoulder. She stood with hands twisted together, her face stretched taut with worry. She had only come halfway into the room.

"She's alive," he said. He stood up. "That door, is it the only means of accessing this room?"

Lauralee gave him a strange look. "Yes."

Erik crossed over to the window in three rapid strides. He jiggled the latch at the bottom and looked through the glass. The window was tightly secured from the inside. It was also a sheer vertical drop of twenty feet to the ground below.

"Who else has a key?" he demanded.

"No one."

Erik noticed that Lauralee still had the ring of keys clutched in her hand. He pointed to it. "And that's been in your possession all day?"

"Yes." She patted the front of her apron. "I keep it in my pocket."

"You didn't leave it unattended at any time?" he asked.

"No."

"Are you sure?"

"Yes, I'm sure," Lauralee exclaimed. "You think that someone broke in here and hurt her?"

Lifting an arm, Erik made a sweeping gesture to encompass the chaos. "What other explanation could there be?"

"Perhaps she's ill, as you suspected. I'll go fetch the doctor."

He hesitated, partly in disbelief that this marked the second occurrence of having to decide whether or not to seek a doctor's aid for Melodie.

"No. No doctor," he said.

"But – " Lauralee began to protest.

"I said no!" Erik's patience had completely unravelled where this woman was concerned. "I will take care of her. If I decide she needs a doctor, I will let you know. Now leave us," he ordered.

Lauralee blinked at him with a dumbfounded expression. "But I – "

Erik advanced on her, his voice a feral snarl. "You have wasted enough of my time. Get out before I physically throw you out." When she failed to move, he roared, "*Now*."

Lauralee picked up her skirts and fled.

Erik slammed the door shut. He allowed himself a few seconds to regain his self-control before returning to Melodie's side. Despite all the commotion, she hadn't stirred.

Erik called her name in increasing degrees of volume to no avail. He then gathered her up in his arms and walked over to the upholstered chair. He sat down, holding her across his lap as if she were a child. The top of her head lolled against his shoulder, and he could feel the chill of her skin beneath the gown. He considered retrieving a blanket, yet he didn't want to release her, even for a minute. The natural heat of his body would warm her soon enough.

"What happened to you?" Erik murmured.

The most logical answer was the one that filled him with the most rage: Wentworth. It was only too easy to imagine that devil somehow maneuvering himself inside – perhaps tricking Melodie into opening the door – attacking her, and then leaving her traumatized in the corner.

Erik rocked her back and forth. He spoke soothingly. "I'm here, Mellie. You're safe. But you need to talk to me. Please." He had to coax her back to reality from the blissful, pain-free world she'd entered.

She remained unresponsive. He found himself humming, and his mouth soon formed the words of a long forgotten lullaby. Crooning softly in French, he prayed for a miracle.

Time slipped by. Erik's desperation became sparked by anger. He wanted to shake her, slap her, anything to rattle her out of this void.

When Erik felt Melodie shift against him, the movement was so imperceptible he thought it was his imagination. Then a small hand crept up his shirtfront. She leaned into him, as if seeking his warmth. In return, he pressed his hands against her spine and pulled her in closer.

"Erik?" Melodie mumbled into his chest.

"I'm here, ma chère."

He met her gaze as she lifted her head up. He was relieved to find her velvety dark eyes clear and lucid. Cupping the side of her face with one hand, he stroked her cheek with his thumb and then dropped a kiss on her forehead.

Melodie stared at him through rounded eyes. "I see you," she whispered.

In the next instant, she hid her face against the crook of his neck. The underside of his chin was teased by the softness of her hair. He didn't know she was crying until he felt the wetness upon his skin. Her near-silent weeping tore at his heart. She shuddered in his arms, clung to his shirt. He could think of nothing to do but rub her back in a circling motion.

As her trembling subsided, Erik couldn't contain himself any longer. "Who did this to you? Who hurt you?"

Melodie's reply was muffled. "What? I don't – "

Erik gripped her chin and tilted it upward so he could see her face. "Was it Wentworth?" he asked flatly.

Her red-rimmed eyes widened with understanding. "You think...oh..." Without completing the statement, she jerked her head away and attempted to jump down to the floor. "Please let me go."

Erik tightened his embrace. "Stop struggling. You're not going anywhere. Not with those feet."

"What do you mean?"

He swallowed a sigh. "They're cut to shreds by the broken bits of mirror you must have stepped on. Do you not remember?"

In answer, Melodie shook her head.

"What *do* you remember?" he questioned.

Melodie spoke in a halting voice. "I remember waking to a world of darkness. No matter how many times I closed and opened my eyes, no matter how hard I rubbed at them, I could see nothing. I was plunged into utter blackness. My greatest fear come true."

She raised a shaky hand. "Then I stumbled out of bed and staggered about. I must have gone a bit mad. That's all I remember, until I heard you singing to me."

Erik's impatience evaporated. He could only imagine her anguish. "Mellie, I'm so sorry. But you've regained your sight."

"Yes, but for how much longer? I have to face the fact that I will go completely blind. It's only a matter of when." She briefly caressed his cheek. "Erik, I thought I would never see your face again."

"That would not be a regrettable fact to most people," he said.

She sniffed, as if offended. "Then I suppose I am not 'most people'. But I am embarrassed about how I've behaved, like a child afraid of the dark."

"You were in shock. It's understandable."

Melodie averted her head.

Erik realized that having come to her senses, she must find the position of sitting on his lap disconcerting. "Let's attend to your feet. I don't want the cuts to become infected," he said briskly.

He carried her over to the bed and arranged the covers around her. "I'll go downstairs and see if there's anything useful in the shop."

As he turned to leave, Melodie tugged at his sleeve. "Wait. What was that song you were singing?"

"A French lullaby."

"It was beautiful," she said.

Erik stood riveted, watching Melodie's hand slide downward until it connected with his. She placed a kiss upon his palm; he relished the contrast of her soft lips against his rougher skin. It was almost laughable, really, the delightful thrill he received at so innocent an act.

"Thank you," she murmured against his hand.

He was out the door and down the stairs before he remembered to breathe.

David welcomed the crisp, autumn night air. Having imbibed a good amount of liquor, he was pleasantly warmed from the inside out. In addition to the hint of brandy lingering on his lips, he could still taste Olivia's kisses.

Olivia Stanton, otherwise known as 'the woman in the red dress', had been his source of distraction for just over a month. Since she had beckoned him with come-hither eyes the night of Blythe's symphony, he had introduced himself to her. They had been inseparable ever since. She came from a respectable family and was already spouting talk of marriage. He had soon learned that her nature was clinging and demanding, yet she coated it with such charm, he didn't seem to mind. But he was not ready for the trappings of betrothal just yet.

David rounded the corner of his street and saw his father assisting his mother down from the carriage. Not wishing to endure another barrage of questions about where he'd been and what his intentions were toward Miss Stanton, David shrunk back into the shadows. He emerged from hiding after the front door of the house closed behind his parents. As he approached the carriage, he halted at the sight of the driver. David grimaced. Olivia had distracted him in more ways than one.

"You, get down from there," David barked. His voice boomed in the tranquil night air.

Taken by surprise, the young man almost toppled from his post before he steadied himself. "Y-yes, sir," he stammered. He climbed down to the ground and stood awkwardly, hands shoved into his pockets.

"What is your name?" David asked. "Jeffrey, isn't it?"

"Jacob."

David took a moment to decide how best to go about this. By no means had he forgotten his mission to uncover Blythe's past; the combination of Olivia's allure and his own inherent laziness had simply delayed matters.

Two days after David had warned Henry about his cousin's nefarious deeds, he approached Henry to ask if he'd spoken to Blythe. The old man's reaction had been snappish to the point of being rude. David had been rather impressed by the fine display of temper, something that he had never witnessed in the usually genial man before. It was obvious that David had struck gold. Other than talking with Ramsey again to obtain more details about that night in Paris, David had not investigated any further.

David began speaking in a conversational manner. "I know my father has been generous in allowing Henry use of this carriage. You've been taking him out fairly regularly, have you not?"

"Yes, sir," Jacob replied.

"Where?"

"To the doctor."

"I see. And when was the last visit?" David inquired.

When Jacob hesitated, David assumed he was wondering how truthful to be. David became more forceful in tone. "Out with it now, it's not a difficult question. A few days? Longer?"

"Longer," Jacob admitted.

"How long?"

"A month, I think."

David raised an eyebrow and said, "Interesting. I suppose he's suddenly been cured of whatever ails him. Tell me, does this doctor, perchance, wear a mask?"

Jacob's bulging brown eyes were answer enough.

Satisfied, David smiled. "Thank you, you've been more than helpful. I will call upon you when I feel the need to take a drive."

"Sir, Mr. Wentworth, please," Jacob yelped. "I can't help you. You have to talk to Henry. He – "

David cut off the lad's frantic ramblings, all feigned good will cast aside. "Do you enjoy working for my family, Jacob?"

The young man nodded his assent, head bobbing jerkily.

"Good," David said. "I trust your mother does also. I know she's worked in our kitchen for many years. Let me make myself very clear." He took a step closer to Jacob. "This conversation stays between us, as well as anything I might ask you to do in future. If you cross me, not only will I dismiss you and your mother, I will make damned sure that neither one of you find work in this city again. Unless living in the street and begging for coin appeal to you, I suggest you follow my orders."

When no further protest was raised, David inclined his head in mock pleasantry. "Enjoy the evening, Jacob."

He headed for the house, whistling.

Sixteen

Melodie suspected that she would never know for sure what had occurred that day.

Upon waking and finding her sight void of any speck of light, her mind had reeled in panic. She rubbed at her eyes, trying to convince herself she was still asleep and dreaming. But her dreams were always comprised of luminous colour, never stark blackness.

She leapt from the bed, and stumbled over her own feet. Losing her sense of balance, she staggered about, arms outstretched. Her palms swept across the dresser. While dimly aware of the mirror smashing to the floor, the sound reverberated in a distant corner of her mind. A scream began to build from the pit of her stomach, gaining strength as it coiled up into her throat; the resounding wail exploded in her brain, but never passed her lips.

Her next memory was the lilting sound of Erik's voice in her ear. Seeing his dear face, even half hidden behind the mask, filled her with the most poignant relief of her entire life. She felt as if she'd been granted a second chance – one that she couldn't afford to waste.

The wounds on Melodie's feet needed almost a week to heal. During that time, she was trapped in her room. Lauralee and Erik took care of her, each in a different way: the former provided food to nourish her body, while the latter aided her with music to sustain her mind.

Melodie noticed the unspoken tension between her two caregivers. If Lauralee was in the room when Erik arrived, she beat a hasty retreat without acknowledging him. Only when Melodie pressed him for the reason behind this odd behaviour did he reveal what had happened. He did not regret his display of temper, but she was appalled and insisted that he apologize to Lauralee. Though he grumbled about overly sensitive females, he extended the apology.

They continued to work on the concerto in her room. While hindered by the lack of a piano, they were still able to make progress. Melodie was grateful for the time spent on composing. If she had been completely bedridden with nothing to do for days on end, she would have gone mad.

After the first week, Melodie was able to walk comfortably for short distances. She couldn't abide being without the piano any longer and insisted on working at Erik's home. Rather than hiring a carriage, he suggested she ride with him. She balked at the idea. She had never ridden a horse before. When he had the gall to teasingly ask if she was afraid, however, she accepted the proposal. With her arms locked around Erik's waist, face pressed to his back, she had the most exhilarating sensation of flying.

Almost three weeks passed before Melodie was fully recovered. She now travelled down that same winding road, but this time on foot. A bag strapped across her shoulder contained her latest scribblings of the concerto. Her cane swung to and fro. She strode quickly, happy to be mobile and independent once more. Sunlight warmed her face in contrast to the cool breeze, leaves crunched beneath her feet, and she wished she could see the reds and golds of the trees in their autumn glory.

There had been no further episodes of blackouts in her vision. Melodie was determined to appreciate every day that she awakened to light in her world. She also vowed to react with dignity whenever the darkness became permanent. Although thankful that Erik had found her when he did, she was horrified that he had first thought her to be dead.

Dead! The complete loss of her vision would be difficult to bear, but it would not signify the end of her existence. She wasn't about to wither up and die, like these leaves that had completed their life cycle and now scattered on the wind.

Melodie held her arm aloft, knowing that she would soon reach the vicinity of Erik's home. As the rough texture of the iron fence met her fingertips, she heard Sascha's ferocious barking from within the house. The sound was dim and muffled, but her heart jumped. The last time she had heard that savageness in the dog's bark had been in the presence of Peter's father. Something was terribly wrong.

She was at the gate when a voice called out to her.

"Miss Mellie, wait."

Melodie halted and turned to her left. "Jacob, is that you?"

"Yes. Sorry if I startled you," Jacob said.

The anxiety in his tone made her uneasy. "That's all right. Is Henry inside?"

"No. It's Mr. Wentworth."

Melodie's jaw dropped. A chill slid down her spine. "David? You brought David here?" she cried. "Bloody hell!" She whirled around, fumbled with the latch on the gate, and flung it open.

"Please don't go in there, Miss Mellie."

She ignored Jacob's plea, cursing again as she nearly tripped on the hem of her skirt. She dashed up the path.

If that bastard has hurt Erik, I'll...

She didn't know what, exactly, but this time, she wouldn't hesitate to jab David in the eye with her cane.

Melodie wrenched open the door and barged inside.

After more than a week of transporting Melodie by horseback, Erik found himself a shade disappointed that she was well enough to walk the route by herself. His reaction was selfish. He didn't wish her prolonged discomfort, but he would miss the feel of her body moulded to his back, her hands clutched against his stomach. Whenever he had asked if she was all right, her reply had always sounded breathless, as though she had been the one cantering down the road.

It made him smile, even now.

A knock sounded at the door. Erik stood and took two steps before realizing it couldn't be Melodie. She would let herself in. Perhaps it was Peter.

Erik reached for his wig on the table. Once it was secured, he put on the mask. The routine was such second nature, he had no need for a mirror. While he had ceased hiding behind these devices when he was alone or with Melodie, he wasn't about to expose himself to the unsuspecting lad.

The rapping came again. Erik opened the door. His gut clenched like a fist at the sight of his unexpected visitor.

David Wentworth returned his stare, his stance casual, as if he had not a care in the world. He wore no coat, attired in a simple white shirt, dark trousers and polished boots. Only his sheathed sword hinted that this was not a neighbourly visit.

Neither of them spoke for several seconds, their gazes unflinching.

David broke the silence first. "Surprised?"

Erik pulled the door open wider. "Won't you come in? I've been expecting you."

Taken aback by this tactic, the younger man's eyebrows knitted together. He accepted the invitation by stepping through the doorway. His gaze wandered about. "Charming."

Erik shut the door and repositioned himself in front of his unwelcome guest. "Why don't we dispense with the pleasantries and get to the point? You're here for a reason."

"Very astute of you. I admire a man who gets down to business. Are you not curious as to how I located you?" David asked.

"No."

Faced with the blunt answer, David seemed on the verge of laughter. "You certainly know how to take the fun out of the element of surprise. Very well. Since you were expecting me, I assume your cousin informed you that we had an interesting conversation."

Although Erik was more than capable of bluffing his way through this scenario, Henry had forewarned him of their 'familial connection' via a letter. While the note had also made it clear that he still did not approve of Erik, Henry had felt it only fair to pass on this information.

"Henry and I talked, yes," Erik said.

"And?" David prodded.

"And what?"

David cocked his head. "You truly are maddening, aren't you. What say you on Ramsey's first-hand account of your kidnapping the star of the Paris opera house? Then there's the crashing chandelier. You literally brought the house down."

"Your friend has me mistaken for someone else," Erik said calmly.

"Really, Blythe, you disappoint me. All it would take is the whispering of a well-placed rumour, and before long, you'll find your career in ruins. The solution to avoiding all this trouble is simple. All it would take is ten thousand pounds."

Erik snorted with disdain. "I should have known this was about money. You can't even be original. Go ahead and start your whisperings. There's nothing like a scandal to sell tickets. I suspect the next performance will be a full house."

Erik was not quite as confident as he sounded. If he did become linked to all that had happened in Paris, the consequences would be devastating. However, he wasn't about to bow to this outrageous blackmail.

Two years ago, he would have slit Wentworth's throat without hesitation or remorse. It was a shame he wasn't that same man; it would have made the situation much more simple.

David was clearly surprised by Erik's nonchalance. "You seriously expect me to believe this cavalier attitude? That you care not for your reputation?"

"Believe what you wish."

The tense moment was interrupted by the appearance of Sascha. Naturally cautious of strangers, she eyed the visitor with wariness.

"Down, Sascha," Erik said. The dog obeyed immediately, lying down with her head on her paws.

David's gaze flickered back to Erik. "Fine," he huffed. "We can play this game your way. It's a shame you'll be dragging others down with you, namely Henry and Melodie. And here I thought you cared for her, especially after the way you rushed to her defence." A smirk played around the outline of his lips. "If the threat of revealing your past doesn't concern you, perhaps I should threaten something or someone more dear to your heart."

Erik kept his control intact, speaking smoothly. "Since you so firmly believe that I caused the disaster at the Paris opera house, you should take greater care. Did Ramsey inform you of the accidental deaths that occurred there? Rumour had it that all of the victims were, in truth, murdered." He hardened his voice. "From this day forward, I suggest you tread carefully. Now, unless you actually have something of value to say, get the hell out of my house."

David's mouth flattened. He took a step to the side, as if moving away, and in the next breath, he lunged for Erik's mask.

Though David was quick, he was no match for Erik's lightning reflex. In one fluid motion, Erik sidestepped the extended hand and clamped on to David's arm. Bending the appendage across the man's back, Erik yanked it upward at a cruel angle. David howled with pain and outrage; he sank to his knees.

Sascha had started barking wildly the moment David had leapt forward. The torrent of sound echoed off the walls, setting Erik's teeth on edge. He bent down to growl in David's ear. "I ought to snap your arm like a twig for that."

Panting, his features contorted into a grimace, David said, "Go on and do it! It will only prove I'm right. That you're a monster."

Erik applied more pressure to the arm. He had the pleasure of hearing David gasp, though he would have preferred a whimper.

When the front door flew open, the sight of Melodie barrelling into the room distracted Erik. His hold slackened enough for David to wrench himself free.

"Erik," she called out.

David raised a questioning eyebrow as he massaged his arm.

Before Melodie could attempt to rectify her blunder, Erik said, "My middle name. It's what I prefer."

"How sweet," David sneered.

Melodie glared in his direction. "What are you doing here, David?"

"Just taking care of some business. What do you say, *Erik*? Why don't we finish this once and for all?"

David's suggestion was vague, but the intent behind it became crystal clear when he caressed the hilt of the sword by his waist.

Erik smiled. "I accept your challenge. Mellie, stay here with Sascha. No, not that way," he said, as David headed for the nearest door. "Out back, through the kitchen. I'll be there momentarily."

The open field behind the house would give them a wide unhindered space. David turned and stalked away.

"What is going on?" Melodie asked. She unhooked the bag from her shoulder and tossed it aside. "Are you fighting with him?"

"I've always found it difficult to back down from a challenge, especially when issued by weasels like Wentworth. Don't worry, I have no intention of killing him," Erik said.

He reasoned that his reassurance was not an outright lie. He had no specific intent to end the man's life. Of course, there was no predicting what could occur during a heated battle.

Melodie made an exasperated sound. "I'm not worried about him, you fool. I care about *you*."

"I assure you, I know how to handle myself. I'm an expert swordsman. A little rusty, perhaps…"

"Erik!"

He chuckled softly. "I'm teasing. I had an inkling this day might come, so I've spent some time re-honing my skills. You have nothing to fear, Mellie. I only ask that you not come outside, under any circumstance. Don't even go near the window. I don't need any distractions."

Melodie hurled herself forward and threw her arms around his neck. "Please be careful," she urged.

Erik returned her embrace, taking a revitalizing breath from the scent of her hair. He then retrieved his sword and joined his opponent outside.

David was restlessly pacing back and forth. Not for the first time, Erik was struck by how David physically resembled Raoul – the fair hair and skin tone, aristocratic facial features, slim build. Yet, as much as Erik had despised Raoul, he had to admit the man had honour; David didn't know the meaning of the word.

"Good of you to finally join me," David stated sarcastically. "I thought Melodie might have talked you out of it. Does she visit often?"

Erik sighed. "Your penchant for conversation is getting tiresome. Let's get on with it."

"I'm merely trying to understand the unique relationship the two of you seem to have. I would almost guess that you're lovers, but I can't imagine any woman wanting you that way. And despite the fact that Melodie has the sweetest lips I've had the pleasure of sampling, I know she's too chaste to consider anything improper."

Erik's distaste for this man made him literally want to spit. He held himself in check. "Your attempt to bait me is obvious. You seem to be stalling for time. Are you reconsidering…?"

The sentence was left unfinished when Erik found himself under attack. Only intuition and speed of reflex enabled him to block the thrust that sought his mid-section. Their swords clashed with a metallic ringing sound. As Erik berated himself for falling victim to the diversion, David stepped back and grinned.

Time to get serious.

Relaxing his body, breathing deeply, Erik cleared his mind of all distractions. His focus narrowed to encompass only David. Erik turned his right side to the enemy. He stood with feet apart, balanced, poised to move. They eyed one another, each waiting for the other to act first.

David leapt forward. He swung his blade with deadly intent. Erik kept his feet close to the ground and easily slid out of the way. After dodging several slashes, he gained a perception on David's style – experienced, impatient, and generally quite good – but not good enough.

With clear irritation, David taunted, "Come on, Blythe. At least make this interesting for me. Or is running away your specialty?"

David lunged with a flurry of thrusts and feints. This time, Erik met him blow for blow, parrying expertly. He nicked David above the elbow. A crimson stain soon marred the formerly pristine linen, like a rose bursting into bloom. Incensed at the sight of his own blood, David attacked again with greater speed and force. Erik held his ground. He ignored the aches that shot to his shoulder with each clash of their weapons. He feinted to the left, and David fell for the trick, leaving himself vulnerable on the other side.

Realizing his error, David began to turn away. He tried to parry the slash. But Erik was too swift, and he struck with ruthless precision. The material of David's trousers flapped open to reveal a nasty gash on his leg; it dripped with blood.

David cried out and staggered back. Erik took pity on him, though it was hardly deserved. "I could have killed you just now, but I didn't. Are you sure you want to continue?"

"Why don't you stop hiding behind that pathetic mask and show yourself as you really are?" David spat. "You're the same monster that destroyed the Paris opera house. Admit it! Did you really think Christine could ever love you? Oh yes, Ramsey told me the details of the sordid story. You've become quite the legend in Paris. Ramsey says, to look upon your face is to look upon Satan himself. Isn't that what Christine saw? Satan?"

Did you really think Christine could ever love you?

The question ricocheted like a bullet through Erik's brain, ripping through any semblance of rational thought. He broke out into a cold sweat and shivered.

Isn't that what Christine saw? Satan?

Erik's grip on the sword tightened until his hands went numb. His breathing was so shallow he might have been dead.

Satan's Son.

Erik glanced up in time to see the figure bearing down on him. The flash of the blade streaked across his vision. Erik deflected the full force of the slash, but not before the tip grazed his side, just below the ribs. He didn't even feel it slicing into his flesh, and resumed the battle with renewed vigor. His self-control was slipping; in its place, a fiery hatred burned. Feelings buried long ago bubbled to the surface again. Erik didn't know if he was fighting David or Raoul, or if it even mattered.

Erik's weapon struck with such power, he drove his enemy back with each blow. David panted, his face twisted with exertion. When David lost his footing and fell upon one knee, Erik moved in for the kill, a surge of triumph coursing through him. Just before he delivered the fatal slash, a cloud of dirt was thrown in his face.

Choking, his eyes stinging, Erik barely managed to block an upward slash that would have lopped off his entire arm. Rather than losing an appendage, his forearm was cut. David scrambled upright, and they crossed swords at the shoulder. Standing toe-to-toe, they glared at each other.

Two can play at that game.

They remained locked in place until David elbowed Erik in the chest. Erik stuck out his foot and hooked around David's ankle, jerking the man right off his feet. David landed flat on his back, arms splayed out. His right hand still clung to the hilt of his weapon.

Erik brought his boot down on the wrist. "Let go of the sword," he said.

"Go to hell!"

As Erik increased the pressure with his foot, a pained expression etched across the fallen man's features. "Oh, I'm sure I'll get there eventually, but it won't be today," Erik said. "Did you know broken wrists take an eternity to heal? You can take my word for it, or experience it for yourself."

When the fingers unfurled, Erik kicked the weapon away. Before David could begin to rise, Erik aimed his sword at the man's throat. "Not yet," Erik advised. "We need to talk first. Your cowardly dishonour actually saved your life. If you hadn't tossed that dirt, I would be speaking to a corpse right now. And a headless one at that," he added.

Erik's lip curled in amusement. "Don't look so shocked. Surely you noticed the angle of my sword's descent toward your neck? In any case, I've changed my mind and decided to allow you to live. I don't need the stain of your death on my hands right now."

His voice became edged with steel. "But I'm giving you fair warning. If you hurt Melodie in any way, as you have so unsubtly hinted, I will hunt you down and kill you. That is a promise. And just to give you something to remember me by…"

With deliberate slowness, Erik pierced David's throat with the tip of his sword. Blood welled and dribbled down into the collar of his shirt. Drawing the tip horizontally, Erik inflicted a wound about two inches long. He made it deep enough to leave a scar; every time David looked at himself in the mirror, he would see the welt.

Satisfied, Erik backed away. "Get up," he ordered.

David rose to his feet. His eyes smouldered with resentment. Erik also saw the flicker of apprehension. He could only assume that his warning had been taken seriously.

As David's gaze shifted to the weapon nestled in the grass, Erik walked over to retrieve it. Erik tossed it to the owner, and said, "Get off my property. If you ever return, you'll learn how I deal with trespassers."

David caught the sword by the hilt. He sheathed it and pivoted around. Erik followed him past the side of the house to the waiting carriage. If the driver was startled by the condition of the men that emerged into view, he wisely showed no expression as he climbed down and opened the door. After David was seated inside the cab, the young man hoisted himself up top and flicked the reins.

Erik watched as the carriage gained speed and made its way up the hill, dust billowing in its wake. Once it disappeared from sight, he turned toward the house with shoulders slumped. Pain and fatigue screamed from every muscle. Though he would have preferred lying down right where he stood, the thought of the woman waiting inside made him trudge forward. His mind felt as battered as his body. When David had mentioned Christine…

Merde! Will you ever stop thinking about Christine, you bloody fool!

He thought he was free of her. Why did she continue to haunt and torment him?

At the house, he exhaled a weary breath and opened the door.

Melodie had passed the time by circling the confines of the room. Sascha had grown tired of the strange behaviour and escaped to her corner in the kitchen.

Occasionally, Melodie could hear a raised voice or the clang of metal upon metal. As she paced, she alternated between twisting her fingers together and digging her nails into her palms.

It took her a while to realize that it had now become silent. Her unease rose to new heights as she wondered what this meant. The creak of the front door surprised her. She began to rush forward, but a chilling thought made her halt. *What if it's David?*

"Mellie."

Flooded with instant relief at the sound of Erik's voice, Melodie banged into the table in her haste to reach him. She chanted his name, and threw herself into his arms. At the sound of metal striking the stone floor, she knew he had dropped his sword. She ran her hands along his chest.

"Are you hurt?" she asked. Even as the words left her mouth, she found a tear in his shirt. A slick wetness coated her fingertips. She gasped. "You're bleeding!"

"It's just a scratch."

"You should sit down," she said. "Where else are you hurt?"

"It's nothing," he insisted.

"Erik…"

Melodie's admonishment was left unspoken when his mouth came down hard upon hers, rendering her speechless in the most literal and figurative sense. She was so stunned, she didn't react at first, limp in his embrace. One of his hands tangled in her hair at the nape of her neck. His other arm encircled her waist, pulling her in roughly, almost violently. She could barely breathe – or perhaps that was the effect of the kiss.

Her heart throbbed in her ears. The swell of excitement and the sound of her own moan surprised her. Her arm wound about his neck, fingers dug into his wig; she wanted to feel Erik's own hair.

As if Erik read her mind, her mouth was released. She saw the flash of his hand removing mask and wig in one motion. Once his lips met hers again, the force of the kiss changed to one of teasing gentleness, coaxing her mouth to part. Her bones seemed to liquefy as she leaned into him. Heat and desire flared from the core of her stomach.

When Erik finally drew back, Melodie had to collect her scattered thoughts. "That was most unexpected," she murmured.

"I couldn't seem to help myself."

Erik spoke gravely, yet she could hear a hint of humour in his tone. She pressed her forehead to his chest. "We still need to attend to your wounds. Sit down, and I'll fetch something for bandages." Although she was enjoying the feel of his arms around her, she wriggled out of his hold. His hand on her shoulder stopped her.

"Wait. We have to talk about Wentworth," Erik said.

"Is he dead?" Melodie asked, her voice flat.

"No. I had the opportunity, but I couldn't do it."

She didn't know whether to be sorry or relieved. "Then you're the better man."

Erik's hand continued to grip her shoulder, the hold almost hurtful. "Mellie, listen to me. You must move back with me."

"What? Why?"

"He's threatened to hurt you. I've warned him against it, but I don't know if it's enough to dissuade him."

Melodie lifted her chin. "He's threatened me before. I'm not afraid of him. Well, at least not so afraid that I'll allow him to run me out of my own home."

"This is different," Erik said. "He'll use you to get to me. Don't make the error of underestimating him. He's more dangerous than you think."

She placed a hand on her hip. "I like living in town. I like my independence. I won't give it up because of David. Besides, he doesn't know where I live."

"He knows there wasn't a carriage waiting for you. He can easily deduce that you walked here, and eventually, he'll find out where you are. Was living here so terrible?" he asked.

"Of course not," Melodie replied. "But it wasn't proper. I know it was my idea, but I was so desperate for your help on the symphony, I would have sold my soul to get it. The situation is different now. I have no excuse to reside here."

"Your life isn't enough of an excuse?"

She hesitated, but obstinacy prevailed. "I won't do it."

"*Goddamnit!*"

Melodie flinched. She was hauled forward by the shoulders to face Erik's fury, impaled by his gaze. "Stop being so damned stubborn! Do you have any idea what it would do to me if he hurt you? I'm not going to lose you, Christine!"

The shouted name hung in the air, suspended and frozen between them. Melodie would have believed she imagined it if she didn't see the horror in Erik's eyes.

Pain squeezed her heart with such unbearable hurt, she thought it might stop beating. Her voice shook. "Do you still love her?"

Erik's eyes closed. He dropped from sight. Melodie felt a tugging on her skirt and realized he had kneeled on the floor, just as he had that night of his confession.

"I don't know what's wrong with me," Erik groaned. "Something about Wentworth reminded me of Raoul. I was plunged into the past again. Forgive me. I would rather cut out my tongue than hurt you."

Reaching down, Melodie found the top of his head and stroked his hair. "It's all right," she said, her voice distant. "I understand if you still love her."

"But I don't," he said, suddenly vehement. "It's you, Mellie. It's you that I love."

Melodie's hand stilled. Her mouth fell open. "What did you say?" she whispered.

"I…"

Erik's voice faded after that singular word, as if he'd been shocked into silence.

Melodie sank down to her knees. She cradled his cheek in one hand, and angled her head until his face came into focus. "I love you too," she said.

Erik's eyes reflected disbelief before melding to wonder. "Mellie," he breathed, his voice husky.

"Erik, just tell me one thing. Who do you see when you look at me?"

Taking her hand, he kissed her palm. "You, Mellie. I see only you. Je t'aime."

Tears blinded her vision. She buried her face against his neck. They rocked in each other's arms, neither one wanting to be the first to let the other go.

Seventeen

Erik had been shocked by his declaration of love for Melodie. He hadn't planned it. It wasn't even something he had admitted to himself. He had blurted out the words without thinking, and frankly, after having endured Christine's rejection, he'd never thought the sentiment would pass his lips again.

While the spoken admission should have been monumental enough to change everything, his routine with Melodie did not alter; however, each time he looked at her, he was consumed by passionate longing, sinful yearnings. Despite those desires, he made no advances beyond the occasional kiss, ever determined to be the gentleman.

Melodie continued to reside on her own. Concerned for her safety, Erik insisted on taking her to and from her home on horseback again. It was better than walking, giving them an advantage should David happen to reappear. David had been thoroughly humiliated, and Erik was certain the man was plotting his revenge. Erik kept his Punjab lasso discreetly coiled within an inner pocket of his cloak.

Erik was filled with contentment and joy, yet a part of him wondered how Melodie could look upon his face and still love him. Months ago, when he had first unburdened his soul to her, she had not fled in fear. Her acceptance of him, despite his murderous past, never failed to astound him.

Whenever plagued with these doubts, Erik only had to gather her in his arms and kiss her. She always responded with ardour; within the limpid depths of her eyes, he could see the love shining back at him.

Though uncertain whether he deserved such devotion, Erik grabbed it with both hands. And like a spoiled child, he held it with fierce possessiveness, for she was his and his alone.

Tomorrow, they would submit the concerto to the managers. The score was complete, and the last two days had been spent polishing it to perfection. Even now, well approaching midnight, Melodie was hunched at the piano, reworking another section.

Erik sat at the adjacent table. He cradled his head in one hand, and gripped the quill with the other. He looked up when she spoke.

"I'm still not confident about this contrasting theme. Perhaps we should try it in a minor key."

"We already did," he reminded her.

"No, that was the next theme."

"We tried it with this one too." Pushing to his feet, Erik stretched out his arms. He came behind Melodie and placed one hand on either side of her neck. He kneaded its base in a circular motion with his thumbs. She hung her head forward with a low moan of approval. Chuckling, he bent close to her ear and said, "Leave it. If there are any adjustments to make, we'll do it during rehearsals."

"You're right," she mumbled. "Don't stop. That feels wonderful."

Erik obliged by continuing his ministrations. "So, what do you plan on wearing?" he asked, trying to keep his tone casual.

"The blue gown."

"That won't do," he admonished. "You can't wear the same dress twice in succession."

She shrugged one shoulder. "The yellow one, then. It's really of no import. And I forbid you from buying me another dress. You've given me far too many gifts."

Erik cringed at the thought of that frilly concoction of a gown. He would have to come up with an alternative plan.

His hands had moved farther apart to massage her shoulders. She reached around to take hold of his fingers. "Thank you. I should go," she said.

"Why don't you stay?" he suggested. "Your room is unaltered."

Viewing Melodie's face in profile, he could see she was tempted. But she shook her head. "No, I'd better not. I'm sorry to make you go out so late. I know you're tired."

Erik didn't realize he was holding his breath until it escaped as an almost inaudible sigh. He brushed aside his disappointment. "It doesn't matter. Gather your things together, and I'll ready Midnight."

Once he'd slipped on his cloak, he stepped out the back door. The air was damp and chilly, making him shiver involuntarily. He didn't look forward to the coming of winter.

Erik supposed there was only one way to end this shuffling back and forth between homes; he simply had to ensure the timing was right.

As David reached up to take hold of the knocker again, the door was pulled open a few inches. He ignored the look of disapproval on the old butler's face.

"I'm here to see Ramsey," David said.

The butler's tone was as frosty as the outside air. "I'm afraid Mr. Farr has already retired for the night."

"It's all right," called a voice from within. "Who is it?"

Recognizing the voice of his friend, David glared at the elderly man and shouldered past him. Ramsey stood in the hallway, attired in a checkered robe and slippers. "David, is something wrong?"

"Hell, yes."

David didn't wait for an invitation. He veered to the right and headed for the drawing room. He strode like a man with a sense of purpose, directly to the crystal decanter of brandy. Only after pouring a generous portion and downing it in several long gulps did he turn around. Ramsey had seated himself on the paisley chaise lounge, his expression bemused.

"Forgive my rudeness. Would you like a drink?" David offered. He tore off his coat and threw it aside.

"No, thank you. But feel free to indulge."

"Don't mind if I do." With a full glass of amber liquid in hand once more, David began to pace the thick carpet. "Well, he's gone and done it. I never thought it would actually happen."

"Dare I ask what you're talking about?" Ramsey inquired.

"My father. He's cut me off."

"Oh."

"Yes, *oh*. In all your barrister wisdom, is that all you can say?"

Ramsey sighed. "This has been brewing for a long time. You can't honestly tell me that you're shocked."

"Of course I'm shocked," David shot back. "I just told you I never expected him to actually do it. I'm his son. He cares more about that little chit than his own flesh and blood."

Ramsey looked confused. "Who?"

"Melodie." David ground out the name. He took another swallow of brandy and relished the burn down his throat. "He tells me how much of a disappointment I am to him, and then has the gall to compare me to a servant girl. I don't care how successful she's become, riding on the coattails of that deformed devil. I've heard it all my life, even as a child. Father always had a soft spot for her."

David glanced away. "Stop looking at me like that. I realize how pathetic I sound, but it makes me bloody furious."

"Sit down, David," Ramsey said. "You're wearing out my carpet."

Feeling a sudden, overwhelming weariness, David heeded his friend's advice and sat down on a chair. He tossed his head and finished the last drop of alcohol, fingers already itching for another glass. "I'm going to lose her, you know. Olivia."

Ramsey shifted in his seat, seeming uncomfortable. "Olivia cares about you."

"Not enough to stand by me when I haven't a cent to my name. You know as well as I do how fickle she is."

"I thought you weren't keen on marriage yet anyway."

"That's beside the point," David grumbled.

Impatience edged into Ramsey's voice. "I don't know what to tell you except what I've been saying for years. Just give your father's company a try, or find some other occupation. Maybe it's time to grow up."

David set down his glass. "I wouldn't have to if Blythe hadn't called my bluff."

"Since you were intending to expose his past regardless, I would hardly call it a bluff."

"Yes, but *he* didn't know that." David pressed two fingers to his temple, and closed his eyes. "In any case, it's too late to appease my father now. I'll never be able to please him, even if I did attempt the business."

"You don't know that."

"Apparently, you don't know my father," David said dryly. "Since Blythe is being uncooperative and he needs a taste of his own humiliation, I've come up with a plan. I need your help."

Ramsey grimaced. "What scheme are you involving me with now?"

"Blythe is having another concert at the Skylon next month. I want to prepare a surprise for him onstage."

"What makes you think he'll be there?" Ramsey asked. "He's a recluse."

The question caused David to cast his mind back to the night of the party at Colin Grayson's home, many months ago. It had been the first time he'd seen Melodie since she moved out, and his first glimpse of a masked figure, bolting away on horseback. Though it had taken a while to make the connection between that mystery man and Michael Blythe, David now knew they were one and the same. He assumed that like most artists, Blythe must possess an enormous ego, to the point of lurking in the shadows to hear his own music being performed.

"Trust me. He'll be there," David said confidently.

"You're playing with fire," Ramsey warned. "The man is dangerous. You've got the scar to prove it."

David flushed. The wound had scabbed over and healed cleanly, but his insides still festered with the need for revenge. Although high collared shirts hid the puckered line of skin from the view of others, he knew it was there.

"Are you willing to help me or not?" David asked, his tone belligerent.

Ramsey glanced toward the ceiling before returning his gaze to David. "I'll probably live to regret this, but I'll admit to being curious. What is your grand plan?"

Allowing himself the smallest of smiles, David began to outline what he had devised for the unsuspecting composer and his lovely assistant.

The next few weeks swept by Melodie like a whirlwind. She and Erik spent their days at the Skylon working with the conductor and the orchestra during rehearsals. She was pleased that everyone treated Erik with respect. While he never spoke of his feelings on the matter, she knew it must mean a great deal to him. He no longer had to shut himself in and hide from the world.

Henry sometimes joined them; he sat on the sidelines and watched the proceedings with interest. He had not seen Erik in some time, and their initial greeting was fraught with tension. By the third week, however, they seemed to have regained a degree of their former ease with each other.

The morning of the concert was ushered in with a bleak dreariness that was typical for November, but a glimmer of sunshine arrived at Melodie's doorstep in the form of a wrapped parcel. Nestled inside the box beneath a layer of tissue paper was her yellow gown. Erik had made arrangements to have it freshly washed for her.

Melodie noticed the dress seemed different. Just to be certain, she laid it atop her bed and ran her palms over the silky surface. Her hands told her what her eyes were unsure of – Erik had somehow managed to alter the dress. It was now a sleeker style, a more mature reincarnation. After trying it on, she was also delighted by the comfortable fit. It had previously been tight around the chest, making it difficult to breathe. She was touched by the thoughtfulness of the gift, but it also made her aware of the imbalance in the scales; he had showered her with so many generosities, yet she had given nothing in return.

That reflection troubled Melodie now as they sat in the carriage on their way to the theatre. They had not spoken since leaving town, lost in their separate thoughts. She nudged more closely to Erik's side and tilted her head against his shoulder.

His voice rumbled from above. "Are you cold?"

"No. Thank you again for the gown."

"And again, it was my pleasure." Several beats of silence passed before he spoke again. "Something is bothering you. What is it?"

His perceptiveness almost made her blush. While she wished to deny it, it would have been useless to do so. "You'll think it foolish, I know, yet I can't help feeling ashamed. You've given me so much, and I've done nothing for you," Melodie said.

"Nothing?"

Erik's voice was coloured with incredulity. He grasped her chin and brought his head down until his face filled Melodie's vision.

"You've given me the opportunity to write music again. Collaborating with you has been…" Erik paused, searching for the right phrase. "It's been like a dream. A miraculous dream. And what of your love and acceptance of a man who never thought he'd find those things in any human being, let alone a wonderful woman? These are gifts that were once beyond my comprehension, but you have made them a reality for me. It's far from nothing, ma chère. It's everything."

An enormous lump swelled in Melodie's throat, making speech impossible. The constriction across her chest could not be blamed on her corset or dress; she was physically ballooned by happiness. She wondered if it was possible to literally burst with emotion. Half-tangled by her cloak, she twisted around and sank into his arms, lulled by the steady beat of his heart.

Henry made the rounds backstage and chatted with some of the musicians. The air vibrated with excitement as they bustled about, tuning their instruments. Sounds of human voices mingled with their musical counterparts to create a unique, dissonant symphony.

As Henry maneuvered through the crowd, one of the managers caught his eye. The press of bodies in the confines of the hallways created a heated stuffiness. Wallace patted at his brow with a handkerchief. His ruddy skin glistened with a sheen of perspiration.

"Henry, I'm glad you came," the rotund man stated.

Henry shook his hand, and said, "I wouldn't miss it."

"Unfortunately, I have rather embarrassing news to extend. There's been some kind of miscalculation with the tickets, and Craig is at the box office right now trying to sort out this mess, but it seems we've oversold the seats. The bottom line is that you currently don't have one, so we were thinking of setting you up on a comfortable chair off to the side. I'm so sorry. I hope that's not overly objectionable."

Wallace had rushed through the entire speech in almost one breath, and now looked close to fainting. He blotted at his forehead again.

Henry responded with graciousness. "I think the aisles might be too narrow. I wouldn't want to pose a danger to the patrons. Why don't I sit offstage in one of the wings? I'll still be able to see and hear perfectly well."

The manager's hunched shoulders relaxed slightly. "Are you quite sure? I feel badly about this."

Henry assured him the arrangement was fine. Wallace went on his way to deal with other matters. Within minutes, Henry was approached again, this time by Erik and Melodie. Erik appeared rather distracted. His eyes darted about as if in search of someone, and he excused himself.

Henry had been so occupied with studying Erik, he hadn't heard Melodie's inquiry. "Sorry, what did you ask?"

"I wanted to speak with the maestro once more. Have you seen him?" she asked.

"No, I haven't."

Finally taking the time to truly look at her, Henry observed that Melodie was glowing; a healthy flush adorned her cheeks, and her eyes sparkled with vivacity.

Henry was struck by a realization. In all the years that he'd had Melodie to himself, she had seemed content. Only now did he comprehend that something had been missing, as if he had been the one too blind to see. She had never exuded such vibrancy, such utter joy for life – not until Erik had entered her world. Despite Henry's misgivings about Erik's past, he had to admit that the man's treatment of Melodie had been nothing but honourable.

"I've never seen you look so happy," Henry commented.

Melodie nodded, hesitated, and then stepped closer to him. "I have something to confess to you. You were right all along. I'm in love with Erik. It's just taken me a long time to realize it. I know you don't approve of him, but I hope that one day, you'll understand."

Sighing, Henry kissed her cheek. "I understand, more than you know. Whom we fall in love with is not a choice."

"He's a good man," Melodie said earnestly. "When you come to know him better, you'll learn to see him as I do. I'm sure of it."

They talked for a few minutes more until Erik reappeared. Melodie began to remove her cloak and asked, "Henry, would you mind locating the maestro for me?"

"Certainly," Henry replied.

Erik interjected before Henry had a chance to move. "Before you do so, if I might have a word with you in private."

Melodie arched an eyebrow. She looked mildly surprised by the request. "You two go on, then. I'll wait here."

Filled with his own curiosity, Henry weaved his way past the throng to find a more secluded area. The dim lighting cast a shadow over the left side of Erik's face. In contrast, his white mask seemed to magically hover in place, one green eye staring from within.

"I believe I can guess your concern," Henry stated.

"Oh?"

"You're worried that David might cause trouble again. I've already spoken with both Mr. Wallace and Mr. Rosenberg. They've warned the staff not to admit him."

"If Wentworth wants to find a way in, I'm sure he'll manage," Erik said. His tone softened with his next words. "But he's not the focus of my thoughts this evening. It's Melodie. I need to ask something of you, and I'm afraid you won't be pleased."

The scene at the entrance of the theatre was one of chaotic uproar. Patrons crowded around the box office window, demanding to be let in. Dressed in an array of colourful silks and taffetas, the ladies stood to one side and chattered with one another. Their gentleman companions argued with the rattled staff.

David took in the commotion with amusement. He could see Craig Rosenberg from behind the glass, gesticulating frantically to one harried-looking young man who appeared to want to crawl beneath his chair. Since Rosenberg would no doubt recognize him from the last event at the theatre, David hoped to remain out of his view.

"This is ridiculous," huffed an elderly man. He slapped on his hat and took the arm of the woman beside him. "Let's go."

The woman refused to budge, her wrinkled face pinched with disappointment. "But I want to see him," she whined. "I've heard he's mysteriously dashing and handsome with that mask."

"Oh, for God's sakes."

David rolled his eyes. He felt a jab in the arm and saw Ramsey chuckling under his breath.

"Are you sure about this plan?" Ramsey asked. "You'll be breaking the hearts of women across the whole theatre. Do you want that on your conscience?"

Ignoring his friend, David looked down to consult his pocket watch. A pair of tickets were thrust into his view. He lifted his head to find the exasperated man before him with tickets in hand. "Here," the man said, practically shoving them into David's palm. "Perhaps they'll be useful to you."

"But I already have a – "

"Throw them away, then. We're done here," he barked, before marching away.

A moment later, the central door to the theatre opened and Rosenberg emerged. "Ladies and gentlemen, please accept my apology for the delay. If you could please check your tickets carefully. In the upper right hand corner, you'll find a small box with a number inscribed. If it is anything other than a 'zero' or a 'one', we cannot admit you this evening."

He raised a hand as disgruntled voices arose. "We will, however, allow you to exchange your ticket for any other showing this season. Those with the numbers of 'zero' or 'one', please come forward. We will open all the doors now."

The surrounding doors were flung open. Most people clamoured forth while others turned away, muttering and shaking their heads. Rosenberg practically disappeared from view, engulfed by the crowd.

Ramsey inspected his ticket. "Looks like we're out of luck. Unless…"

His voice trailed off as David held up his newly acquired tickets.

David grinned.

Erik walked along the plush carpet and led Melodie to their seats in the front row. His gaze flickered over the heads of the audience as they talked in hushed tones. He could feel a sense of anticipation in the air. Erik draped his cloak along the back of his seat before sitting down.

Aware of his movements, Melodie asked, "Wouldn't you be more comfortable with your cloak backstage?"

He had not told her of the lasso tucked inside. "It's very dear to me, custom-made by the finest tailors in Paris. I would rather keep it close. I'm more concerned with where Henry is seated. He should be here with us."

Melodie waved a hand in a dismissive gesture. "He doesn't mind. He says it reminds him of when we used to sit in the rafters, except he doesn't have to worry about the height. He liked the privacy of it, but not the distance to the floor."

The start of the performance had already been delayed, and the patrons were restless. At last, the members of the orchestra and the conductor filed onto the stage to a round of polite applause. First on the programme was a short, lyrical piece by Saint-Saëns. After that, the violin soloist emerged to perform the concerto.

Erik's eyes narrowed as he regarded the young man. He was interesting to look at – tall and gangly, with crookedly imperfect features. Most curious of all were his eyes, a pale icy blue, and hair that was so blonde it was almost white. Unfortunately, Erik found his musical sensibility to be less than desirable. His technique was proficient, but he lacked the sensitivity to fully bring the rich romanticism of the concerto to life. If the managers had permitted it, Erik would have played the piece himself. Since that hadn't been an option, he had no choice but to endure what would no doubt be a lacklustre performance.

Feeling a pressure on his arm, Erik glanced down at Melodie.

"Promise me you'll try to enjoy this and not be overly critical," she whispered.

She was well aware of his opinion on the violinist. "I'll try," he said.

Erik leaned back in the chair, closed his eyes, and attempted to relax. As he anticipated, the performance was good, but not spectacular. At least the orchestra was in fine form, and he took pleasure in hearing the notes that he and Melodie had created.

When it was over, applause erupted from all around. Rosenberg made his way up to the stage. He introduced the soloist, who bowed deeply.

"And now, ladies and gentlemen," Rosenberg continued, "it gives me great pleasure to welcome the composer to the stage, Mr. Michael Blythe."

Fresh applause filled the theatre as Erik got to his feet. A strange light-headedness arose, making him sway slightly off-balance. He reached for Melodie's hand.

"This is your moment," she said.

"Our moment," he corrected her. "And you're coming with me."

Melodie linked her arm through his and allowed him to lead her onstage to join Rosenberg's side. Erik blinked as he faced the masses. As they clapped with thunderous enthusiasm, he remained enveloped in a dream-like state.

Movement at the corner of Erik's eye caught his attention. With a stab to the gut, he was plunged back into reality.

David was climbing up the stairs, approaching fast.

Rosenberg spoke out of the side of his mouth. "Excuse me, but I must ask you to leave the stage. Please return to your seat, sir."

David disregarded the manager. He lifted his arms and faced the audience. "Ladies and gentlemen, if I could have your attention."

Scowling, Rosenberg's eyebrows shot up as recognition set in. "Hold on, I know you," he began to say.

His words were overridden as David once again asked for quiet.

Melodie's hand tightened around Erik's arm. "Is that David?" she asked, her voice tinged with disbelief.

Erik said nothing. Perhaps it was a blessing that his lasso was out of reach. No matter how much the patrons enjoyed the concerto, he didn't guess they would empathize with his desire to garrotte Wentworth's neck. Silence descended on the theatre as everyone became aware that something unusual was happening.

David spoke loud enough to ensure his voice could be heard from every corner. "I feel it is my duty to inform you all that this man, Michael Blythe, is a criminal running from his past. Do you not wonder what lies behind his mask?" He flung out his arm to the side. "Many of you know my good friend, Ramsey Farr."

Erik recognized the man that strode forth from the other end of the stage. Ramsey's gaze met his briefly and then settled back on David, who continued with his speech.

"Two years ago, Ramsey was in France at the Paris opera house. During the middle of a performance, there was an explosion, and the chandelier crashed down to the stage. Fire broke out. The theatre was destroyed, and countless people perished. This was no accident. Legend told of a hideously deformed man who haunted the theatre, responsible for murder and mayhem. Ramsey saw this monster with his own eyes, saw him kidnap a helpless woman. He fled Paris and escaped to London."

David pointed to Erik. "That madman stands before us now. Michael Blythe."

Unsettled murmurings swept through the audience. David bellowed over top of them in order to be heard. "What have you to say against these charges, Blythe?"

Erik stared at his foe. The capability of speech seemed to have deserted him. He was trapped. And David knew it.

David turned to face him. "If you're innocent, you won't object to the removal of your mask."

Though he immediately regretted it, Erik took an involuntary step back. As he felt the pull on his arm, he remembered that Melodie was still attached to it. Erik thrust her toward Rosenberg.

"Take care of her," Erik muttered. His thoughts spun. If he refused to take off his mask, it would be a damning admission of guilt. He had to think of something.

When Erik spoke, his words rang clear and strong. "The reason for my mask is my own affair and no one else's. While I'm sure Mr. Farr was a witness to the events you described, I was not the culprit. You're trying to condemn the wrong man."

"Prove it!" David unsheathed and brandished his sword. Several women screamed. Alarmed outcries echoed about. "Remove your mask, or I will do it for you," David threatened.

Erik tried to use David's own antics against him. "I don't feel the need to prove anything. You're the one waving your sword in a public forum against an unarmed man. Which one of us is acting like a madman?"

David's face was twisted by frustration. He sprang forward with a sudden roar of rage. Erik braced himself for the impact, but was thrown backwards. Orchestra members cried out and scrambled to get out of the way.

It took all of Erik's strength to hold the man at bay; he blocked David's arms with both hands. They twirled in an absurd parody of a waltz. Music stands and chairs went flying as they careened about. David managed to wrest one hand free and clawed toward the mask. Erik threw his head back to avoid the grasp. They spun around again in a clumsy pirouette.

It took several seconds for Erik to register the increased intensity of screaming that filled the theatre. His eyes widened with horror. Hungry golden flames were consuming the red velvet curtain, spreading higher and higher. During their struggle, a gas lamp must have been knocked against the fabric, instantly igniting it.

Even David's grip had slackened as he took in the view. Erik seized the opportunity by backhanding the man across the face. David was sent reeling.

Erik raced forward and grabbed the curtain. He yanked, pulled, desperate to bring it down before the flames reached the ceiling. Visions of the smouldering ruins of the opera house tormented him. He couldn't allow the same tragedy to occur here.

Thick smoke billowed. Erik choked in a spasm of coughing. His eyes watered. The radiating heat was incredibly intense. Despite his furious endeavour, the curtain failed to release its hold. His muscles strained as he increased his tenacious grip. When he felt a presence at his side, he turned his head.

It was Ramsey.

The man took hold of the drapery and with their combined efforts, it finally ripped and came tumbling to the floor. Ramsey stomped across it with his feet. Erik used his hands to roll the fabric in on itself to smother the flames. Realizing that Erik was having more success, Ramsey stooped to copy the technique.

Both men were left heaving for breath when the fire was extinguished at last. Their eyes met. Neither of them said a word, their expressions mutually unreadable. Erik broke the contact first. He pivoted around to examine what was left of the stage. Everyone had disappeared. The floor was covered with scattered sheets of music and overturned chairs.

Erik heard a groan from the far side of the stage. He found Rosenberg slowly rising to his feet.

"Where is Melodie?" Erik asked, his voice sharp.

Rosenberg rubbed at his jaw. "I don't know."

"What do you mean, you don't know?"

"I...I'm sorry," Rosenberg stammered. "He came at me with the sword. I thought he was going to kill me. He struck me across the face, and I must have passed out for a minute. He wouldn't hurt her, would he? I don't understand what's happening." He sounded dazed. "What he said about Paris, is that true?"

Erik turned his back on the manager, afraid that he would strangle the man with his bare hands. His fingers curled into fists, clenched so tightly they trembled.

When he found Wentworth, he vowed to finish matters once and for all.

Eighteen

"If you're innocent, you won't object to the removal of your mask."

Only when Melodie tasted blood did she realize how deeply she was biting her lip. She mentally cursed David with a colourful string of words; Henry would be appalled by the extent of her vocabulary.

She felt Erik step away from her, and then she was propelled into the arms of another man.

"Take care of her."

Hearing Erik's curt instruction, her mind rebelled against being cast aside, yet she understood the reason for it. Rosenberg's hand was warm on her shoulder; she took no comfort from its presence.

When chaos erupted around her, she clutched at the sleeve of the manager's jacket. "What's going on?" she demanded.

Rosenberg guided her further across the stage as he spoke. "They're fighting. I can't believe this is happening."

She heard the pounding of feet, could feel the floorboards vibrating as people fled for the wings. "Is he all right?" she asked.

"Who, Blythe? He appears to be holding his own." Rosenberg sucked in a breath. "Oh my God."

Shouts and screaming filled the air. Melodie's pulse jumped. "What? What is it?"

"Fire. The curtain is on fire. We have to get out of here," Rosenberg said.

Feeling his tug on her arm, she tried to shake off the pressure of his hand. "No."

"Melodie, please. We have to go."

She could smell the smoke now, could almost taste it, acrid and bitter. Her eyes stung as she dug her heels in. "No. I'm not leaving him," she insisted.

Rosenberg gasped. Before Melodie could ask what was wrong, a blurry shape filled her vision. Her forearm was captured in a bruising grip, and she heard the manager grunt. "Mr. Rosenberg?" she called.

She was almost hauled off her feet. Dragged along by an unknown captor, she tried to wrench herself free. "Stop! Let go of me."

"Let her go, David," said Henry's furious voice.

He confirmed Melodie's suspicion of the mystery man. She heard the slap of an object striking flesh, followed by a thud to the floor.

Alarmed, she cried out, "Henry?"

Once again, she was jerked forward. She struggled against David's grasp. "What did you do to him? Henry!"

Melodie raised her free arm and raked her nails across David's face. She should have expected it, but the force of the blow across her cheekbone stunned her. Her resistance ebbed as she was forced along. She stumbled several times over the hem of her dress. Though she attempted to keep her wits about her, she was unsure of where they were. "This is madness, David. What are you doing?"

David spoke for the first time. "Something I should have done long ago."

Melodie was spun to the right, her hand smacked against a railing. "Climb," he ordered from behind her.

"No. I refuse to go any farther," she stated.

Fingers seized her chin, forcing her to look at an object placed inches from her nose; it was the glinting blade of his sword.

"Start climbing, or I will slit your throat where you stand," David warned.

Any doubt that he was serious was erased when his face came into focus. His bloodshot eyes reflected a chilling intensity that she had never seen before. Perhaps he truly had gone mad.

Melodie shivered. Forcing one foot in front of the other, she began to ascend the staircase. Each step took her farther away from Henry and Erik.

An idea came to her. Melodie threaded one hand through her hair and undid the clasp of her hairclip – the one Erik had given her. She enfolded it in a fist, slid her hand down the front of her skirt, and let it go. She heard a faint clattering sound. David did not make a comment, so she could only hope he had not noticed.

She prayed that Erik would find it. And in turn, that he would find her.

Erik headed for the nearest wing of the stage. The area was not well lit, and he tripped over something. He glanced down.

"Henry!"

Erik knelt by the body lying prone on the ground. His gaze took in the bloody gash that marred the older man's temple and then came to rest on the eyes – eyes that were open, staring into space. He placed two fingers on the side of the man's neck.

Henry was dead.

With a heavy heart, Erik murmured, "Je suis désolé, Henry."

He had no doubt that Wentworth was responsible for this. That bastard was completely out of control.

Erik grimaced, and stood up. He continued to make his way to the back corridors. His emotions were on the edge of skittering out of control, but he had to remain level-headed. He couldn't allow anger and fear for Melodie's safety to cloud his logic.

The area backstage was deserted, the complete silence almost eerie. David could have taken Melodie through several possible routes: to the rear of the theatre through the stables, around to the front, or through the side entrance. As Erik tried to decide on the most likely choice, his boot crunched down on something. Normally he would have kept on walking, but instinct made him stop.

It was Melodie's hairclip.

He picked up the object and turned it over in his hand. While it was possible that it had simply fallen out of her hair, it might also serve as a clue to her whereabouts. Melodie was clever. She could have deliberately dropped it.

Taking a look around him, Erik spied the nearby stairs that ascended to the roof. There was no escape that way. Surely David would not have chosen that dead end.

Erik took three steps toward the rear corridor and then halted. He returned his gaze to the staircase. Some unnamed force tugged at him, lured him toward the roof. But if he was wrong, too much time would be lost. The hope of finding her would dwindle to an impossibility.

"*Merde,*" he muttered.

He slipped the jewelled ribbon into his pocket, next to the lasso that he'd retrieved from his cloak. Then he ran up the stairs.

Melodie gasped at the shock of cold air that assaulted her senses. She hugged her arms against her chest. Wind whipped at her hair. She wasn't sure if it was the force of the wind, or the strain of the endless flight of stairs that stole her breath away.

David took hold of her arm again and led her forward across the roof. Though she wanted to resist, she didn't. At this point, it would be a fruitless endeavour. When he stopped, he released her arm.

"David, talk to me," she implored. "Why did you bring me here?"

"We'll see if Blythe is successful in stopping the fire. I rather hope he is, as I don't relish the thought of being consumed by flames. Either way, my miserable life will come to an end tonight. And so will yours."

As the meaning of his words sunk in, Melodie's mouth parted. Her shivering intensified until her teeth started chattering.

"You're drunk," she accused. "You don't know what you're saying."

David laughed. "Yes, I'm drunk. That's why I have the courage to do this. My life is in ruins, and it's your fault."

"*My* fault?" she said, incredulous. "You can't blame me for the failings of your life. That's absurd."

"Is it? You've been a thorn in my side since the day Henry brought you home." He sounded like a petulant child.

"So you're going to kill me? You may be many things, but you're not a murderer."

"Your faith in me is charming. My father has always said I've never set a goal for myself and achieved it. Maybe it's time I proved him wrong."

Melodie fell silent, contemplating all the disadvantages against her. Never having been on the roof before, she was unfamiliar with the layout. She didn't have a weapon, not even her cane. And as much as she hated to admit it, her lack of sight was a serious problem. She could think of only one solution.

She had to convince David that he still had a life to live.

Erik opened the door. As he peered out into the darkened stillness of the rooftop, his eyes adjusted to the wan light. He heard a voice carry on the wind.

He breathed a soundless sigh. Melodie was speaking, though he couldn't see her.

Erik took cover behind a lone statue. It was the only adornment on this roof, and he was grateful for its presence. He could assess the situation without being seen.

Erik craned his neck and saw Melodie and David, mere steps away from the edge of the roof. He wondered if she realized how close to the precipice she was.

"You're wrong," she was saying. "Your father loves you."

"Please, spare me the platitudes," David sneered.

As they talked, Erik's gaze flickered back and forth between them. David still gripped his sword, though it was pointed downward and did not seem an immediate threat. While the lasso would have been Erik's preferred means of wringing David's neck, he couldn't use it while Melodie was so close. He had no other weapon to consider except one that he had not exercised in many years.

Erik hoped it wasn't rusty from disuse.

Melodie continued to drone on about his father, but David was barely listening. Instead, he thought about how disastrous this night had turned out to be. His cheek still throbbed from the blow Blythe had dealt him. And despite David's earlier words to Melodie, he wasn't entirely confident that he could go through with this plan of extinguishing both their lives. It wasn't the first time he had considered it, but he had never come this far before. He should have consumed another bottle of brandy to further dull his doubts.

David regarded Melodie through bleary eyes, struck by how beautiful she looked tonight. He realized, with a strange sort of clarity, that he both loved her and hated her. It was the same mix of feelings that he'd believed he reserved only for his father.

The revelation loosened his tongue. He started rambling about his woes – his disinheritance, his loss of Olivia, his lifelong battle to please his father.

Melodie never interrupted him, seeming to listen with a sympathetic ear. Even through his alcoholic haze, David knew that was wishful thinking; still, it made her all the more endearing.

Movement in the corner of his eye distracted him.

Blythe emerged from the shadows, an inky silhouette save for the unearthly radiance of the white mask. David almost took a startled step back. He caught himself in time, sweat breaking out on his brow. He had deliberately brought Melodie to the roof's edge, but he wasn't ready to take the plunge just yet.

David grabbed hold of Melodie, swung her around, and held the sword to her throat. He addressed his uninvited guest. "I know your reflexes are quick, but it will take less than a second for me to kill her. I suggest you stand back. You were successful in stopping the fire, I presume?"

"Yes."

"Of course you were. I suppose you're the hero now. How splendid for you." Although he spoke sarcastically, David was lucid enough to appreciate the irony.

"I understand, you know, how you feel about your father," Blythe said, his tone gentle.

"Don't try to patronize me. You know nothing about it."

"I know only too well. You've spent your entire life trying to please him, yet no matter what you do, it isn't good enough. After an eternity of trying, it's simply easier to give up. He's your father, a powerful figure, someone you both love and hate. I understand because I've been there, but it doesn't have to be like this. You don't need him, David. You can forge a life on your own and move far away where no one knows you. You can start over without answering to anyone. It can happen, but it starts here. All you have to do is put down the sword. Put down the sword, David."

David stared at the composer, directly into eyes that shone with impossible brilliance in the dark of night. David was trapped in that gaze, unable to glance away. And yet, he felt at ease. He didn't want to look away. He wanted to obey. The voice was compelling, reverberating in his mind with a calm, clear command.

Put down the sword, David.

David's grip on the weapon began to relax. His arm dropped. Though David didn't see Blythe's mouth move, he could hear the musical voice.

Good, David. Step away from Melodie.

Thudding footsteps and a shout echoing through the air jolted David out of his trance. He blinked.

"David, don't be a fool. What are you doing?"

At the sight of Ramsey, David lifted the sword again and pressed the blade flat against Melodie's neck.

David glared at Ramsey. "You traitor. And you have the gall to call yourself a friend."

Erik suppressed his urge to groan aloud. He had been so close. Like a puppet master, he'd manipulated David's strings, bent his will. If he'd only had a few seconds more, Melodie would be safe in his arms.

"I am your friend," Ramsey said.

David continued to glower at him. "I saw you leaping to Blythe's side to help him. No friend of mine would have done that."

"You would have rather seen the theatre engulfed in flames? A repeat of the Paris disaster?"

"Yes."

Ramsey appeared shocked by the answer. He spoke quietly. "Then I'm sad to say, perhaps you're right. No friend of mine would hope for something so evil."

"I'm glad we understand each other," David said. He turned his gaze to Erik. "Your trickery was impressive. Is that how you made Melodie care for you?"

Erik couldn't stop the pulse that came to life beneath his eye. "It's not too late, David. You can still walk away from this."

"I'm not under your spell any longer," David spat. "Don't waste your breath. Say goodbye to your Erik, Melodie."

Erik's eyes bulged at the swiftness of David's motions. Melodie was there, caught in David's grip. In the next instant, she was gone, her scream slicing through Erik's heart.

David had pushed her off the roof.

"*NO!*"

Erik's anguished cry exploded from his throat. He barely noticed that David was hurtling toward him, sword held high. Erik didn't stop to think; he acted from sheer hatred.

Blocking the downward slash with one hand on David's forearm, Erik punched him in the face with the other. David's head snapped back, yet he continued to cling to the sword. Rage gave Erik more than enough strength to wrench the weapon away. He plunged the blade, almost to the hilt, straight through David's gut.

Erik cursed himself for every opportunity he'd had to end this man's life. If he'd only heeded his base instinct – the murderous impulse that lurked within – both Henry and Melodie would still be alive. Now she was dead, and something within Erik shrivelled up and died too; his world had been reduced to a lifeless void.

David's face slackened in an expression of shock. With fierce satisfaction, Erik shoved him backwards, and a savage thrill tore through him when he tossed the body over the edge.

Erik panted for breath, chest heaving, and a roaring in his ears. As quickly as the thirst for revenge was sated, despair rose to take its place. The agony of it ripped at his insides, threatened to shred his sanity.

When Erik heard the familiar voice floating up from below, he thought his plunge into delirium was complete.

He looked down. His jaw fell open.

"Mellie!"

Several stone gargoyles protruded from the face of the building. Melodie was hanging on to one of them with both hands. Directly beneath her was air, a hundred feet of nothingness that ended with the cobblestone streets of London.

Erik dropped down and lay on his stomach. Edging out as far as he dared, he stretched his arm. His fingers splayed, wiggled, but he was just shy of reaching her. "Mellie, give me your hand."

"I can't," she said.

"You can."

"No, I can't!" Desperation laced her voice. "I can't support myself with one hand. I'm barely hanging on. Please help me. Don't let me fall."

Erik understood the problem. The stone was wider than the span of her palm, making it difficult for her to grip it. She was literally hanging on by her fingernails.

Erik slid forward another inch. It still wasn't enough. When he moved again, he started to topple over. He tried to back-pedal, and only succeeded in throwing himself further off balance. He felt a tug on his jacket. For a hair-raising moment, he was suspended in mid-air. Then he was being pulled back to the solidness of the roof.

Erik jumped to his feet. He extracted the lasso from his pocket and ripped off his jacket. He didn't even bother to thank Ramsey for bringing him to safety. When he started tying the lasso to his waist, he noticed the blood on his hands. David's blood. He wiped it off on his shirt.

"I need you to lower me down," Erik said. "I'm a few inches short of reaching her."

Ramsey gaped at him. "With that thin little rope? You're a big man. It can't possibly hold – "

"It can, and it will," Erik interrupted. As he tied a firm knot, he prayed his claim was true. "It's stronger than it looks. Here. Wrap it in your fists." He thrust the other end of the lasso into Ramsey's palm.

Ramsey sounded panicked when he spoke. "I don't know if I can do this. You must outweigh me by at least – "

Erik cut him off again. "You only have to support me for a few seconds until I can pull her up myself. There's no other way." He seized the man's shoulder. "But if the rope starts to slip, and you think you can't do it, yell out to me. I'll try to bring Melodie up to you somehow. Grab on to her, and let me go. If the choice is my life or Melodie's, you must save her. Understand?"

Ramsey nodded. "Yes."

Erik flattened himself down once more and reached out. He dropped lower. "I'm coming, Mellie."

Melodie's voice was reduced to a whimper. "I can't…can't hold on."

"Just a second longer, love. I'm almost there," Erik urged. He strained to close the gap. At last, he clamped on to each of her wrists. "Got you. Ramsey, start pulling back," he called out.

Erik's stomach lurched. His grip was slipping on her left wrist. Blood had trickled down from her injured fingers, making the contact slick. He tried to squeeze harder, but the slide continued until he lost the battle.

Melodie screamed, now dangling from a single limb.

Erik ground his teeth together. His muscles wrenched in pain as he contorted himself. Stretching back with his free arm, he was relieved when he felt the stone of the roof's ledge. He scrabbled for a firm hold with one hand while maintaining the tenuous connection with Melodie.

His grip on Melodie's right wrist began to slip.

"Erik!"

Dear God, help me.

Sweat trickled down Erik's temple. "Don't worry, Mellie. I've got you."

Seconds ticked by, the equivalent of three heartbeats. Erik could have sworn his heart ceased altogether. Within the first beat, he knew he had no alternative but to grab Melodie's arm with his other hand. In the next, he stretched himself out, and momentum propelled him downward. He had failed; they were both going to die. In the final beat, he felt his leg being yanked, and he was dragged up.

The three of them collapsed on the rooftop. Ramsey tumbled over onto his back. Erik gathered Melodie into his arms, holding her so tightly, he may have crushed some bones. He shut his eyes, and buried his face against the side of her neck.

Finally drawing back, Erik extended his arm toward Ramsey. They shook hands. "I am in your debt," Erik said. "Thank you."

As if unable to speak just yet, Ramsey dipped his head in acknowledgement.

Melodie remained hunched over, trembling. Erik reached for his crumpled dresscoat and draped it over her shoulders. He took a moment to undo the lasso from his waist, thinking it ironic that the weapon had been used to help save a life.

Melodie's voice was small when she broke the silence. "David?" she asked.

"He's dead," Erik said.

She showed no reaction to the news at first. Then she grasped his sleeve. "Henry. He hurt Henry. We have to make sure he's all right."

Erik stiffened, his mouth going dry. "Mellie, I have to tell you something."

"He's badly hurt, isn't he. That bastard. I'm glad David is dead." Melodie's tone was venomous.

"It's worse." Erik hesitated. "There is no way to make this any easier, so I'm just going to say it. Henry is dead."

Melodie took a sharp intake of breath. "What? He can't be."

"He is. I found him myself," Erik said grimly. "He suffered a blow to the temple. Depending on the intensity and the precise location, it's a means of killing a man. Wentworth probably used the butt of his sword."

"You found him?"

"Yes."

"Then you're wrong," Melodie stated.

"Mellie…"

"*You're wrong!*" She leapt to her feet and threw off his jacket. "Take me to him."

Her eyes were wild and glassy, her voice brittle as ice.

Erik was afraid she would shatter in her next breath.

"I'll take you to him," he said.

Melodie clung to her belief that Erik was wrong for as long as possible. Hope carried her down the stairs and enabled her feet to keep moving. When they reached level ground, she heard people milling about, but couldn't distinguish what they were saying. Her only focus was getting to Henry; everything else shrunk to an odd buzzing in her head.

Erik halted and murmured near her cheek. He was the only person she seemed to hear clearly.

"We're here," he said.

Melodie knelt down and stretched out her arm. She found the curve of Henry's shoulder. Following the downward slope, she traced a path that led to his hand; it was unnaturally cold to the touch.

She jerked her own hand back as if burned, and clutched it to her chest.

Erik's breath warmed her ear. "Mellie, the Inspector is here and wants to talk to me. I'm not leaving you. I'm just a few feet away, all right?"

Melodie nodded. Leaning forward, she brought her face close to Henry's. She needed to see him, his dear, wrinkled face. Though it was marred by a hideous gash and streaks of dried blood, she only saw the kind soul of the man that had raised her with love. He was dead. And she would never get the opportunity to call him 'Father'.

She stayed on the floor, unaware of the passing time. It rather surprised her that she was so calm. In fact, she felt nothing at all. No pain. No grief. Not even an urge to cry.

What kind of a woman am I?

Erik returned to her side. "Are you ready to go?"

"What will happen to Henry?" Melodie asked.

"The authorities will take care of him for now."

"Do you think he suffered?"

"No, I think it was quick," Erik replied. "Mellie, let me take you home."

"He should have a blanket," she said. "He's cold, and he's not fond of the cold. He always liked summer. I know it makes no difference, but I hate for him to be so cold. Will someone bring him a blanket?"

Melodie knew she was babbling, yet she couldn't seem to stop herself.

A new voice joined in. She recognized the owner to be Ramsey. "I spoke to the Inspector. You're in the clear, Erik. How is she?" he asked.

"Henry needs a blanket," Melodie informed him.

"A blanket?" Ramsey repeated.

"Yes."

"I'll take care of it," he said, his voice kind.

Satisfied, Melodie kissed Henry's forehead. "Goodbye...Father."

Time seemed to leap forward. Melodie gradually became aware of her surroundings – a rhythmic rocking motion and cushiony seat beneath her. She didn't remember getting into a carriage. She was nestled against Erik, wrapped in his jacket. Her hands were cold, and her fingers throbbed with pain. Reaching into a pocket for warmth, she found a small, velvet-covered box.

"What is this?" she asked.

"It's for you, but the timing isn't right," Erik said, sounding uneasy.

"For me?"

Erik took the box from her. An object came into focus before her eyes; it was a ring, a sky blue stone with diamonds set on either side of it. "It's beautiful," Melodie said. Her voice sounded strange to her own ears, flat and emotionless.

"I asked Henry earlier in the evening for, well, for permission to marry you," Erik explained. "And he granted it. But as I said, the timing couldn't be worse. You don't have to say anything. We'll talk about this some other time."

"Some other time," she parroted.

Frowning, Melodie wondered what was wrong with her. She vaguely understood that she must be in shock. Talking was tiring. She didn't want to talk anymore.

More time escaped from her. She realized the carriage had come to a halt. Erik assisted her, and when her feet touched the ground, her queasy stomach revolted. With a moan, she said, "I'm going to be sick."

After Melodie finished retching, Erik scooped her up and carried her into the house. Sascha greeted them with a wagging tail, but Erik couldn't stop to give her the attention she sought. He would have to make it up to her tomorrow.

Melodie's behaviour worried him. She lapsed into long periods of silence in which she didn't seem to be aware of anything around her. When she did speak, it was stilted and mechanical, as if her spirit had been extinguished.

Once upstairs, Erik set Melodie down on his bed. She sat upright, staring ahead, listless and unmoving. Erik tore off his shirt and tossed it on the floor, glad to be rid of the bloody linen. He also removed his mask and wig. Pulling on a fresh shirt, he didn't bother to button it. He was more concerned with tending to Melodie's wounds. Her hands and arms were a mess. Several fingernails had ripped off, and the undersides of her arms were scraped raw. He guessed that when she fell near the gargoyle, her arms had grazed along the stone until she managed to grab hold of it.

Erik shuddered at how close he'd come to losing her.

Within minutes, he'd retrieved a pitcher of water, basin, soap, and clean cloths. He used some of the cloths to cleanse the cuts and then wrapped her hands and arms in the makeshift bandages. Exhaustion was creeping up on him, but he ignored it. He sat beside Melodie, rubbed at his face, and regarded her.

"Can you undress yourself or would you like me to help you?" he asked.

"Yes, thank you," Melodie said.

Emitting a sigh, Erik began the task of removing her dress. The last time he had tried this, he hadn't gotten past the corset.

When he'd finished, her dress, corset, and stockings were hung over a chair, her shoes placed underneath. Melodie sat on the bed in her chemise. Erik supposed that a true gentleman would have guided her to her own bed; however, he didn't trust her to be alone tonight. He wasn't about to let her out of his sight.

"Try to get some rest, love," he said, nudging against her shoulder.

After Melodie lay down on her side, Erik climbed in and arranged the covers around them. He turned on his side. Curving an arm atop her waist, he shifted close to her back. Sleep would not come easily to him tonight.

He kissed the top of her head and began to hum a lullaby.

He awakened to two distinct sensations; he was alone, and something was wrong.

Flinging out an arm, Erik felt the coolness of the sheet beneath his fingertips instead of a warm body. He lit a candle and stepped into the hallway. The door to Melodie's room was closed, but he could hear her sobbing. His gut twisted at the heartbreaking sound.

Erik knocked on the door and let himself in. "Mellie?"

Within the glow of the candlelight, he saw Melodie huddled on the bed, curled into a tight ball. Her face was burrowed into the pillow, her cries muffled. At the sound of his voice, she lifted her head.

"I'm s-sorry. I didn't want to w-wake you," she said, her voice thick.

"It's all right."

"I can't seem to s-stop crying."

Erik set aside the candle and ventured closer, unsure of what to do. Perhaps she wanted to grieve in private.

"Erik?"

"Yes?"

"Would you mind h-holding me?" Melodie asked.

Erik sat down on the bed, leaned back, and stretched out his legs. Melodie crawled into his arms. She wept against his chest. As the sobs became less forceful, she said, "I can't believe he's dead. It isn't fair."

Tears leaked from her eyes, even as she swiped them away. "There's so much more I could have said to him. Now it's too late. I loved him so much. He died trying to protect me."

Erik said nothing. He stroked her hair, rubbed her back. For a while, the only sound was their breathing until Melodie spoke again. "I didn't thank you for saving my life."

"I'm just grateful you had the bravery and strength to hang on for as long as you did," Erik said. "When I thought I lost you..."

His voice faded; he couldn't complete the sentence without feeling sick.

"Are you in trouble with the authorities?" she asked.

"No, Ramsey was most helpful. He gave a statement about what happened on the roof. And when the Inspector questioned me about the accusations that Wentworth had made about Paris, Ramsey stepped in and said that he had been mistaken. That I wasn't the man responsible for the disaster there."

"He said that? How remarkable."

Erik shared in her surprise. He'd never expected this turn of events. "Indeed. Perhaps he's trying to atone for participating in David's plots."

"Erik, back in the carriage, was I dreaming or did you show me a ring?"

Erik swallowed at this change in topic. "No, you weren't dreaming. It was very real."

"What did Henry say when you talked to him?" she asked.

"He said that while he's loved having you for a daughter, he's always wondered what it would be like to have a son. Then he said he looked forward to the day when he could officially call me 'son'."

Melodie looked up, eyes awash with fresh tears. "You do realize," she said, "that you haven't officially asked me? Ask me the question, Erik."

"Now?"

"Mmm hmm."

Erik's heart began to thud faster. He tried to clear his throat, and only succeeded in sounding strangled.

"Melodie, would you do me the honour of marrying me?"

She kissed each of his cheeks before answering.

"Yes," she replied.

They continued to hold each other until Melodie's eyes closed, her breathing deepening. Erik watched her sleep. Eventually, his eyelids grew heavy, and his head lolled back.

He dreamed of slipping the ring on her finger and calling her 'wife'.

Epilogue

Melodie sat on the couch, legs curled beneath her, absently running her fingers through the fur on Sascha's head. When she and Erik had returned earlier in the evening, Sascha had been wandering throughout the rooms, issuing periodic whines from her throat. Puzzled at first, Melodie then guessed that the dog's sensitive nature had picked up on the changes that had been made within the house. Most of the furniture and household items had been moved to their new home this morning. This would be their final night in Erik's cottage.

Melodie had moved back with Erik following the night of the concerto to recover both physically and mentally. While she had enjoyed her independence, it was a comfort to be close to him again. Erik managed to be supportive without being stifling.

Albert Wentworth paid them a visit a fortnight after the tragedy. Looking haggard, he seemed to have aged ten years since Melodie last looked upon his face. First, he informed Erik that he bore no ill will against him for having caused David's demise. He was shamed by his son's actions, especially regarding Henry. Albert then announced that he wished to transfer his late son's trust fund to Melodie. Stunned, Melodie refused the offer, but Albert was insistent. She agreed to consider it.

Melodie discussed the issue with Erik. He stated that pride did not make him fond of the idea, but it was her choice to make. While she did not know how much money was involved, she imagined it was a generous sum. She decided to accept the gift and put it to good use.

They intended to continue composing together. The security of the trust fund would enable them to choose commissions that were of true interest to them, rather than accepting every offer in order to survive. Some of the money would go to Peter so he would have the opportunity to attend school. And in the back of Melodie's mind, she dreamed of opening her own music school; one that would welcome any child interested in music.

She and Erik were both fond of his rural home, but neither of them felt it would be wise to remain. They had deceived the townspeople by claiming to be uncle and niece. Once they were married, the truth would be revealed and make their situation too difficult. They also reasoned that their new life together should begin in a new home.

They found a townhouse in London that was larger than the cottage, yet still modest in size. Melodie was thrilled with the location. While she had enjoyed her stay in the country, she had missed the city life. It was even close to the Skylon theatre, where they were promised to receive more commissions. Erik conceded it would take some time to be comfortable dwelling there, but he also liked the idea of the amenities of central London; he still retained his taste for fine wine, tailored clothes, and exceptional music.

Now, on the eve of her last night in a place that had become home, Melodie contemplated how she'd run through a gamut of emotions today – her wedding day. They had chosen to be married in a private ceremony. While she had managed to hold back her tears during the exchange of vows, by the end of the 'husband and wife' proclamation, they'd overflowed down her cheeks. Joy and sorrow had created a bittersweet combination, seeming to split her in two. If Henry had been alive to share in the moment, she would have been whole with perfect happiness. She had consoled herself by believing he was there in spirit. And in fact, he had been there in name; they had taken his surname of 'Blythe'.

The feel of hands brushing Melodie's shoulders made her smile.

"Are you ready to go upstairs?" her husband murmured in her ear.

Melodie's pulse quickened at that simple question. "Yes, I am." When she found herself lifted in his arms, she couldn't contain a giggle. "What are you doing?" she asked.

Sascha emitted a single bark, as if indignant that Melodie was being taken away.

Erik chuckled. "Sorry, Sascha. I'm afraid you'll have to stay here." He began walking toward the stairs. "I realized that I neglected to carry you over the threshold when we came in. Carrying you upstairs will have to suffice."

Melodie nuzzled at his throat. Her fingers played with the fine hairs at the base of his neck. "I'm not complaining," she said.

Erik set Melodie down on her feet, unable to tear his gaze away from her – his wife. His mind seemed unable to grasp that this was real. He had surrounded his bedchamber with candles, and their combined radiance cast a soft luminance over Melodie. She was a vision in her simple, ivory dress, dark hair sleek and flowing down her back. Caressing her cheek with one hand, he traced over the freckles that she hated and he adored.

"Are you nervous, love?" Erik asked.

"No. Yes. A little," she admitted. "Are you?"

"Terrified. But somehow, I think we'll manage."

In a little over a week, it would be Christmas. Erik had never celebrated the holiday before, never understood the appeal of it. But this year, circumstances were different. His whole life was different.

With the exception of the prayers his father had forced him to recite as a child, Erik had asked for God's assistance more times since he'd met Melodie than in his entire lifetime. Each time he'd appealed for help, his prayers had been answered. Erik wasn't ready to start attending church on a regular basis, but he did acknowledge that some divine intervention must have brought this woman into his life.

Since the time he'd been born, he'd been set on a course into darkness. In various fleeting moments, he'd glimpsed the occasional flicker of light and hope. Those moments, however, had been too brief to dispel the shadows. Only now did he see a new path before him, bright with a constant, unwavering glow – a path of love.

"Erik?"

Melodie brought her hand to his cheek – the twisted, ravaged one – and stroked it gently. "Is something wrong?" she asked.

"No," he replied. "For once, everything is as it should be. More than I ever hoped it would be."

Erik pressed his lips to her palm. Entwining her fingers with his, he led her by the hand and said, "Shall we go to bed, Mrs. Blythe?"

"Finally," Melodie said. "I thought you'd never ask."

Glossary of Words and Phrases

fils de...	son of…
je suis désolé	I'm sorry
je t'aime	I love you
ma chère	my dear
mademoiselle	miss
merde	swear word
putain	swear word
salaud	bastard

LaVergne, TN USA
16 December 2010

209062LV00007B/115/A